Let Your Hinged Jaw Do the Talking

W0006648

Tom Johnstone came to fiction writing rather late in life, and so pursues it with the quiet desperation of someone conscious of the relatively short time he has left. He is the author of the collection *Last Stop Wellsbourne* and three novellas, *The Monsters are Due in Madison Square Garden*, *Star Spangled Knuckle Duster* and *The Song of Salomé*. His short stories have also appeared in such publications as *Black Static*, *Terror Tales of the Home Counties*, *Nightscript VI*, *Body Shocks* and *Best Horror of the Year Volume 13*.

tomjohnstone.wordpress.com

Let Your Hinged Jaw Do the Talking

a collection by

Tom Johnstone

T Johnstone

The Alchemy Press

Let Your Hinged Jaw Do the Talking © Tom Johnstone 2022

Introduction © Colleen Anderson 2022

Cover and art © Peter Coleborn

This publication © The Alchemy Press 2022

First Edition
ISBN 978-1-911034-15-5

Published by arrangement with the author

All rights reserved. The moral rights of the authors and illustrators of this work have been asserted by them in accordance with the Copyright, Designs and Patents Act1988

No part of this publication may be reproduced, stored in a retrieval system, or transmitted, in any form or by any means without permission of the publisher.

All characters in this book are fictitious and any resemblance to real persons is coincidental.

Published by
The Alchemy Press, Staffordshire, UK
www.alchemypress.co.uk

Contents

Acknowledgements

"A Heart of Stone" originally appeared in *Making Monsters*, 2018

"Creeping Forth Upon Their Hands" originally appeared in *The Ghastling, Book 12*, 2020

"Cuckoo Flower" originally appeared in *The Alchemy Press Book of Horrors 3*, 2021

"Face Down in the Earth" originally appeared in *Terror Tales of the Scottish Highlands*, 2015

"In the Hold, It Waits" originally appeared in *A Book of the Sea*, 2018

"Let Your Hinged Jaw Do the Talking" originally appeared in *Nightscript 6* (2020), then subsequently in *Best Horror of the Year, Volume 13*

"Mum and Dad and the Girl from the Flats over the Road and the Man in the Black Suit" originally appeared in *Supernatural Tales* #33, 2016

"Slaughtered Lamb" originally in *The Eleventh Black Book of Horror*, 2015, then subsequently in *Best Horror of the Year, Volume 8*

"The Chiromancer" originally appeared in *Supernatural Tales* #36, 2017

"The Cutty Wren" originally appeared in *A Ghosts and Scholars Book of Folk Horror*, 2018

"The Fall Guy" originally appeared in *Twice Told: A Collection of Doubles*, 2019

"The Topsy Turvy Ones" originally appeared in *Terror Tales of the Home Counties*, 2020

"Coffin Dodger", "The Lazarus Curse", "Professor Beehive Addresses the Human Biology Class" and "Zombie Economy" all appear here for the first time © 2022

Thanks

I have many to thank for the creation of this collection, from the Jolly Brewer pub where I scribbled out most of the title story, and Victoria Leslie whose fairy tale workshop kickstarted it, to William Shaw and Jane McMorrow of the Bookmakers, the author-friendly pop-up bookshop where I wrote much of "Zombie Economy". The published stories in this volume go back several years and during that time I have had so much help and encouragement from friends in the dark fiction writing community: Priya Sharma, Anna Taborska, Stephen Bacon, Laura Mauro, Kit Power, Simon Bestwick, Tracy Fahey, Rosanne Rabinowitz... The list goes on and on and I apologise for anyone I've missed.

Many of these stories originally appeared in various publications, so I am indebted to the following editors and publishers: the late Charlie Black, C.M. Muller, Rebecca Parfitt, David Longhorn, Paul Finch, Gary Fry, Ellen Datlow, Rosemary Pardoe, Robert Morgan, Mark Beech, David J. Howe, Djibril Al-Ayad, Emma Bridges, Peter Coleborn and Jan Edwards. Peter and Jan also allowed me to talk them into publishing this collection, so thanks to them for publishing and editing the original stories here for the first time. As mentioned elsewhere, "Zombie Economy" benefited from vigorous and rigorous beta-reading from Anna Schwarz and Colleen Anderson, but I also made use of the linguistic skills of Lucie Lorenz when writing the French dialogue. Finally, thanks to Miranda Morris for the Desmond Tutu gag in "Professor Beehive Addresses the Human Biology Class" ...

Dedication

To my mother and father

Introduction

The Devil's in the Details

Imagine you live in a suburban neighbourhood, where neighbours chat over the fence, actually borrow cups of sugar and will walk with a glass or bottle of wine to the neighbours to sit on the porch and watch the sunset. Perhaps you live there now.

Children play games in the yard; dogs chase balls and a few hummingbirds thrum about in the cooling twilight. It's warm enough that you go for a walk, to stretch your legs after dinner. Night pulls up its bedsheet and the first stars spark the indigo sky. You relax in the peaceful laziness of your safe neighbourhood.

Then you notice that the shadows cast by the streetlights seem to create inky nothingness and ... is that a strange scratching or rattle you hear? You glance over your shoulder, not too concerned. You shouldn't have had that extra glass of wine – that's all.

As you stroll further you have this sense that something is following you. You turn a circle, but it is only you and a tabby crossing the street. Then the scrape sounds again, closer, and was that a puff of breath on your neck? You stop and turn. There is nothing. You turn back and it is right in front of you –

This is Tom Johnstone at his best, the master of the slow reveal, where every story builds mystery toward a disturbing otherness. It's what we've been afraid to voice, that these bastions of UK culture and society hide darker inclinations. What happens if you just lift the flap a bit and peek beneath? Gentleman's clubs, boarding schools, penny arcades, ventriloquist dummies, simple postcards from abroad, a belligerent ex-cop, the innocence of discovery, a child gone mad and a mad child – what crawls and scuttles forth is not a knife-wielding maniac. No, it is more insidious and burrows into our minds, to settle under the skin and make us shiver and think.

It's what we've always worried, that what seems too good to be true is in fact a sham, that our worries and fears are more than just stress and anxiety from overwork.

Johnstone pulls a deft thread through the skin of the weird, giving it a tug now and then. His exploration of what is considered the first zombie film, *White Zombie*, fleshes out each character, the possessed and dispossessed alike, in "Zombie Economy", and reveals that everyone is a watcher of another's fate.

The guilty are not always punished and the innocent not always saved in "Creeping Forth Upon Their Hands", "Face Down in the Earth" and "The Fall Guy". In each of these tales there are real and flawed people who tangle with history, whether it's that of their ancestors or their own past secrets. "Professor Beehive Addresses the Human Biology Class" and "The Topsy Turvy Ones" make manifest what the acts of others can create.

Every character is so vivid you'll swear you met the person down the street or in your regular pub. "Mum and Dad and the Girl from the Flats over the Road and the Man in the Black Suit" and "A Heart of Stone", as in many of Johnstone's tales, wind the character into ever more twisting turns and, like the best of *Black Mirror,* holds up a lens on what "the devil's in the details" means when we overthink.

Eldritch things that walk on their hands, strange sentient plants and mythic wraiths out of the Gaelic mists – the scope of Johnstone's work leaves a trail that will never look the same. This is the best stew of weird fiction and firmly establishes him in the genre. Tread carefully as you read lest you stir up too much.

—Colleen Anderson

Let Your Hinged Jaw Do the Talking

"Dance with me," he said.

"You're bold," she said.

That was what Mary loved about him, though. He was bold, but not too bold.

Old too, but not too old. The Brylcreemed silver hairs combed back over his head stretched like the rain-slicked roads out of the small town.

I say "Mary" but I mean my mother. It helps if I call her "Mary". That makes it a story.

He was in Carluke on a business trip, he said. She didn't ask what his business was. That was one of the first things she learned about him: that it didn't do to ask too many questions. If she had done so she felt sure he'd have said something like, *Ask me no questions and I'll tell you no lies.*

Instead, she let him let her do all the talking. He asked her about herself and she told him, about how her pregnant mother walked from Lanark to Carluke after Mary's father died in the pit explosion. He was a good listener, nodded in all the right places. When she spotted him smiling she said, "What?"

"Nothing. I like your accent."

She looked away, embarrassed by the glint in his blue eyes and the way he smiled at her, kept looking at her mouth when she talked.

"I thought you wanted to dance," she said, pursing her lips. It was his turn to look away.

"I didn't do very well the first time. This is nothing like the tea dances back in Sidcup."

She had to admit he was immaculately turned out. His arms felt strong even if his feet were all over the shop, his fingertips probing the small of her back as if searching for something. Looked like he had money too, even if something about him made her wonder *for how long?*

If I'm honest, she probably just wanted a way out of there. That was what he was.

"Don't worry," she said. "You'll get better with practice."

~~~

A diamond ring and a trip to Gretna Green later and she was the lady of the mock-Tudor manor with the wax fruit on the table. Not exactly Eltham Palace but an improvement on the pebble-dash poverty she was used to.

But the garage was his castle.

It didn't matter to her. The grounds were extensive, dominated by gigantic twin conical conifers, a sundial in between. At least I remember them as gigantic from when I was a child.

I also remember how frightened I was of that upper-crust ventriloquist doll on the television variety show.

But I can't remember why.

It will come back to me, I'm sure.

That's why I'm writing it down. Turning it into a story helps me make sense of it. When you're young the grownups are always telling you stories. If it isn't fairy tales at bedtime, it's their own personal stories. "How I met your father/mother". After a while they get all mixed up in your head and you can't imagine your mother ever having a life before your father, before…

~~~

"Dance with me," I said.

I didn't expect her to say "yes", thought she'd slap me for being forward, phrasing it as a command like that. But I soon saw that wasn't the way of things up here. You dancing? You asking? *All very rough and ready in this Scotch provincial hall, the girls around her whispering to her and giggling when they caught me looking.*

I knew she was a free spirit, but I also knew I was going to make her my princess.

Bit like me, Daddy?

Bit like you, sweetheart. But different.

She was such a free spirit. I thought of her as an untamed lass, dancing barefoot among the smoke and coal dust of these streets full of granite houses under granite skies. Would I be able to tame her? Did I even want to? But I didn't worry about that for now. I just let her do the talking, danced with her on my two left feet.

And did you, Daddy?

Did I what, sweetheart?

Tame her?

No sweetheart. I never did. You know your mother. No one ever could.

~~~

Fast forward twenty-five years or so to my own marriage. I didn't meet my husband at a tea dance or ceilidh, but somewhere between my workstation and the water cooler. Things always look more romantic through the filter of the past. There's barely an old film or television clip from my dimly remembered youth but makes my tear ducts swell with an ache of longing and nostalgia these days. And I've no doubt, if we have children of our own, we'll spin our meeting into a fairy tale for them.

Our eyes met over the fake potted plant…

Maybe we could tell them about the time I screamed my head off when he suggested we watch a film about Ray Charles. Eventually he managed to calm me down and we finally established I'd got the blind soul singer mixed up with the Seventies variety act Ray Allen and Lord Charles, the very duo that gave me the screaming ab-dabs back when I was seven. Of course, they weren't your usual television double act. For starters, one of them was made of wood.

But that was part of the trouble.

~~~

"There, there, sweetheart, don't take on so. He's not real! He's just a vent's doll… A ventriloquist's doll, like the ones in the warehouse. Look, the man's doing the talking for both of them, see? His mouth isn't moving but the doll's is, so it looks like His Lordship's doing the talking."

My father had switched the TV off by now and was trying to tickle me while poking fun at the puppet's airs and graces. I could still see it in my mind's eye: the hinged jaw snapping open and shut like a gamekeeper's trap, allowing clipped aristocratic one-liners to escape, the lips always fixed in the same wide grin; the glass eyes rolling, one knowingly monocled, the eyelids lowering slyly, then rising again to reveal the fixed stare that so terrified me. The manikin sat on the man's knee, like a child, but its dapper tweed jacket and silk cravat and barbed insults suggested an urbane man-about-town. If this was a child it was a creepily precocious one.

Father sat by my bed until I went to sleep that night, reassuring me the dummy wasn't a real person, couldn't really talk.

"So the man was … letting the doll do the talking?"

This was the only time he got angry with me, that evening, stiffening at the way my words echoed his tale of the Wooing of Mary, glaring at me with the same hard blue ice-chip eyes he'd worn when he told me never, but never, to go in the garage.

~~~

Yes, that would be a funny story to tell the kids, if we ever have them.

Well, not the last bit.

Just the bit about me getting into a lather over Ray Charles. Ben would tell the tale without all the creepy stuff about the dummy or the garage, as a way of enabling them to laugh at how kooky their old mum is!

~~~

My father should have known I'd react like that to the dummy on the telly. Because that's the thing I've remembered that I previously forgot: the time he took me to see his toy warehouse.

It's odd he was so tight-lipped about it when he first wooed Mary. I mean, toy wholesaler! It's not as if he was an arms dealer or something.

He never took me again after that first time.

Maybe if it had just been one of them.

But rows and rows and rows of them lined up on the shelves, glass eyes staring at me from the shadows, a dust-specked finger of sunlight poking through a small window picking out a pair of them.

Maybe if the eyes hadn't moved.

It could have been an employee of Fox Bros. lurking behind the shelves playing a practical joke.

On a four-year-old girl?

That's almost more frightening than the thought of one of those wooden things taking on a grinning, unnatural life!

But that's too awful to contemplate, so let's go with the idea that Barry Giles or Beryl Mott or one of the others thought *I know! Let's scare the boss's daughter into screaming hysterics! That'd be a great idea!*

Maybe the eyes didn't move at all. Eyes can follow you without moving, can't they? That's what they say about portraits, right?

So let's consider the scenario again: an impressionable rather highly strung child, a dimly lit warehouse full of vents' dolls, a father busy with his work, child foisted upon him by a mother at her wit's end.

You'll be all right here, princess. Lots of toys for you to play with. Keep half an eye on her, would you, Beryl? I've got a meeting with my accountant.

Beryl's eye wasn't on me, not even half of it. I later heard she had her eye on Barry Giles.

But dozens and dozens of other eyes *were* on me.

~~~

15

Fast forward ten years or so to my Troubled Teenage Years, the years of rebellion. Derek and Mary having delayed parenthood for a decade after their nineteen-fifties wedding, out of the deeply ingrained prudence they both shared, this was bound to be a fractious time.

And when I came home from university sporting a "Support the Miners" badge it was "Don't get me started on that Scargill beggar" from him.

And Maggie? Wouldn't hear a word said against her. She'd helped hard-working strivers like him, unlike those ruddy socialists on the other side. And as for the ne-er-do-wells like that brother of his, who'd never aspired to much, there was opportunity for them too, if they'd but take it.

"Take Sidney," he went on and those blue ice-chips flashed in his eyes. "I offered him a share in the business but he wasn't having none of it. I still call it Fox Brothers, in hope he might have a change of heart and come on board, but he'd rather wallow in drink and self-pity over in Sidcup.

"Wouldn't he, Mary?" he called through the serving hatch.

I wasn't sure what I was expecting from Mary. She was usually full of blunt pithy Caledonian wisdom, but not this time. I willed her to throw me a lifeline, perhaps invoke her father, buried under tons of rubble and fossil fuel, but she remained tight-lipped, fussing around her kitchen domain in her lilac twinset while the father-daughter row took place, cleaning every pot and pan and surface to within an inch of its life, until each one reflected a face as rigid as wood or wax, mouth shut like a trap.

~~~

Derek Fox went to his grave not knowing what really happened.

There were rumours it was an insurance job, that warehouse inferno. In the end they arrested Uncle Sidney for the crime. He protested his innocence but the judge and jury were convinced by the prosecution argument that he'd always resented his brother's success and burned the place down to get his own back.

I know better.

Years later I visited him in prison and he told me he never wanted anything to do with Derek's business, or any of the other vile unnatural things his brother got up to. He pleaded with me to help him get out of jail. I just told him to stop saying those things about my dear father and left with his cries for help ringing in my ears.

There were other rumours too, about the fire, wild talk of screams coming from inside, but that's just nonsense. The place was empty of the living. I made certain before I scattered petrol around like holy water, trying not to look at those accusing eyes on the shelves. After I let myself in with the key I borrowed from Derek's study, avoiding their glazed gaze was the first thing on my mind, after disabling the alarm of course.

Don't look in their eyes.

Don't look in *her* eyes.

It was for her sake I did it. It was the only way I could think of to free her. Because that was what *really* terrified me all those years ago.

Not just the glassy eyes staring at me.

But her staring at me out of one pair of them, in particular.

Now I'm no longer four years old it seems odd to say, at the least, to have a dummy so closely resembling my mother in looks and dress, even down to the lilac twinset it wore, sitting there on that shelf in the shadows at the back of the warehouse.

But there she was.

And throughout the rest of my childhood I could never shake the conviction that the resemblance was more than just superficial, that she herself, or at least some vital part of her, had been staring panic-stricken from those eyes, pleading for release. It was only when I reached my adolescent years that unformed unease about the world and my place in it changed into a certainty about the source of my alienation and its remedy. It was only then that I knew what to do.

The argument about the miners' strike and her reaction to it confirmed the suspicions I'd harboured since I was old enough to entertain such thoughts: that the woman I'd always thought so feisty and indomitable was in fact well and truly under the thumb. Her sharp tongue was a sham concealing a lack, a sliver of something missing from her, cut out of her and hidden somewhere dark and musty.

She must have entered that forbidden garage. She must have seen what was in there.

After breaching that inner sanctum he had to silence her, and she never spoke of it until after the fire. Everyone thought the trauma of this catastrophe had brought on her illness, but that wasn't what she raved about during the delirium of what my father would only call "brain fever", shooting me accusing looks as if it were me responsible for her condition.

Which I suppose I was.

She was burning up, a reaction to the drastic measures I'd taken to bring her back to herself, as it were. The high fever she was running might explain her ravings about "the woman in the garage … the hand neatly cut off at the wrist".

What was Mr Fox doing in there? Making her, or unmaking her?

I call him Mr Fox to make a story out of it, of course, because it enables me to make sense of it.

My lovely kind gentle daddy, who soothed my night terrors, even if he was arguably responsible for them, cutting up women, cutting out part of my mother and putting it into a ventriloquist's doll! When you put it like that, it seems unthinkable.

But if you call him Mr Fox and her Mary, that's a different matter.

It's like when he told us his war stories. My mother

would scoff at some of the more far-fetched ones, purse her lips at the risqué ones about furtive encounters with girls who spoke but a few words of English. Yes, how she'd turn her face away from his apologetically kissing lips after some of those!

But when spinning yarns about storming the beaches of Normandy he edited out the worst of it, the bodies or bits of bodies floating around in the churning waters, just telling us about tearing up onto the shore dodging bullets. There he was, fantastic Mr Fox, surviving a massacre by the skin of his teeth, getting out with maybe a singed brush, the rascal.

But to Mary's ain folk he was something more than that. They all came down when they heard, a small army of uncles crammed into a battered transit van, all built like the outdoor privies in their backyards. Men in black donkey jackets with coaldust ingrained in the very pores of their skin that made their faces into brooding scowls, they crowded into that antiseptic room, mobhanded.

My father cowered outside as if they were more frightening than the Nazis strafing the beach as he put his head down and ran for it through the surf. When one of them came out to report on her condition – "There's been an improvement," was all he said – Mr Fox tried to sit me on his knee like a shield, his arms grabbing at me, his mouth pleading. "Come on, princess, sit on Daddy's knee!" Fully grown, I shook him off as the miner stood and stared at the scuffle, but then Mr Fox muttered some words that came jibing out of my mouth even though he was not close enough to manipulate invisible wires in my back.

"Why couldn't you help my grandmother when she walked barefoot to Carluke?" The words came streaming out like vomit though I tried to hold them back with my teeth, gritting them in a dummy's grimace. *Gottle o' gear, gottle o' gear!*

"Princess!" said Mr Fox, in a tone of scolding indulgence, laughing it off desperately. "What a thing to say! She's got a sharp tongue this one, just like her mother! Still, nothing like a child's simple cruel logic, eh…?" he added pointedly, still apparently convinced I was one.

My eyes pleaded with my great uncle to see these were not my words, but he just shook his head at the whole contemptible display my father and I were staging. He turned his sooty face away, saying, "She was too proud to accept our help." Then he walked back into the private hospital room.

He didn't want to leave Mary there with her uncles. But one of them came out and said, "Best if you went home and got some rest, Mr Fox", and he didn't argue.

~~~

We never saw her again. They took her back to Lanark. She must have improved enough to travel.

He went downhill after that, visibly shrivelling in her absence, whatever magic he might have possessed fading from his eyes, their blue ice-chip glint dissolving to a watery shimmer. Sitting there those last few months he looked no more alive than when he was laid out in his suit one overcast morning in April. Trying to make me sit on his knee must have been the first sign of the decline that later saw him asking who I was and where Mary was.

"Has she gone out to the shops?" he kept asking.

Coffin Dodger

As Sykes crouches down to check the mower's cutting height, he sees the dead child's name.

The sight is disturbing enough to distract him from his annoyance at having to make this laborious adjustment.

He thought he'd be able to get away without altering the height when he began on the open area near the cemetery entrance, but it wasn't long before he had to start mowing among the tombstones and face the perennial problem of the mower getting stuck between them. That's when things got a lot harder.

There's enough space for a pedestrian mower to pass through the gap – a normal mower, not this one, a pea-green John Deere C52 KS with a chute to allow the cut grass to escape. It still gets clogged up though. If only *he* could escape. He shouldn't still be doing this job at his age. He'll probably be doing it when he dies. The divorce settlement gave Marsha the house and the kids, but he still has to pay for both as well as his own meagre flat and existence, all out of a wage that's barely enough for him to live on. To think, he used to be someone. Not many people knew who he was, but that job gave him a certain status. That it should come to this! Slaving away in the heat to mow a miserable cemetery…

The chute has a metal flap, angled downwards to make sure stones caught in the blades don't fly out and hit passers-by. Not that they're much of a problem in this churchyard, tucked away on a quiet lane off the road out of town – just as well, as once it's snagged on a few of the gravestones the chute is angled up rather than down so wouldn't offer much protection. Sykes is sweating already from struggling to get the machine past these obstacles, and it's only been about fifteen minutes since he began. The sun's not fully up yet, but it's going to be hot, he can tell, and he's still got the rest of the bloody place to mow. He's barely started and he feels like he's done ten rounds with Conor McGregor.

The grass is too long for the height of cut it's on, but he's damned if he's going to raise it, he decides. As well as the troublesome chute, this model's got another feature designed to give the user ball-ache. In order to adjust the height of the deck, you have to move four levers individually, one for each wheel, and he can guarantee at least one of them will be stiff and stubborn and refuse to shift, especially when his hands are already sore and slippery with sweat from the effort of handling the machine.

It's only a matter of time before the John Deere C52 KS chokes on a particularly long thick clump of grass, stalls and grinds to a halt. As if it's sulking, or staging some passive protest, like some crusty sitting in the road outside a nuclear base or quarry or oil refinery, the mower refuses to start again. Repeatedly pulling the starter cord is fruitless. The engine must have flooded or overheated.

At least with human demonstrators, in his previous life he could have grabbed the irritant by the dreadlocks and dragged them over the tarmac to the waiting meat wagon. Since the ignominious end of that former career he's had to use more softly-softly measures when dealing with the recalcitrance of machines, though kicking them does sometimes help ease the stress. In this case, as he waits for the engine to cool down and the fuel to settle in the tank, whichever is the cause of the mower's malaise, he relents and finally lifts the deck, shifting the levers into a higher position none too gently, one by one.

That's when the name on the tombstone catches his eye.

It takes Sykes a while to place the name, but it's there somewhere in his memory. From many years back. The trouble is, at his age, remembrance of things past is a far from exact science. It doesn't help that he's lived so many different lives, been so many people. Having savagely jammed the levers governing the height of the deck into place, he raises himself creakily back up to his full height and wipes sweat away from his brow.

But it isn't just the physical exertion of adjusting the mower that's causing him to perspire. He looks at the name again. And then he remembers.

James Albert Dance.
17th April 1964 – 21st November 1968
Sleeps with the angels.

It's a child's grave.

But it can't be the same one. It must be a coincidence.

"Hey, Grandad!" A boy's voice shouts.

He looks up towards the source of the insolence, cursing himself for doing so. A cheeky young face grins back from a boy in a grey hooded top, perched on a mountain bike stopped on the pavement. His odious little mates chortle at the jibe, sitting on their own flashy-looking bikes. Sykes is working next to a wall that overlooks the road, but the ground is high on the cemetery side, exposing him to the scrutiny of passers-by as though he's standing on a raised stage. For a few long seconds his eyes meet the boy's.

"Coffin dodger!" That's the parting shot as the bikes speed away leaving behind the echo of their riders' taunting laughter.

Back in the day he'd have nicked that one so fast his feet wouldn't have touched the ground. But the boy's head would have – hard and repeatedly.

Snarling these thoughts aloud, his teeth grinding together so hard he feels like his jaw will break, Sykes sets himself to renewed attempts to restart the mower, as if each stroke of the starter-cord might yank the memories from his head. Finally, a protesting groan from the engine drowns the recollection in a cloud of fumes as the chute expels the remaining fragments of grass and dust from its maw. Momentarily, the grey plume forms itself into a shape that might be a child's, or perhaps a woman's, as it begins to grow in size, but he closes his eyes and shakes his head to dispel the impression – or perhaps in preparation for a sneeze brought on by the machine's dusty exhalation. The need to sneeze passes along with the tide of recollection, and when he opens his eyes again the cloud has dispersed. Yet, despite shutting out most of what happened, one of the memories has settled like a dandelion seed, shaken off its mother plant. His jaws work, teeth grinding fragments of dust, spitting them out of his mouth. But he can't rid himself of the memory of the name.

After all, it's what he called himself for a while.

Operation Jackal, they called it: something to do with a hit man in a Frederick Forsyth thriller who used the stolen identity of a dead child as cover.

Sykes wasn't an assassin of course. His job was to *prevent* acts of subversion. Not that he expected any thanks for his pains. Which was just as well because he wasn't going to get any. What he received in the end was quite the reverse. Condemnation. Persecution, even, for acts he performed in the line of duty, back when his name was James Albert Dance, not Robert Alan Sykes. The name he picked from the Register of Births, Marriages and Deaths shared his date of birth, but unlike him the child didn't live past the age of four.

It's strange to see this date inscribed on a tombstone. But he isn't going to dwell on it. As with all his problems his solution is the same. To leave it behind him. No looking back.

He has finished mowing this part of the cemetery, anyway. Time to move on. Besides, if he glanced over his shoulder he might see more clearly the small figure he just glimpsed out of the corner of his eye.

Sykes is relieved to see that these tombstones are older than the ones where he saw Dance's name. These headstones are so encrusted with patches of mustard-yellow and ash-white lichen you can't see what's written on them anyhow. It must be the heat that makes the substance look wet, as if the splodges were the result of a small child finger-painting. For a moment the thought of his own children is unbearable. Limited access has stunted his relationship with the two children he sired with Marsha.

The other mother and child, he has no contact with whatsoever. "Who *are* you, James?" he remembers Imogen shouting, the last time they spoke. "Should I even call you James? Or is it another name you answer to?"

One thing he likes about this job: when his thoughts and memories get too loud he can just drown them out with some noisy industrial machine, like a lawn mower or strimmer or hedge trimmer. When he's working in the park, and a member of the public approaches him with some enquiry or other, it can be difficult for them to secure his attention when he's operating one of these devices, ear-defenders clamped over his head. He uses this to pretend not to hear them.

In this cemetery there's no one around to bother him. The last human voice he heard was the boy who shouted at him from the road, but his mowing pattern has taken him away from there, deeper into the cemetery. Away from people and their endless demands on his attention and time. That's one of the reasons he consented to take on this mowing job. Even when he was a beat cop he was never very good at fulfilling the day-to-day public-facing obligations of the job. Undercover work was more to his taste, allowing him to blend into the background at the meetings he infiltrated, the way he'd merged anonymously into the thick blue line when more openly policing demonstrations in London. But even if his features registered with any activists there, no one recognized him in the small town to which his handler sent him when he was part of the Special Demonstrations Squad. That's when he met Imogen. Things got rather more complicated when he started dating her. But she was a key activist and his orders were to get as close to her as possible.

"Yes, *that* close," his handler said.

"Is that allowed?" he wondered, a tremor in his voice betraying his excitement.

"Don't worry about that." The handler's eyes narrowed. "Just make sure she doesn't cotton on to who you really are."

But he was wrong to think they'd back him up when she did. He remembers how betrayed he felt when his lawyer told him Imogen was pressing charges.

"Rape? How can it be rape? She was screaming my name out when we fucked!"

"Screaming for you to stop?"

"No, she definitely wasn't doing that." He spat, allowing himself a little smile, and returned the solicitor's stare with a self-satisfied glare of his own.

"Which name?" the solicitor asked. "Which name was she screaming?"

He looked down. It had been "James", of course.

"Rape by deception..." the lawyer muttered. "She thought she was having sex with someone else."

"Well, she seemed happy enough, whoever she thought she was doing it with."

"Robert, I'm only asking these questions because you'll get them and much worse in court."

"If it gets that far."

But his bravado masked the sensation of powerlessness, like sinking in sludge, like being a kid again at the mercy of the whims of adults who could be kind or sadistic depending on who it was and what mood they were in. It was this that first drove him to seek a career in the police. Having that uniform, that authority, was the most obvious way for someone from his background to have power over his life, and over the lives of others.

...back my name.

The voice jolts him out of his thoughts and memories.

It's high-pitched but sort of a cracked voice, so close it could be inside his ear. How else would it have penetrated his ear-defenders?

He releases the dead man's handle. The engine falls silent.

He takes off his ear-defenders.

Listens out.

Silence.

He wonders if his bike-riding tormentors from earlier have come back to play some prank upon him. There are plenty of hidey holes in this isolated spot, behind tombstones and in shady overgrown corners. Not only is much of the uncut grass almost waist high, but the yew hedges are unkempt and smothered with old man's beard and elder. That's the problem with volunteering for a task like this, a job in a lonely place. Not for the first time, he wonders why he agreed to it; no one else in the parks department wants to do it. With a rather fatalistic kind of symbolism, there's a convention that it's generally those approaching retirement age who work the cemeteries, put out to pasture in a horticultural *memento mori*, as if it's the penultimate stop on life's train journey.

He hears a tapping, like someone knocking insistently on a wooden door, but higher pitched, faster. It's as if someone's trying to remind him of something. Surely it's only the compulsive rhythm of a woodpecker's rapping beak. Better that than a raven or a crow, he supposes. He looks about him, sees the vast expanse of tall grass that still needs cutting. Time to crack on. There's plenty to do and he won't finish it off standing around.

He thought he might take this job slowly, draw it out so it might fill a couple of days, but he's beginning to think he'd like to get it done and out of the way today so he doesn't have to come back tomorrow.

He glances down and sees it. There it is again.

James Albert Dance.

It can't be in two places at once. Two different corpses

with the same name perhaps? Another unlikely coincidence, and anyway the date and mawkish message are the same:

    17th April 1964 – 21st November 1968
    Sleeps with the angels.

He must have gone back on himself. That's what it's like, mowing sites like this, sometimes going round and round in ever-decreasing circles, or backwards and forwards like a mental patient compulsively pacing up and down a hospital corridor. After a while it all blends into one, the graves included.

And always this sentimental fluff about "sleep". So many of those under the earth here "fell asleep" according to the carved writing on their headstones, a phrase that contains the disquieting suggestion that they might wake up.

As he ventures deeper into the cemetery, down to the unkempt yew hedge that divides this realm of the dead from the world of the living, he sees movement in one of the elder bushes overhanging this dark corner where the graves are so close together he can barely guide the mower between them. He ignores it at first, thinking it must be the wind or a small animal such as a fox disturbed by the intrusion of his infernal machine. But then he thinks he can hear that human voice again, high and cracked, just audible over the roar of the mower's engine.

He releases the dead man's handle, allowing the machine to fall silent again, to listen for the voice.

Nothing.

He really must be losing his mind.

The mower refuses to restart this time, as if punishing him for his foolish credulity. Perhaps it's just as well. He'll need a strimmer to do most of this area with its jam-packed tombstones. He begins dragging the machine's battered carapace back over the uneven ground towards the path that leads to the churchyard entrance where he parked the van, hoping those kids who taunted him haven't vandalized it. But before he reaches the van he hears that squeaky voice again.

Give me back my name.

"Can't do that." His own voice sounds alien to him, swallowed up by the overgrown vegetation. "I've already done it. Stopped calling myself that years ago."

He hears a faint childish chuckle. Must be one of those damned brats laughing at him for talking to himself. He feels hotly ashamed, addressing a voice that must be internal. The laughter's high-pitched but cracking like an adolescent voice breaking, or one coming from a mouth choking on graveyard soil.

The brittle chuckling continues. Sounds like his foolishness is cracking someone up. Or maybe *he's* just cracking up.

Again, an elder bush shifts as if stirred by the wind, even though there is none. The air is still as death. He glimpses what could be a small boy's fragile form tottering towards him, but he can't be sure – the figure's half-hidden behind leaves and branches. Then small hands push the springy branches aside to reveal the hint of a face.

The little of it he sees is enough to make him step back in horror. His ankle catches on the low iron railing around one of the graves. He stumbles backwards. Falls onto a horizontal stone slab with a fissure bisecting it. Time seems to slow down as his weight splits the whole thing apart and he feels himself being sucked down into the earth. The thought of becoming trapped under the slab, with loose soil pouring into his mouth, spurs him to scrabble for purchase on the sides, but it isn't enough. It only makes things worse.

The pressure of his flailing legs and pummelling feet on the two pieces of stone slab force them open like a twin trapdoor, and he falls between them, the two pieces forming a lethal V that start to crush his chest and spine in a pincer movement. Hot panic shoots through him, his breathing comes out in laboured gasps as if his lungs are anticipating the asphyxiation that awaits him should he succumb to the gravity inexorably pulling him down into the grave.

Sykes looks around wildly for a potential rescuer, calling out in a strangled voice. He'd even take help off that brat, despite the hideous face he glimpsed bobbing above its tiny body. But he can't see the child now. Maybe it's behind him. The idea of it being there, out of sight, unable to see it approach or whatever it's doing, is almost more frightening than the prospect of meeting it face to face. He ignores the stabbing pain in his chest, pushing from his mind the image of a splintered rib piercing his lungs. Bracing himself against this agony he twists around to look behind. But all he sees is another eulogy to a somnolent departed relative, and his movement only hastens his descent into the crushing maw.

Hysterically, he wonders if these people who allegedly "fell asleep" were even actually dead when interred. He imagines eyes opening in stifling blackness, shredded fingernails clawing at smooth, nailed-down oak, lungs fighting for diminishing air under tons of soil – a fate he may be about to share the way things are going.

This prospect gives more urgency to his plight. His adrenaline goes into overdrive as he steels himself to break free. Endorphins mask the pain of ribs he silently prays are merely bruised rather than broken. His feet bicycle the subsiding soil in the grave, like those of a drowning man treading water, in a futile attempt to find a foothold, but he feels his strength failing. The only things preventing him from sinking right into the grave are the crushing slabs and his own sweat-slippery hands grasping the railings on the edge of the tomb.

He hears the death-rattle of loose soil beneath him, shifting, dropping. But there is a glimmer of hope: the easing of the pressure on him from the pieces of slab, which have opened a little wider in response to his descent, no longer crushing him so much, and now beginning to release his torso from their deadly embrace.

Using the grave's iron railings, he's able to lever himself up out of its maw, pulling his legs up through the gap, then using his feet to push himself out of it and on top of one of the pieces of slab, which supports him just long enough to escape before they slide back into the black chasm below. He rolls over onto the grass next to the grave, flopping face down on the ground, sucking at the air like a landed fish, tasting fragments of dirt and dust between his teeth, probably from the slabs that just almost crushed him.

Flailing around for a purchase to raise himself from the ground, he senses someone or something looming over him. At first, he thinks it's the mower, which he left there when he tumbled into the yawning grave. But there are two shadows on the ground below him. The human one is about the same height as the mower's. He hears a crackly little chuckle before it speaks.

Give me back my name, and you can...

He turns to face this newcomer. Short plump legs in white socks and buckled shoes, the kind a small child would have worn decades ago. Sykes raises his head to take in the short flannel trousers and mouse-coloured duffel coat. The clothes remind him of his own childhood in the late sixties and early seventies. Finally, he makes himself look the figure full in the face...

Give me back my name, and you can have your...

While the body is that of a child, the face is something else entirely. His first glimpse of it made him back away, and his second closer look almost has him repeating his pratfall into the grave, the yawning grave beside him. It's a dreadful old man's face, thunderhead purple, twisted with malevolence and hate, a recipe leavened and soured with terror and panic and bitterness and loneliness. Stark lines fracture its features into a monument to trench warfare, while the eyes blaze with a pitiless lustre.

It's like looking in a mirror, but one that enables you to see yourself anew.

Give me back my name, and you can have your face back!

Sykes' hands move instinctively to his face, as if to check it's still there, which it is of course. He laughs at himself for ever thinking otherwise, and at the figure for suggesting its absence, causing pain to complain loudly in his injured chest. The chin feels smoother than it ought to.

"You're welcome to it!" he snarls at the child with his face, laughing with hysterical relief at his escape, heedless of the agonies this drives through his crushed chest. "Anyway, like I said, it's not mine to give. Gave it up years ago..."

He fires up the John Deere C52 KS and shouts, "You can have it!"

Coffin dodger, the figure taunts him in its dry chuckling voice.

Knuckles white with rage on the dead man's handle, he drives the mower straight at the figure, expecting it to disperse into the dust it came from. Because that's what it is, he decides, an hallucination brought on by the heat and the dust from the dry grass, forming into a small human shape, acting upon his brain. But when the mower is about to strike the figure, which he now sees wears a grey hooded top, not a mousey duffel coat after all, it pleads with him.

Sorry Mister I was just joking please don't please...!

Yet he keeps going, knocking the ghost-child to the ground. He feels the blade catch on cloth and snag on flesh and grind on bone as he forces the mower over the lumps of a body that twitches and whimpers. *This won't do the chassis any good*, he thinks ruefully, *but it is what it is*.

Eventually, he gets the John Deere back to the van. It looks a sorry state. Battered to fuck, and it'll need a steam clean to get the blood off. He climbs into the cab and adjusts the rear-view mirror to check his reflection. He touches his chin too, which still feels way too smooth. But it would do, he realises, as he sees a four-year-old child's face staring back at him.

Cuckoo Flower

14/04/22: 06.43
Always Use the Correct Nozzle, Lucy!
Yes, it sounds a bit obvious. I should know this by now. But sometimes I still need reminding, especially at those times when I haven't been sleeping too well.

So here's a recap on the importance of using the correct nozzle in my line of work. Full cone for spot treatments, deflectors for overall coverage. You wouldn't catch me using one of these for fungicide or insecticide work, especially not after I'd used it for weedkilling. That way madness lies. Not to mention, killing the patient. You can triple rinse, quadruple rinse, quintuple rinse, and there's still a chance there might be some herbicide left in the knapsack and on the nozzle. Maybe just a single droplet, but at the strength I'm using the consequences could be catastrophic.

In any case, that would be the wrong sort of nozzle. You use *hollow* cones for fungicides and insecticides, for a finer droplet spray.

For this job, I'm using an air induction nozzle, also known as a bubble jet. It draws air into the liquid stream, reducing the number of smaller droplets and aerating the larger ones to aid their dispersal. I need maximum coverage for this job, with as little drift as possible. The last thing I want is off-target application, especially given the product I'm using, but I do want to make sure I hit the target crop.

Hard.

This time I'm going to kill it outright.

14/04/22: 07.12
The World According to Terence Quick

I remember the man who taught me all I know about nozzles and knapsack sprayers.

Terence Quick, with his round pink smiling face: a cricket ball with steel-rimmed spectacles. That was how I thought of his head, the smile curving around it as though following its circumference. Grey fleece over a shirt and tie, above grey Sta-Prest slacks. After each pearl of wisdom had dropped from his lips he'd sit back in his chair and clasp his hands over his stomach, smile that satisfied smile, and ask the assembled students in his gently modulated Devonshire lilt the rhetorical question: "Are you happy with that?"

How I hated him.

But I did so in the same way as I hated my driving instructor, a man I came close to punching on one occasion.

And like my driving instructor, he got me through the test.

14/04/22: 07.46
Pre-Start Checks, Lucy!

I'm out into the jungle again soon. When I say "jungle", I mean the polytunnel.

But not before I've carried out the pre-start checks. Again, this is kindergarten stuff which I nearly forgot in my eagerness to get cracking.

First, having donned the Operator's Protective Garments, white disposable coverall, teal nitrile gloves, steel-toe-capped rubber boots, mask and respirator, you depressurise the tank to make sure no residue of a previous application lingers in the lance, which would leak out when you remove it to check the filter inside the hose.

Then you proceed to the dry checks. Examining the outside of the tank for cracks or abrasions, checking the pump handle is working correctly, removing the lid to examine the filter and the inside of the tank, including the pressure chamber as well as the lid itself. When replacing the lid, it's important to ensure you don't cross-thread it. To do so would mean leaks and possible contamination, to yourself, the ground around your feet, and quite probably the water table beneath, too, especially if you're carrying out your checks near a drain, as well you might be.

Because next come the wet checks.

You fill the tank with six litres of water and repressurise the tank. This should reveal any leaks you haven't spotted with your visual inspection. Assuming there are none, proceed to the pattern check, spraying a sample into a measuring jug with the nozzle in a vertical position so you can see if the water's fanning out evenly. If it doesn't, if it splutters and makes a mess of the whole thing, it could mean there's some blockage in the system and you need to go back to the drawing board. If not, you're good to go for a practice swathe on the concrete to ensure it's giving a good even spread. But first you have to pick the tank up, shaking it at a forty-five degree angle to see if the water splashes out from any hitherto undetected leaks.

You are now ready to calibrate your applicator!

Are you happy with that?

The way I'm going I won't be started before eight—

15/04/22
A *Round-Up (Get It?) of the Arguments*
For and Against Glyphosate

I didn't rule out glyphosate to begin with. Arguably it is effective against *Reynoutria japonica*. That's Japanese knotweed for any lay person or persons who might read this. I say "arguably", because there is a 2014 report by Rosemary Mason suggesting the notorious weed has developed resistance to Monsanto's flagship product. The report's full of wild claims and political rhetoric amid some pertinent arguments, at one point asking, somewhat bizarrely, "Why does David Cameron hate Wales?"

I imagine Terence Quick's response to such a document.

His lips would curl upwards at the corners until his smile curved around the contours of his face like the stitching around a cricket ball. Perhaps he'd make some quip about tree huggers or knotweed fanciers, and we, his students, would all laugh along. We were there to learn how to use such substances after all. He'd raise a hand to still our laughter, reminding us there *are* dangers associated with such chemicals, even comparatively harmless ones like glyphosate! Such hazards, he'd go on to say, are the reason why we must take extra care to follow the COSHH assessments, check the specifications on the product label, carry out the right calculations on the calibration charts, fill in the application records, et cetera. Blah blah blah. Never mind the COSHH assessments, I felt well and truly under the cosh when I underwent the training under Quick's tutelage.

Returning to the 2014 report.

While Mason may sound like a tin-foil-hat-wearing crank from my previous comments, she does have letters after her name and so I don't dismiss all her findings out of hand, despite some of her more eccentric outbursts. The main thrust of her argument goes something like this: glyphosate was originally patented as an antibiotic, but it also kills off beneficial bacteria in the guts of human beings. Hence her concerns about traces finding their way into the food chain via spraying on or near vegetables. Then there's the issue she raises about Japanese knotweed's resistance to this herbicide, leading to its re-emergence as a "super weed". After a concerted large-scale attempt to eradicate the plant using glyphosate in Adirondack National Park, Upstate New York, persistent regrowth despite the treatment led to experiments on rhizomes from historically treated and untreated sites. These trials, recorded in August 2015 at the ESA Centenary Annual Meeting in Baltimore, seem to confirm this pattern of resistance.

When I tried glyphosate on the as-yet-unnamed plant I discovered in the Philippines, the results were initially most satisfactory. A polytunnel containing about two thousand square metres (that's roughly half-an-acre in old money) of lush shining vibrant green plants with their unusual red globe-like flowers, slowly turning to brittle grey-brown husks.

Well, that was easy, I thought.

It may well be asked, why was I so keen to find a way of destroying this plant in the first place, to the extent that I brought back specimen samples with me to England in order first to cultivate it, then subject it to various herbicides.

I'm not sure I can answer that one, except to say I was fascinated by the plant.

During my field trip to the Philippines, I noticed the invasive nature of the plant, which the locals called the "Cuckoo Flower". Its ability to overwhelm and suppress all the other competition made Japanese knotweed, let alone bindweed or old man's beard, look like a timid shrinking violet by comparison.

Cultivating it under test conditions was not a problem. I soon found it had easily colonised the polytunnel.

And the glyphosate seemed to have done the trick when it came to killing it off.

Or so I believed.

Plants Playing Possum?

I went in there six days after the application to remove the withered stalks, which were shrouded in a fine powdery mist of dead, decaying plant matter. That's when I noticed the patch of green under the dead brown skin of one of them, peeling away like a flake of paint as I began to tug it out.

I stopped pulling before the roots became loose, not that this would have happened easily. I could feel the plant resisting my exertions, as if the harder I pulled, the stronger the roots held on, pulling back with equal and opposite vigour, my sweat-slick hands sliding off the slippery stalks in the intense humidity in there. At first I dismissed this as my imagination, until I saw the green.

Perhaps I should have gone ahead and ripped it out then and there, the others too, piled them onto a bonfire and turned a flame thrower on them. Then again, I'm not certain it would have done any good.

All my wrestling with one of the plants seemed to make it greener. I wondered if the plant was reviving. Then I realised it was worse than that. It wasn't coming back to life as I pulled. It was just that more scraps of dead brown skin were falling off as I did so, exposing the green underneath. It had never died. It just wanted me to think so. The brown shrivelling, the grey dust, they weren't symptoms of chemical poisoning.

They were a disguise. It's a phenomenon known in the biological lexicon as thanatosis, a concept from zoology rather than botany.

Or to put it another way, the things were playing possum.

Maybe they sensed that if they did this I'd go away, leave them alone long enough for them to, I don't know – it seems insane when I write it down – make their escape.

As soon as they sensed this stratagem had failed, the scales fell away. All five hundred or so gorgeous abominations emerged in their luscious treacherous glory. I'm aware my language is becoming somewhat unscientific, but those words came into my head as I watched them standing there, stately and triumphant, like a phoenix from the ashes, times five hundred. Their glossy green leaves stretched out and their deep red globe flowers bobbed above a carpet of papery mothwing shrouds, lying there like a child's discarded Halloween costume, or lovers' strewn clothes.

~~~

Yes, I really must temper my language.

It's all there in the photos attached to the official document for anyone who really wants to look. With any luck, that's the only place they'll be able to see them.

Looking at those globes, I think again of Quick's cricket-ball head. Maybe I should name the plant after him, something ending with *globosa terenciana*.

I suppose I should name it after me too: so *Luciana globosa terenciana*. In shape, the red flowers do resemble the yellow ones on a *Buddleia globosa*, the more commonplace buddleia's less invasive relative.

Are you happy with that, Lucy?

Hmmm. Not sure I am.

If my suspicions about these plants (?) are correct, maybe I'm not so happy to have my name attached to them.

29/04/22
When is a Plant Not a Plant?

I think I've killed them this time. It's been two weeks now, and they really, *really* are dead. The paraquat did the trick.

Are you happy with that, Lucy?

Yes, I know. It's banned in the EU. Not that this country takes any notice of that these days, but the government's hankering after the good old days of lax health and safety standards hasn't quite filtered through to reintroducing such things onto the market here. Good thing I smuggled some in when I returned from the Philippines. Clever of me, eh, Terence?

Well, I thought I was very clever until I went back home for the first time in days and read reports of other botanists first sourcing and transplanting, then taking similar measures against, these plants all over the world. My first reaction was to feel a bit put out that I hadn't been the first to discover this new plant, as I'd thought. I should have published and peer-reviewed my findings before I destroyed the plants. Not very rigorous scientific practice, Lucy! But I have been under a lot of strain with these plants (if they are plants). It might have affected my judgement. Maybe I was a little hasty. Or maybe…

Yes, I know this is going to sound insane, and I can imagine how Terence would react if I came up with a theory like this in his class. He'd give a smug little smirk and hold it up to the ridicule of the rest of the students.

Wouldn't you Terence? Well, you're not here now, are you? So you wouldn't understand what's happening to me, that I'm starting to think the plants (if they are plants) are playing tricks with my mind.

Then it hit me.

When it did, I knew I'd have to rush back to the polytunnel in the middle of the night.

Yes, I'd better do that —

30/04/22: 00.16

Empty.

My first thought was that the application was so strong it didn't just kill the *Luciana* (I still think of them as that, whatever the other botanists might call it – as if it's *my* discovery, my creation even, to my pride or perhaps shame…). Maybe the paraquat destroyed it utterly, so all the plants rapidly decomposed and disintegrated.

To nothing?

Well, why not? After all, I did use all the paraquat in the bottle. Well, not quite all, but over half.

But I didn't really believe this hypothesis.

I shone my torch around the polytunnel, my hands shaking, making the disc of light bounce and judder over the shining plastic, finally falling to the earth to illuminate the empty space. There was no trace, not even a fine powder to indicate the plants had once been there. Just bare soil.

I wondered if a gang of thieves came and dug up the crop. The plants might be extremely valuable to some collector or rival botanist, even dead! But there were no footprints in the soil, no marks at all apart from where I surmised the roots came free. The disturbance in the earth was minimal, suggesting it wasn't the result of hardened criminals hurriedly and messily digging over a plot to drag my *Luciana* from the ground, but of something gently, patiently easing the roots free from their earthly prison.

Maybe even something easing its own roots out.

But that's ridiculous. Plants can't move. They're not animals.

Or maybe that's what they want me to think. Just like they wanted me to think they were dead. And I was certain they *were* dead! I cut layers and layers away from a random selection of the brown husks to check there was no green hidden underneath. And if they were animals, that would be bloody agony!

~~~

And yet … they're gone, Lucy.

Maybe you didn't really want to kill them at all, your precious *Luciana*. Maybe you just told yourself they were dead to make yourself feel better about your recklessness in cultivating them.

Oh, stop this! They say talking to yourself is the first sign of madness. Who knows what that makes writing to yourself…? But is it any more insane than the other ideas I'm entertaining? Such as, if a plant could feign death, that would be the ultimate camouflage.

Not quite the ultimate.

Now, if an animal could pretend to be a plant…

I must stop thinking like this.

~~~

I'd shone the torch around the field looking out for signs of movement, perhaps thieves making off in a van full of dead plants. The shaft of light did pick out something moving. It looked at first like a human head bobbing in the beam, round and red like Terence Quick's but completely featureless. So, the plants *did* escape!

Ridiculous, I told myself.

I thought the more likely explanation was that some seed escaped from the polytunnel when I opened the door and started a new infestation outside.

30/04/22: ?

Well, I could deal with that tomorrow – there was still that almost half a bottle of paraquat left.

No, not now. There was still some paraquat remaining in the bottle. It's empty now. Because of what I saw outside the polytunnel.

I'm waiting for it to take effect so I won't have to live with the consequences of what I've done. I wave the torch around again. More of the bobbing heads appear to blush in its light. Hundreds of them. I don't know what frightens me more: the thought of them departing the polytunnel *en masse*, or the idea of them reproducing so quickly in such large numbers to replace the dead or missing ones. Or maybe it's the manner in which the male plant pollinates the female that leaves me sickened and desperate. As I watch and listen I imagine the creatures' glossy-green trunks swelling as they gestate. I hope the whispering sighs I hear come from the friction of leaf brushing against leaf, stem grinding, rubbing against stem, flower kissing red spherical flower, rather than from those obscenities expressing the pleasure of their writhing, with something approximating to actual vocal cords.

Now I'm the one blushing and gasping at the sight and the sounds, feeling faintly horribly aroused, as well as nauseous, even enviously thinking, *Well,* somebody's *getting it...* And thanks to my final libation in this lonely place, I've now guaranteed I'll die never once having experienced what they were enjoying, the joy of mutual carnality.

I think about this as I observe the cuckoo plants, no longer caring that I know what manner of beings they really are, much less that I'm observing their dalliance, not really blushing at all, altogether heedless of me, so passionately wrapped up in each other as they wantonly copulate on the bare, dirty earth.

It shouldn't be long now.

I hope the pain isn't too terrible.

Professor Beehive Addresses the Human Biology Class

"Ah, things were so much simpler back then," mused Shawcroft.

"Back in the day." I smiled, swirling the whisky around in the tumbler: a fine single malt.

He hadn't aged well but he disguised it reasonably effectively: hair combed back slickly over his pale domed scalp; round glasses with tortoise-shell frames encircling his eyes hiding the worst ravages of middle age; a dove-grey pinstriped double-breasted suit, immaculately pressed, with a white handkerchief folded into a perfect triangle nestling in the top pocket and a pink carnation in the buttonhole. All no doubt intended to convey the impression of the dapper man-about-town. The impression I formed was more overweight Bertie Wooster gone to seed, a man out of place in this age.

But I was the one who looked incongruous in his club. I was surprised they let me in at all. No small amount of special pleading on my behalf persuaded its gatekeepers to relax the admission code.

"Back in the day," he echoed, his eyes so misty behind those circular lenses that I could imagine them steaming up and making his blue eyes look more watery than they already were.

I sensed where this was heading. Shawcroft was going to wax lyrical about our time at B— School, "the best days of our lives" or something of the sort. I carried on smiling vacantly. I knew that kind of thing was expected of me. I wouldn't be here otherwise. Just as I wouldn't have been there had it not been co-educational.

"So, did you go into Classics in the end, Henry?" I asked, remembering his close bond with our Latin master George Beattie, or "Professor Beehive", as we called him – because of the way he droned on, of course, his voice a low burr that buzzed on the sibilants. But Shawcroft didn't join in with the name-calling.

Shawcroft had his own nickname among the rest of the class: "The Postman". Beehive was always sending him off on errands, usually to Rutland Sandhurst, Head of Science. Shawcroft was one of the few pupils he managed to recruit to take a Latin A Level. Beehive's air of indifference and soporific tones sent most of us to sleep until he would wake us with a snap of his ruler on the desk of whichever miscreant was unfortunate enough to attract his attention by snoring or other obvious signs of slumber. Sometimes the steel rule caught the edge of a carelessly placed finger, adding the reputation of a sting to the rationale for his moniker. Perhaps he knew what we called him because he also wore a yellow-and-black striped tie.

The Postman never slept in class. He seemed captivated by Professor Beehive's honeyed words. So much so that the Latin Master lined up his protégé for an academic career in the field, hence my inquiry. Of course, it was well-known that Mr Beattie preferred Greek to Latin. However, this subject wasn't on the curriculum at our relatively middle-brow co-educational private school. So he took Shawcroft under his wing, giving the boy personal tuition in Ancient Greek language and literature, art and culture, civilisation and, of course, philosophy. The rest of us mere mortals had to make do with *amo, amas, amat,* taught by rote in that monotonous voice of his. I often thought it was his own boredom at instructing us in the language of what he perhaps saw as the less intellectual of the two ancient civilisations that rubbed off on us, and coaxed us into a light doze in that stuffy room.

Shawcroft still didn't answer my question. He was

gazing distractedly around the vast room, its oak panelling lined with portraits of old men, some in black suits, some in ermine gowns; and the wooden shields from which the heads of big cats stared glassily, each one frozen in a roar more shocked than fearsome, as if petrified in mid-leap through the wall.

"Not everything has changed," I suggested, following his eyes with my own, as they took in Sir Robert Walpole, William Pitt the Younger, Gladstone, Disraeli – prime ministers punctuated by pumas and panthers. Despite their blunter dentistry and better-manicured fingernails, these civilised men seemed somehow redder in tooth-and-claw than the beneficiaries of the taxidermist's art on either side of them.

Perhaps that was the idea.

"But did you…?"

"Carry on with Classics?" His eyes finally met mine again, almost as glassy as those in the heads lining the wall, if more mobile. "No." And he gave a little shiver, enough to stir his handkerchief and make it tremble like a ghost. He straightened it, then reached for the black iron poker to stir the embers in the vast fireplace that served our huddled oxblood armchairs, before using a pair of tongs to place another log on the fire. "Don't you find you feel the cold more as you get older…?"

I shook my head. "I'm outside a lot in my line of work. Must have made me immune to it, I suppose."

He nodded and I noticed him peering at me as if checking for traces of dirt on my clothes. Our chance meeting on the street had seen him as immaculately turned out as ever – and me in my mud-spattered work clothes. "Ah, Robin! What a turnup for the books! How the devil are you, old friend?" Etcetera, etcetera. We exchanged phone numbers and agreed to continue the reunion in these more salubrious surroundings, where Shawcroft's ministrations now reinvigorated the fire, its flames now infusing his tense-looking face with a sickly lustre.

"Well, I'm *not* immune," he muttered. "As for the Classics – I eventually decided … they weren't for me. Went into the family firm of stockbrokers instead."

"I see." I stared at the flames a moment. "But you and Beehive?"

"Like the Greek Civilisation and the Roman Empire: ancient history. Let's just say I rather lost interest in the field once I was away from his influence."

The fire was roaring now. Its blazing reflection in his glasses made it impossible to make out his eyes anymore so I couldn't see if the faint smile on his lips reached them.

"And how about you, Robin? What are *you* doing with yourself these days then?"

He'd successfully deflected the focus of the "catching up" back to me just before I could protest something along the lines of: *But what really happened? You were all set for Oxbridge!* That had been the talk of the common room, though it was generally acknowledged this future was only possible for Shawcroft with the benefit of Professor Beehive's tutelage.

"I'm a gardener." I smiled.

He blinked.

"Oh really? Where?"

"Back at our *alma mater*," I replied, watching to see if his smile slipped. It didn't but I still couldn't see what his eyes were doing. "Funny how one's life goes round in circles sometimes."

"Indeed," he agreed, and I wondered if he was thinking the same as I was, that this trite little phrase referred as much to this impromptu get-together as to my employment situation. "So, what's happened to Old Gruntworth? I'd have thought he'd have retired by now!"

"If Grimesworth ever retired I think he'd fall down dead on the spot. Some people… It's just their work that's holding bodies and souls together, I sometimes think. But what was it some of the prefects used to say about him? '*He* knows where the bodies are buried'." I mimicked an exaggeratedly deep but recently broken adolescent male voice, full of bravado and affected worldly wisdom. Seeing the look on Shawcroft's face I swiftly added: "They meant metaphorically, of course."

"Quite… But how did you end up in the gardening game – and back at the old school, to boot?"

~~~

Grimesworth was that all right (*I began*). "Old school", I mean. When I first started on the school gang, he was still mowing the playing fields by hand with a giant Mastiff. That's a lawn mower, by the way, not a grass-eating dog: a pedestrian cylinder machine. It wasn't just that he felt that a "proper groundsman" oughtn't to rotary cut the playing fields of such an illustrious establishment as B—, with its reputation for producing world-class sportsmen at the rate Bernard Matthews churns out turkey burgers. After all, the grounds maintenance department long ago invested in a Hayter ride-on lawn mower, as well as a tractor with cylinder attachments. But Grimesworth also insisted on box-cutting all eleven football pitches, and the fifteen rugger ones, too. That was one thing neither the tractor nor the Hayter could do, just scattering the grass about for someone to rake up, something no one ever had time to do. While Grimesworth was the head gardener, those gigantic machines lay idle, mothballed in the shed. If anyone objected he just grunted at them, a characteristic sufficiently well-known among the student body to warrant his nickname.

To begin answering your question, Henry, remember I was a day pupil and my home village was a twenty minute drive from the school, public transport pretty much non-existent. My common entrance results didn't merit a full scholarship though my parents unsuccessfully petitioned the Bursar for a reduction in fees. They managed to find a lift to the school for me with a local chap who worked near it, a softly spoken Welshman named Tony Llewellyn, who lectured at the nearby sixth form college and whose son

David was an apprentice with the school grounds maintenance gang. David was as quiet and unassuming as his father, with hair in the fashion many young men wore it in those days, short and parted at the front and sides, shoulder length at the back.

Our journey took us over the Somerset levels, often shrouded in pale mist and crisp frost. As you said, things were so much simpler then. Men were men, and winters were winters. None of this identity politics and global warming nonsense to muddy the waters, eh, Henry? Llewellyn dropped us both near the gardeners' mess room, where I remained until the school opened and lessons began, with nothing to do but stand there shivering as I watched them stoically getting ready to carry out their daily tasks. That was how I first met Grimesworth, still a relatively spry forty-three years old then. He took pity on me on the coldest days, inviting me to wait in the mess room and warm myself for a while by the three-bar electric fire that heated their quarters.

"I was worried there'd be icicles forming under your nose if you stood out there much longer," he'd say as I thawed by the damp donkey jackets drying near the fire.

At first I felt awkward standing in the corner as the taciturn men sat on their sofas, reading newspapers whose brash garishness was a stranger to my parents' breakfast table. But as time went on I overcame my shyness enough to ask them questions about the work. Grimesworth in particular took a great deal of pleasure in answering me, perhaps seeing in me the germs of an interest that would eventually lead me back to this place.

In the end, I began to feel I belonged more there in that mess room than I did in the classroom. It's not easy being one of the few day pupils in a school populated mainly by boarders. I often yearned to be one, imagining it was like one long slumber party. In particular, I solemnly wished I boarded in Ash Tree House, perhaps sharing a dormitory with Diana Harrow, generally agreed to be the loveliest girl in the school. It makes me laugh now to think of how I imagined life in that girls' boarding house – like some sort of softcore version of Malory Towers, populated by nubile young ladies in pale diaphanous nightdresses, playfully exchanging endearments, chastely (or perhaps not!) kissing each other lightly on the mouths, pledging eternal friendship, all shot through a lens tastefully smeared in Vaseline.

~~~

Noticing Shawcroft's beetling eyebrows shoot up from his spectacles, I broke off from my narrative. Perhaps it was time for another drink. I certainly needed more lubrication and it occurred to me that he might need a drop of the hard stuff to help him process what I'd just said. I always suspected he had feelings for me, even at school, and judging by his eagerness to get me alone here he might take my inability to return them rather hard.

He must have taken the hint, at least about the drinks, for he stirred from his seat. His head turning, I saw his eyes for the first time since I'd begun my reminiscences, no longer hidden by the reflected glory of the flames in his glasses.

It wasn't a pretty sight.

"I'll come with you," I said. "See what they've got."

"Very well then," he replied.

He seemed a little put out but after what I'd seen in his eyes there was no way I was going to leave him alone with our drinks. Their purchase took place amid an uneasy silence between us, odd looks passing between him and the barman. There had already been raised eyebrows when I first entered the club at Shawcroft's invitation. He explained at the time that the "fairer sex" were allowed in as guests, but it was unusual to say the least and usually took place under the auspices of a monthly "Lady's Night".

Once we'd returned and settled back into our wing-backed armchairs he broke that silence, saying, "I never believed the rumours about you, Robin. I thought it was all

... you know, children being vicious. I thought perhaps..."

Maybe you didn't want to believe them, I thought. Maybe it pleased you to assume that since no other boys took any interest in me, nor I in them, I was somehow "available" – just because you bothered to talk to me.

~~~

It was hardly the ideal place to come out (*I continued*). I already felt a misfit as a day pupil, lacking that sense of community in shared adversity that comes with boarding. Though I wished I boarded in an unthought-out way, I'm glad I didn't, knowing what I do now.

But as to the rumours, I was terrified someone would find out something to confirm them and it would get back to my parents. So I kept my feelings about Diana Harrow and her long willowy limbs, her dark haunted eyes and darker tresses, to myself, and I made sure you and I were joined at the hip to try and replace those rumours with the one that *we* were an item. It didn't work of course, if anything backfiring horribly but my secret remained safe from my parents. It wasn't their anger that frightened me, rather their disappointment. It hardly mattered. I found other ways of disappointing them after I'd left that place for the first time. I'm talking of course about the manner of my return.

In the highly charged hothouse of the school I felt my slowly gestating inclinations were under constant scrutiny, and not just that of the prurient interest of my own age group, I had sometimes sensed. But the gardener's mess room was a brief sanctuary from that in those chill mornings. Although it was an intensely masculine environment, full of the tang of sweat and tobacco, as well as the sweet aroma of wet cut grass as we drew closer to summer, I never received any inappropriate attention from Grimesworth and his men. While they didn't handle me as a Dresden shepherdess, they respected my girlhood. The only unease came from an uncomfortable sense they were holding back from any uncouthness they felt might offend female ears, an unspoken sense of "Mind your language, boys. There are ladies present..."

As unformed as my sexuality was, there was a clear direction of travel. Perhaps the whispered gossip about it became a self-fulfilling prophecy. The softly gleaming curves glimpsed between certain pages of the gardeners' lurid newspapers were a guilty pleasure. Then there were the stable girls. I couldn't get a lift home with David and his father because they kept different hours, so I had to crouch in the back of Major Bray's Land Rover, listening to his twin sons bickering and snickering in the passenger seat. The major, stiff-lipped, flat-capped, steel-wool haired, ran the school's equestrian centre. As I waited for him to march his tweed-clad square-bashing shoulders out to his mud-spattered bone-rattling vehicle, I stood by the gate surreptitiously watching the stable girls mucking out the stables, jodhpurs chafing against strong thighs. Eventually the Major would bark an order to me to jump in the back of the Land Rover, booting me out of my daydream, leaving me worried he'd caught me staring at his female employees and would say something to my parents. As far as I know he never did, too tightly focussed on his own concerns and keeping to his own regimented routine, I suppose. But at that age, you think everyone can see your most embarrassing inmost thoughts. You think anyone's even interested. It took me years to grow out of that delusion. I still haven't entirely done so but at least I'm aware of it now and can master it.

Do you remember Mr Sandhurst's human biology classes? No, I don't suppose you do. You managed to skip them in order to pursue personal tuition in the Classics with Mr Beattie, to almost universal bewilderment. Why would anyone want to be excused from such a joyous occasion? Most saw the class as an opportunity to snigger at its subject matter and to speculate amusingly on the perversions of its teacher. For he too had a nickname. And when I remember that, it's part of the reason I'm thankful

I never got my wish to be a resident of Ash Tree House. For "Randy Sandy" was the housemaster there.

There was one time you graced that class with your presence, the time Sandhurst invited Beehive to address it. But you weren't there for the sessions that led up to it, and perhaps you weren't even aware of his nickname, insulated by your special status from the cut-and-thrust of the classroom banter that reigned supreme under Sandhurst's tutelage. That lascivious white-haired old fox! I can't imagine any self-respecting institution putting him in charge of Ash Tree's hen house now. But as you said, things were so much simpler back then. Obviously not simple enough for him, though, because he ended up in jail.

So you missed out on the bawdy farce that passed for sex education when Sandhurst was in charge. I particularly remember one occasion when Diana Harrow was the centrepiece of the entertainment, though I'd rather not recall it in detail. That was when farce nudged against tragedy. Let's just move on from it actually…

~~~

"Another drink?" Shawcroft offered, seeing my head in my hand, covering my face.

"No. No thanks." I was aware my voice sounded brittle, even a little snappy.

"Are you all right?" he asked.

"Yes. Fine. I'll be okay in just a moment."

"Look, if you don't want to talk about it…"

"No, it's all right. The incident you witnessed – Professor Beehive holding forth about Aristophanes and hermaphrodites and so on – doesn't make a lot of sense without it. So I'll tell you what happened."

I mastered the emotions threatening to overwhelm me, then continued.

~~~

The previous lesson, we'd dissected the genitals of a female rat, lying spreadeagled in some kind of sickly yellowish fluid. Predictably, some pupils had to excuse themselves in order to vomit. Even more predictably, much was made of the girls doing this, proof of the weakness and sentimentality of our kind even though plenty of boys succumbed to nausea, too. The hardier ones mocked these weaklings as honorary females, and I was quietly proud of myself that I didn't fulfil the stereotypical expectations of my sex, though a little disappointed in Diana, to see her making a rapid exit for the girls' toilets. I'd always thought – or perhaps hoped – she was made of sterner stuff than that.

I was still congratulating myself on my fortitude at the beginning of the following lesson when I saw a group of boys huddling around James Snodgrass, who was entertaining them with his latest cartoon. Some shot surreptitious glances in my direction. Snodgrass was generally considered a loser but had managed to ingratiate himself with the school's alpha male caste thanks to his abilities as a draughtsman, in particular his uncanny talent as a caricaturist.

From the glimpses I could make out, his latest masterpiece was a parody of *Snow White and the Seven Dwarfs*, featuring myself in the starring role and the grounds maintenance gang as my miniature companions – with a crudely obscene twist. These horticultural dwarfs were servicing "Snow White" in various ways, those unable to find room at her temple waiting in line, jaws slack and drooling, eyes wide and eager, pendulous-tongued, and priapic. It seemed my attempts to quell any rumours of my Sapphic orientation had been all too successful leading them to redirect their lewd speculations in another direction.

Shuddering internally and burning with sick shame at the vile drawing, but determined not to show it, I lowered my eyes. I could feel theirs on me, hearing gleeful whispers to the effect that Snodgrass had struck comedy gold in the form of my scarlet cheeks. At that moment, Sandhurst strutted through the door, crow's wing gown flapping.

Snodgrass quickly hid the artwork under his exercise book and his fan club rushed back to their nearby desks. But far from frowning suspiciously or raising a questioning eyebrow at the conspiratorial clatter generated by their hurried return to their places, the biology master smirked indulgently at boys being boys. Perhaps he noticed me looking at him, for he wiped the grin from his mouth and, as if he had forgotten himself, swiftly assumed a more serious expression, though there was still a glint of mockery in the cold blue eyes.

"Well, class," he began, "I trust you've all recovered from the effects of last week's practical." He paused to allow time for laughter, then raised a long-fingered hand to silence it. "A scientist must subdue human feelings to the greater good of … acquiring knowledge. Diana Harrow, step forward please."

She did so, obediently, ignoring the wolf whistles and catcalls from the group who'd huddled around Snodgrass. Her hips swayed as she did so but she wasn't playing to the gallery. It was just the way she always walked. I could see from the frightened expression she tried to master when she turned to face us that she took no pleasure in this attention. In that moment I knew she was terrified of Sandhurst. She stood there, staring straight ahead as he circled her, his arms clasped behind his back like an army officer inspecting an unkempt subordinate.

"Diana here has been to matron a few times with her little ailments lately," he said in sardonic tones. "I'm wondering if it's an attempt to avoid certain duties required of her around Ash Tree House. Or it might just be a reaction to last week's practical. Then again, it might be something else… Who knows? The workings of the female body, indeed the female mind, are a mysterious thing. Consider Diana Harrow…"

He circled closer now, his right hand extended, so he could almost touch the sweeping curve of her hip. If he was another pupil, one of the boys that is, it struck me he would certainly have broken the "six-inch rule".

There was complete silence from the previously rowdy class.

"Still a girl, mentally, emotionally and ... legally. Yet according to my observations, physically a woman. What is the reason for her sickness, eh?"

He regarded her for a moment, his eyes fish-like, wide, pale and unblinking. The breathless hush continued before he went on. "Unfortunately, I can't cut her open like our poor rodent friend to discover it."

This he almost spat out, and I saw her eyes widen, her lips parted in a sobbing gasp. Poor Diana. I could hear the antique radiator ticking like a bomb, then: "Sit down, Diana," he said, as if in disgusted despair at her. "Carry on, class. Write up last week's practical. I have some ... errands to run."

And with that he was gone in a blur of black, his face the bruised purple of thunderheads, distorted by who knew what passions. As Diana stumbled back to her desk, a wounded thing, she passed close to mine. Impulsively, for I'd never plucked up courage to speak to her before, I whispered, "Well, I thought you were very brave, Diana."

I regretted it immediately. As if my attempt at kindness were the final pressure on the crack in the dam made by others' cruelty, she burst into floods of tears.

"Oh well done, Ribena," hissed Felicity Mordant, using a nickname I acquired when my first period began unexpectedly in the girl's changing rooms and I had to beg her and her chums for a sanitary towel. "Now look what you've done!"

The Mordant clique then began ostentatiously comforting her. They clucked around her in a sisterly cluster, occasionally turning their heads pointedly towards me, shooting me venomous glances. I could just make out Diana between them, her face covered with a curtain of hair. For the rest of the class I did not dare to look at her.

Perhaps I should have done, for it was the last time I ever saw her.

~~~

Finally, noticing I'd paused again in my reminiscences, Shawcroft cleared his throat. "Well, I expect you'll be needing another drink after that," he offered.

"I'll get them," I said.

He opened his mouth to object, but he could see from my expression I was adamant. I knew I couldn't really afford the club's prices but after what I'd seen in his eyes before, I wasn't going to let him buy the next round.

When I returned from the bar and settled back into my armchair, I asked him, "Did Beehive discuss with you what he was going to say to us?"

"A little," Shawcroft ventured, avoiding my gaze.

"Well?" I persisted. "What did he say?"

He sighed. "I don't know, Robin. I mean ... I can't remember."

"Come now, Henry. You *were* their little go-between, after all!"

"Yes, yes, yes, like in the Hartley novel. But 'the past is a foreign country' and all that, and... Well, rather like the chap in that, I was a bit too young to understand what was going on. Those messages they passed to each other through me might as well have been in Latin or Greek or Double Dutch for all I knew of what they contained. Anyway, I never read them," he added quickly. Beads of sweat bedewed his scalp. It must be the heat of the fire and of the excellent malt I'd bought him.

"But you were rather good at Latin and Greek, if I remember."

"I didn't live up to Beattie's expectations, I fear, Robin. Memory was never that good. Still isn't. You'll have to remind me..."

"Well, it was all very odd. Sandhurst had given us a quick rundown of origin stories of the sexes. Adam's rib, etcetera. Then he introduced Beehive, who came in with

56

you trooping after him like an obedient puppy. Beehive read a long passage from Plato's *Symposium*, in translation mercifully, where Aristophanes is explaining his theory of how human beings were originally doubles, literally joined at the hip, elsewhere, too, then cloven in twain by an angry god as a punishment for some original sin. No doubt you could understand it in the original Greek, eh, Henry?"

"What…? Oh no, not me, Robin. I was never terribly good, really. I can't understand what the old fool saw in me. I must have been something of a disappointment to him."

"You're too modest, Henry. I'm sure you could have gone on to greater things if you'd stuck at it."

"Oh no. Not me." He stared at the fire with a faint smile of complacent defeatism. "It was my memory, you see. Always my memory. It always let me down, that bit of the old brain box."

"Still, I'm surprised you don't recall anything about his big presentation. It was pretty memorable. It certainly made quite an impression on me even though I was only half-listening. I was more preoccupied with wondering where Diana was, sick with jealousy at the thought she was off somewhere playing truant with Harry Barclay…"

"The captain of the Under Sixteen rugger team," Shawcroft put in. "It was well-known they were having it off."

I smiled through the cramping sensation in my belly that image still brought on.

"So you do remember *something,* then!" I pointed out. Shawcroft lowered his head, shaking it half-heartedly, that strange insipid smile on his lips again.

I decided not to press the point, continuing instead. "But it was more than just sex for those two. That was what made it hurt so much, like a kick in the gut from one of Major Bray's stallions, the feeling I got that they were made for each other. Like two halves of one of those hermaphrodites that Zeus carved in two, reunited at last.

That was all I could think about when Professor Beehive was telling us about Aristophanes and his theory."

"Well, they'd broken the six-inch rule all right," Shawcroft remarked, and there was something unpleasant about his tone. "By rather more than six inches, going by what I saw of Barclay in the showers once," he added with unnecessary prurience that made his voice tremble. Finally he composed himself. "I thought they'd both been expelled."

"So did I at first, when they weren't back at school the next day, the next week, even. My fevered imagination saw them caught *in flagrante delicto*, then sent home in short order. And yet it seemed unlikely they'd have expelled *him* outright. Her maybe. She was only a scholarship girl, after all, a bright kid from a poor background, there to make up the numbers, to help secure the school's charitable status. Not all that popular with the other girls, either. All the cliques of wealthy princesses envied her natural beauty, resented her for having the temerity to be clever, too. He, on the other hand, *would* be missed the next time Mr Speed needed to send him out to lead the team to glory, win another cup for the school. And then there were the different ways they'd have been viewed. Her in disgrace, but him just doing what comes naturally to a red-blooded male, chalking up another notch on his bedpost. But she was more than that to him, and him to her, too. I suppose it was inevitable but I'll never forget the day it happened."

"What happened?"

"Oh, come now, Henry, if you can't recall that your memory really *is* failing. The police cars, the search of the grounds…"

"I suppose I must have been off that day."

"…the announcement in assembly the following day that Mr Sandhurst was taking leave of absence; then the following week that he wouldn't be returning…"

"Oh yes, of course. Excuse me."

Briskly, he got up to use the lavatory, leaving me

musing on my memories, staring into the dying fire. When he returned I resumed my narrative.

~~~

Life went back to normal eventually, in so far as anything could be described as such in that place. Of course, it was all over the news, what they found in Sandhurst's study, the images and literature. We'd all suspected it, eh, Henry? I'd always wondered if Beehive was involved in whatever he was up to. Those little notes you passed, those errands he was always sending you on, maybe they had something to do with it…?

Oh, don't look so blank, Henry! All right. I know. I know. You were too young to understand. To the pure, all things are pure and all that.

But they never found them, did they? Alive or dead.

Sandhurst pleaded guilty to the sexual offences, the possession of indecent material, but he was adamant he knew nothing about the lovers' disappearance. The prosecution blew a lot of hot air about his obsession with Diana, that he discovered she was pregnant, either by him or by Barclay, found them together, etcetera … flew into a murderous rage. But they didn't have the bodies let alone any other evidence beyond the circumstantial so there was no murder conviction.

He got out after a few years with good behaviour, though he'd never work as a teacher again. A broken man by all accounts.

And as for the rest of us, we all went our separate ways. I don't keep in touch with my old school pals, but certain names do crop up from time to time in the public eye: sportspeople, celebrities, politicians. James Snodgrass is now a cartoonist for the *Daily Mail*. Felicity Mordant became a lobbyist and polling analyst, working for Lord Ashcroft. But what about Professor Beehive? What about you? What did you get up to?

Nothing to say?

~~~

Shawcroft just sat there staring into the flames, the same bland smile playing on his lips. I continued.

~~~

That Beehive was involved seems obvious to me now. But Sandhurst must have protected him, refusing to name his associates. How very noble of him...

After university, where I was an unexceptional student, I drifted into unemployment for a while until my father offered me a job in his antiques business. I tried it for a couple of years but it wasn't for me. I don't know if this caused him disappointment or relief. Perhaps a bit of both.

I made contact with David Llewellyn, and through him found out that there was an opening on the school's grounds maintenance team. It wasn't the most auspicious career for someone of my education and background, and yet it felt a like a kind of homecoming, which helped to alleviate the nagging sense of guilt I felt towards my parents for all the sacrifices they'd made, for so little return, it seemed.

"Welcome to Dad's Army," said David, when I returned to the mess room that had been my refuge during my school days. He'd filled out a bit from the skinny lad I knew as a girl, not much older than I was. As I looked around I saw what he meant. All the others were in their sixties, the same band of men who'd worked there since I was a teenager. There was Grimesworth, his face raw and ruddy behind his huge snow-white walrus moustache.

"Hello Robin," he growled amiably. "Yes, I'm still here. Don't look so surprised! Too old to work, too poor to retire – that's me."

Though I had little experience of this kind of work, full training was provided and I took to it with enthusiasm. I soon learned how to mark out football, rugby and hockey pitches from scratch, using string, pegs and tape measures. I enjoyed working out in the open air, with my own thoughts and memories for company, even if not all of them were particularly pleasant ones.

I preferred it to sitting in the mess room during tea breaks, listening to the sound of Grimesworth snoring, sometimes starting awake with a terrible expression, as if from a bad dream, demanding to know what that awful sound was that nearly gave him a heart attack. I suppose he meant the scrabbling bumping noises on the low roof. David would laugh good naturedly, reminding him it was just squirrels or birds running about up there, or cones landing on it from the thick conifers crowded around, planted to conceal our unsightly yard from the prospective parents who toured the grounds on one of the school's numerous open days. He'd glance sharply at me as he reassured Grimesworth of this, as if warning me to corroborate the story, and I would hastily nod in the old man's direction my endorsement of David's explanation. I couldn't tell if he noticed, for his tired eyes seemed to be long ago and far away.

It was not long after starting the job that I began seeing Diana Harrow again, first in a dream, dressed like the Disney Snow White, but with fairy-tale gown, torn and besmirched with filth. I watched, helpless, as shrivelled leech-like things with grinning old men's faces battened on her various orifices until she was little more than a husk.

The second time was before match day. I wasn't dreaming on that occasion. Well, I was awake, at any rate. Grimesworth had sent me to renew the markings on the pitch where the Under Sixteen rugby team were scheduled to crush some spotty Herberts from the local academy to a bloody pulp. It was his last week in the job before he retired, and he never liked going to that end of the playing fields, anyway.

In the chill morning I pushed my marker laboriously on its three trundling wheels along grooves left by the "burning in" of the lines. October mist blurred the edge of the school's land where sports turf met the line of trees that delineated the boundary of the playing fields.

It was there that I saw her, sharply and clearly defined

even in the mist, her dark eyes and raven hair just as I remembered them.

I abandoned the lines and made for her.

She was gone by the time I reached the spot but I noticed what was growing behind where she'd been standing.

An ash tree.

That's where I'll tell the police to dig. They'll wonder how I know, of course, probably think I'm mad at first. That was where *you* were supposed to come in, Henry. I'd always suspected you, and hoped your conscience would spur you to confess, but you haven't been very forthcoming so far, and now you've gone all quiet on me. I'd been following you for weeks but it suited me to let you think it was a chance meeting.

Behind the cordon they'll build their funny white tent, where they'll place the withered two-backed skeletal thing they'll find in the makeshift grave, the two bodies joined first by love, then permanently so, pathetically huddled in an eternal embrace.

How do I know what's down there?

Not just from the type of tree, but what's carved in the bark. It's lost its clarity over the last thirty years or so, but you can just about make it out if you know what you're looking for: the heart with the arrow through it framing "JB 4 DH". This was their special place, as you found out when you went on one of your solitary rambles around the school grounds late one summer evening.

You've always thought her so pure, yet here she is rutting away with that rugger bugger, making the beast with two backs. You see them entwined in its green shade and think miserably how no one will ever look at you the way she looks at him. You will never be one of the ones who cannot take their eyes off each other, can't keep their hands off each other. In a sudden silent rage you find the rock nearby – and the strength to lift it. Drop it on the back of his head as one of her widening eyes stares up from under him, his skull crushed, her body trapped beneath his bulk, fighting a losing battle for breath.

After a time you go back there, see what you've done. You panic, run to fetch Beehive, your only real friend. He comes back with you to the place, stares at the half-dressed figures lying quite still in their final clinch in the hollow of gnarled roots where you found them. With an odd benevolent smile on his face he asks you to stay there while he gets help, saying everything will be fine, the school looks after its own, deals with such matters in its own way. He returns with a needle and catgut from Matron, and Grimesworth carrying a spade. While the head gardener digs a large deep hole, Professor Beehive sits cross-legged and performs a weird ceremony over the dead, muttering phrases in Ancient Greek in his strange droning buzz as his crabbed hand snatches the needle back and forth, back and forth, in an arc like that of a conductor's baton. When he is finished he rises from the ground, dusts himself off, takes a Polaroid of his handiwork, and tells you no one must ever speak of this. "Grimesworth's first loyalty is to the school," he tells you when you glance at the burly figure labouring away nearby. "Isn't that right, Grimesworth?" he calls to the hunched figure outlined by the blood-red dying sun, who replies with a small sad and scared nod. As the three of you drag the heavy canvas sack towards the hole you realise Beattie is quite mad and you are lost forever.

That's my theory anyway. It's as good as any and it's the only one that makes sense to me. I've embroidered it a little with a few imaginative flourishes.

But I don't hear you protesting your innocence. Perhaps you're exercising your right to silence. You'll need it when the police arrive. I'm off to phone them now. I waited until Grimesworth retired both from his job and from life, the latter closely following the former, as I had expected. I didn't see any reason why he should be caught up in this.

Nothing to say? But then you're not in much of a position to do or say anything right now. You see, while you were off powdering your nose in the little boy's room, I was powdering your drink with the substance I found in the pocket of the dove-grey jacket you left on your chair, the stuff that was meant for me, I think. I may have only got a low 2.2 for my biochemistry degree, a "Desmond" as the cool kids used to call it, after the South African Archbishop, but I know what it is. I also know that others have gone missing wherever you've lived.

That reminds me, there's something else I need to do, something to do with chemical alteration of the sensibilities. The trouble is, I've forgotten what it is. You see, I have memory troubles, too. This phrase keeps coming into my head like some half-forgotten childhood lullaby: *Take one every mealtime, with food.*

I found something else in your pockets when I went through them – the crumpled old Polaroid photo you must have found in a drawer in Beehive's study and impulsively stole and kept as a souvenir. When at last he noticed its absence he interrogated you about it, but you already had an excellent schooling in acting the innocent, as you thought with a sly little smile of what it depicted and the power it gave you over him: the lovers forever entwined, taken when they were still young, freshly killed, stitched together like two conjoined twins in a carnival freakshow bottle, as if to reunite the two separated halves of a primordial whole.

I'll put it back there for the police to find. But did I find it in your pocket, or did I put it there in the first place?

Memory can be so deceptive.

The Chiromancer

"Penny arcades not your thing, Willy?" asked Bertie, affecting an air of innocence, breaking the uneasy hush that had fallen in the smoking room of the Regina Club.

At any moment the four men sitting there expected it to be broken by the mild commotion of a police raid. The bobbies would likely just take everyone's details and go. It would all be terribly inconvenient and rather humiliating, but everyone would just give fake names and addresses to avoid exposure. You did get the odd officious one who had a thing against "their sort", but mostly the officers didn't question the credentials offered. After all, Brighton coppers were notoriously corrupt, and given the subs Regina charged, as like as not its proprietor had the means to come to some sort of understanding with the law.

The Regina Club had a fairly respectable clientele to protect. Take these four: Wilfred Purslane, literary agent; Harold Jenkins, retired partner in a firm of solicitors; Frederick Miles, turf accountant; Albert Wood, actor, resting. Admittedly, the latter's more precarious profession, which at present obliged him to survive on National Assistance, stretched the definition of respectable a little. Come to that, so did Miles's, living as he did on the proceeds of games of chance and at the whim of the Brighton racecourse gangs. Yet when you loved as they did, it didn't do to be too picky about the company you kept, though you always had to be careful.

They all had secrets, over and above the (to them) obvious one they all shared. As they grew old in each other's company they felt more and more inclined to open up about their lives, spinning yarns about their youthful escapades, in the relative safety of the Regina's marble halls, that might be tall tales. Teasing out these other secrets was Bertie's peculiar talent (the reason why Freddie paid his subs!). He'd often do this with an apparently innocent off-hand remark, like the aforementioned one referring to Purslane's curious reaction to the fortune-telling machines in the penny arcade on the promenade.

He knew too well that Wilfred was a tough nut to crack, clamming up whenever Bertie tried to probe his early life. He was aware that Purslane had worked for Jenkins many moons ago, but Harold wasn't exactly forthcoming about that either. When Bertie saw the look on Wilfred's face in the penny arcade he knew he was onto something, he wasn't sure what. All he knew was, the literary agent had gone pale when he saw what was in there. It wasn't the laughing sailor dummy in the glass case, though that was unnerving enough, with its fixed grin and nodding head and peels of manic glee. Purslane had been staring at the two machines opposite that one: another glass case with a cyclops-eyed gipsy fortune teller poised, hand out-stretched, next to a contraption that claimed to read your palm and print out your destiny, illustrated by a representation of a giant hand, carved up into segments radiating lines, each one of which matched a word such as "fame", "love", "riches" and so on to each of the portions of the palm, advertising a kind of mechanical chiromancy.

They'd all been promenading along the seafront, taking the air, killing time before dinner. Bertie had suggested popping into the arcade as a "hoot". It had seemed less so when Wilfred had turned round and walked out in apparent umbrage, leaving the other three wondering what he was in such a funk about. By the time they'd had a few port and lemons at the club it was all forgotten until Bertie brought it up again. Now they all sat eagerly awaiting Purslane's reply.

"No, dear boy," he said, with sardonic emphasis on the endearment, glaring at Bertie over the rims of his half-moon spectacles, "they're not my thing at all. And yes, there is a story behind it, as I suppose you're all hoping. It's to do with my twin brother Nathaniel, and how he started my career as a literary agent. Indirectly, of course."

"Good grief, Willy!" Freddie Miles exclaimed. "I didn't even know you had a brother – still less a twin brother!"

"Nathaniel Purslane…" said Bertie, his eyes wide. "Isn't he – ?"

"Nathaniel is dead," Wilfred rapped out.

In the ensuing silence he took off his half-moon spectacles, then proceeded to clean them meticulously with a white silk handkerchief from the top left-hand pocket of his black pin-striped suit jacket. He took a sip from his glass, lit his pipe, and began his tale.

~~~

I could see from the start that the police wouldn't be able to shed any light on his passing. The force was rather over-stretched with the Brighton trunk murders. So I took it upon myself to carry out my own investigation. I felt I owed it to him to try and discover the nature of the forces that drove him to his end.

He was found hanging from a beam in the ceiling of his digs in Kemptown. The toppled-over chair seemed to indicate suicide, another reason for the police to ignore it. Those stolid bloodhounds had no one else to hunt.

I did feel a certain sense of guilt. Shouldn't I have been acting as my brother's keeper? The truth is, we had less in common than you might think. Though we were twins I am right-handed, unlike him, and the differences didn't end there. While I toiled away at Cribbins and Jenkins he had rejected such bourgeois trappings in favour of a life of literary obscurity. Our father subsidised his writing and academic scholarship with a meagre private income. But the last time I communicated with him he had been full of optimism about some rare and valuable manuscripts he had unearthed.

Trying to keep things light, I said, "So you're going to

be able to earn your own keep at last, old chap!"

His reply suggested he was less than impressed by my attempt at levity. "Ah yes, Wilfred, Father's little treasure, the hard-working solicitor's clerk. When these beauties see the light of day the price they'll fetch might rival even your princely salary!"

I sniffed, taking in the squalid surroundings of his lodgings. I had no wish to remain in the draughty yet somehow musty room for much longer. I heard fitful scratchings that sounded like they came from somewhere behind the peeling wallpaper. *Still, hardly surprising that place has a rodent problem*, I thought.

I didn't say anything about this though. Instead, I said, "I take it from your new-found enthusiasm for literary archaeology that you haven't managed to find a publisher for your own masterpieces. Have you tried sending them to that Campbell Thomson woman? I've heard her anthologies are terribly popular, you know!"

My reference to the *Not at Night* series was perhaps a little too provocative but sometimes Nathaniel sorely tried my patience with his insistence on pursuing the most obscure avenues in the field of what he was pleased to call "weird fiction". He just needed a good agent to steer his dubious talents in the right direction. Needless to say, my advice fell on deaf ears. Now was no exception.

At the mention of the editor's name he spat loudly and wetly. The resulting expectoration became entangled in the strands of his beard. This at least served to protect the already filthy floor.

"Why ever not?" I asked. "God forbid, but you might even make some money…"

He wiped his mouth with a greying handkerchief grasped in nicotine yellow knuckles, and said acidly, "Thanks so much for your kind advice. I know what you think of my work: the semiliterate scribbling of a third-rate money-grubbing hack. I don't lecture you about your fondness for young sailors – oh yes, I've seen some of the dives you haunt! Don't worry, Wilfred, I don't report what I've seen to Father. I'd be grateful if in return you would keep your attempts at literary criticism to yourself!"

~~~

"Dives? The cheek of it," said Bertie with mock indignation, his eyes glancing around their opulent surroundings. "Still, I suppose young Nat Baudelaire might have had a point. You did have to slum it back then, didn't you, Willy – couldn't afford to live it up in places like the Regina Club…"

"Indeed," said Wilfred, cocking one eyebrow laconically. "And I wasn't too keen on Pater finding out about my secret peccadilloes, so —"

"And sailors at that! You're such a cliché, Willy."

"Are you going to keep putting your tuppence worth in, Bertie, or are you going to let me get on with this tale?"

"All right! All right!"

"As long as you *do* get on with it," grumbled Harold. "And *do* get a move on," he added. "At this rate our esteemed hosts are going to shut up shop before we find out what this has to do with the penny arcade…"

"Yes, well, we'll all find out a lot quicker without interruptions," put in Freddy. "Though I have to ask: were those his and your exact words? If so, your memory's remarkable – such an ear for dialogue!"

"That's a matter of opinion," muttered Harold, though to be fair, Wilfred's talent in this regard was somewhat superior to that of his late brother, who was notorious for his long paragraphs of floridly descriptive prose, unbroken by the more mundane rhythms of common everyday speech.

"I find as I get older, memories from twenty years ago or so are very vivid," Wilfred said, rather stiffly, "particularly the ones surrounding the death of my brother…"

Freddy glared at Harold and asked Wilfred, "Anyway, what did you say to that?"

~~~

Oh, a rather cheap remark, I confess. "Well, you needn't come bothering me for money then, old chap." Or something like that.

He just sneered back. "Oh ... I won't be needing it, Wilfred."

But I was already heading for the door that hung loose on its rusted hinges. In the coming weeks the true meaning of his words was to become clearer to me. You may remember the story: obscure writer and scholar unearths undiscovered masterpieces by Shakespeare, Marlowe, Webster, Middleton and the like. I dare say you're all expecting me to say how I rushed around to his garret when I heard this and congratulated him on his good fortune, like any normal loving brother would have done. I'm ashamed to say that any happiness I might have felt at his success was somewhat overshadowed by the fear that he might gloat over the comparison between his new wealth and my continuing drudgery in the offices of Cribbins and Jenkins.

~~~

(Harold Jenkins looked about to say something, open-mouthed as he was – something like, *Who are you calling a slave driver?* Or perhaps, *How dare you! After all I've done for you!* might be more his style. Bertie just gestured him to silence. As for Purslane, he barely even glanced in Jenkins's direction, as if the effect of his choice of words on his former employer was a matter of indifference to him.)

~~~

So that less than amicable exchange about Nathaniel's literary and financial prospects was the last conversation we ever had.

But what I wanted to know was, why would he commit suicide when he was on the brink of wealth and great acclaim? I knew that riches were not uppermost on Nathaniel's list of priorities, and it was clear that he wasn't interested in success in the way I would understand it.

Somehow it fell to me to sort through his effects, such as they were. So I once again found myself inside Nathaniel's lodgings, where poor ventilation added to the odours of stale perspiration, incompletely dried laundry, and inadequate plumbing – plus the fragrance of the fluids expelled by the body *in extremis*, a sweet subtle nutty, slightly cloying aroma mingled with the acrid stench of ammonia that somehow put me in mind of gentlemen's public lavatories. Conventional I know, to associate sex with death, but there we are.

There was something else as well, something I recognised from my most recent visit to my brother's squalid abode: a musty ancient smell of dry leather. At first I put this down to all the leathery old books weighing down the creaking shelves lining the walls.

In the silence of that room, with dust motes cavorting in what little sunlight managed to penetrate the greasy smears on the tiny windowpanes, I heard it. It was the same scratching noise that I had assumed was a rodent infestation during my previous visit. It now appeared to be coming from behind a jerry-built partition wall adjacent to a door, locked apparently rather more securely than the poorly hung one serving the apartment as a whole. What instinct prompted me to investigate the source of the noise I shall never know. First, I needed to find the key to the sturdy door.

I made for the mahogany bureau, a family heirloom that I suspected had never known the tender caress of a duster while in my brother's possession. He had crammed the poor neglected object with countless yellowing papers, curling at the desiccated edges, and scrawled with what I knew to be his own handwriting. There was a notebook too. As I leafed through it the dry rattling of the pages echoed the scratching.

Nathaniel's spidery handwriting was not easily legible, but from what I *did* manage to read it appeared to be some kind of journal.

~~~

At this point, Wilfred delved in his inside pocket and produced a leather-bound notebook whose dog-eared pages were yellowed like the tobacco-stained walls of one of Brighton's seedier public houses. Taking another sip of his port and lemon, he leafed through it to find the relevant page and began to read.

~~~

I now know I shall never amount to anything now beyond derivative mediocrity. I once valued originality above all things. Latterly, I have come to realise that this obsession was futile. One can only play the cards one is dealt; the important thing is how one plays them. However, drawing on one's literary antecedents is one thing. It's quite another when a publisher sends back a manuscript, marking in red ink whole passages that, he points out, I have unwittingly lifted wholesale, indeed "word for word" from another's work. It is the influence of that abomination *I acquired from Madame Crowley, I feel sure. The literary forgeries It created were to be the means of freeing me from the yoke of want, so that I could write my own work unhindered. But far from freeing my muse, It has killed her off for good, leaving me only capable of plagiarism of the most abject and slavish kind! This is the end for me, I fear.*

~~~

"Oh, really!" muttered Jenkins.

The others all looked at him, questioning his interruption.

"Exhibit A!" he said. "When I was at the bar, I was always fully briefed before I went into court but I was never so well-prepared as you are, Wilfred, my poor little drudge. And yet we're supposed to believe you weren't expecting to have to play the *raconteur* this evening until young Albert here prompted you."

There was a long silence as Purslane stared back at Jenkins, with his pale blue eyes. "I always carry this notebook. Perhaps some of us are *always* readying ourselves for a court appearance, Harold."

He lowered his gaze to the papers and began to speak again, though not reading from them this time, but rather addressing their author.

~~~

Oh, Nathaniel, it distresses me to think that you took your own life because you felt you had become somehow bound to literary mimicry. Rather ironic when one considers the venerated poets and playwrights whose work you forged! Take the Bard: a magpie if ever there was one, stealing unashamedly from Holinshed, Seneca and others. But what do I know, dear brother? A mere scrivener such as me!

Something else was at work: the influence of this "abomination" he mentioned, and a certain Madame Crowley.

I looked through the bureau where I'd found the notebook. It was then that I noticed two other items in one of the drawers: a pack of tarot cards, and a key that looked as if it might well fit the lock to the adjoining door.

I was reluctant to try the key, hearing again the uncanny scratching behind the wall, which sounded far more regular and purposeful than the febrile scuttling of a mouse or rat in the wainscoting should. Putting off opening the door, I pulled a card from the pack. Aptly enough, it was the Hanged Man. The figure in the picture was suspended upside down by one foot, his blonde locks flowing down toward the earth – a rather more protracted and impractical way of doing oneself in than the one employed by my brother, I imagine. As I opened the pack another card fell out: a business card advertising the services of "Madame Crowley, Palmist, Clairvoyant and Dealer in Curios", together with an address on Elm Grove.

I snorted. No wonder Nathaniel lost his head, consorting with such charlatans! Nevertheless, I placed the card inside my breast pocket. If nothing else, my brother's collection of occult books might fetch a good price there.

The steady scratching behind the partition wall

continued and despite my misgivings I found myself unable to put off trying the door any longer. The key fitted and the heavy door swung open.

All I could think when I opened the door was: *Good Heavens! There's one of J. Alfred Prufrock's ragged claws...*

(Yes, dear brother, I wasn't quite the Philistine you habitually made me out to be, just because I rejected the life of squalid literary poverty you chose. I might not have been one of the *avant garde* but I was familiar with the works of Mr Eliot! And when bewailing your inability to write anything original, you might have done well to look to his example. I understand the fellow was rather keen on incorporating whole passages of other people's work in his verses and it didn't seem to do *him* any harm!)

It's funny, isn't it, the peculiar thoughts that come into one's head when one's faced with the incredible. There the thing was, scribbling away at *The Verie True and Tragical Historie of King Harolde*, Act V, Scene III, or whatever it was, and all I could think was, *it's a left hand!* Hacked off at the wrist, blackened parchment skin, ghastly yellow talons, but the thing that really set my teeth on edge was, *the beastly thing's writing with its left hand!*

And how different from my brother's nearly illegible scrawl! As if to underline this, the hand was pain-stakingly copying the text from a draft in Nathaniel's scribbled handwriting.

I could see that the five-fingered horror had nearly finished its counterfeit blank verse masterpiece, but I couldn't stand the scratching of its quill any longer. Nearby lay a wicker cat basket. This I snatched up and avoiding touching the hand I unceremoniously scooped up the thing, spilling its ink pot in the process, and tipped it to the back of the basket, snapping the hatch shut. I watched the ink pool around the interrupted iambic pentameters of the *Verie True and Tragical Historie*. This was one lost manuscript that was going to remain unfinished!

It had occurred to me that Nathaniel's new literary gold

mine might turn out to be counterfeit but I hadn't imagined he'd had a helping hand, not one of *this* nature, at any rate. As the hand in question scrabbled around restlessly in the cat basket I wondered if this Madame Crowley he mentioned might be able to shed some more light on my brother's death. I began flicking through the journal again, looking for earlier entries that might mention her. Before too long I found myself reading an account of a séance conducted by her and her associate Professor Solomon Silence. According to Nathaniel's account, he had attended the event in order to research a story he was working on. They sounded like a classic pair of fraudulent spiritualists: Madame Crowley playing the medium's part, speaking in tongues and rolling her eyes back in her head, while this Professor Silence character stage-managed the whole sorry farce.

Then I heard the hand scrabbling and squirming for release, and thought of its loathsome febrile movements like those of a chopped off newt's tail, remembered the lengths I'd gone to avoid touching the grisly relic, and shuddered. How did this moving dead thing sit with my natural scepticism about the occult?

I turned the page, looking for the sequel to this encounter.

~~~

"I see we're to be treated to another lengthy passage from Exhibit A!" grumbled Jenkins, as Purslane once again leafed through the journal. "Wilfred, I'm beginning to think this is a rather elaborate practical joke you and young Albert have cooked up between you. All this incredible nonsense about an animated severed hand, indeed! I've got to hand it to you though – forging a whole notebook, staining the pages with tea, it's a lot of trouble to go to! In all my years at the bar I never—"

"Please, Harold," said Freddie. "I want to hear!"

~~~

The shop on Elm Grove was closed, so I didn't expect an answer when I gently rapped on the door. Yet I could see a shape dimly outlined behind the glass in the doorframe, and seconds later it opened. There stood Professor Silence. Without a word he ushered me inside. The only sound was the tinkle of the bell attached to the door, to alert the proprietors to the entrance of customers, who I imagine are few and far between.

Madame Crowley sat in a wing-backed chair, her eyes slits, her plucked epicanthic eyebrows arched so high they almost reached the top of her domed forehead, where a crown of thin greying hair sat like a tortoiseshell cat.

"Ah, Mr Purslane," she breathed, without opening her eyes.

"Madame Crowley," I murmured, hardly daring to raise my voice in the dead silence of the room, darkened by the closed curtain over the shop front. Around me in the dim light I could make out various forms of occult paraphernalia adorning the shop window, the walls and certain cabinets. A pentagram hung on the wall, alongside a parchment of runic symbols and a framed but faded portrait of a bald middle-aged man with intense staring eyes, wearing a wing collar. His face was familiar to me. It looked as if the room doubled up as an antique shop and a medium's parlour.

Madame Crowley's eyes fluttered open and she noticed me gazing at the portrait of the man I now recognized as Aleister Crowley.

"No relation," she smiled, "though I was one of his army of lovers in my younger days. Marriage however was not high on the Great Beast's list of priorities…"

Her smile grew wistful, but the black berries of her eyes flashed when she saw my sympathetic expression.

"So why did I take his name?" she asked rhetorically, as if seeing the question in my eyes. "I simply thought it had a better ring to it than Miss Alice Smithers, for my chosen vocation."

"You were going to show me something, were you not?"

"Ah yes, I believe I was," she replied lethargically. "Solomon! Solomon!" she called, waving her long thin hand listlessly.

Professor Silence, who had disappeared into a back room of the shop during this exchange, padded back in as soundlessly as he had disappeared. He licked his fingers, slicked his flowing hair back behind his ears, and donned black leather gloves. Then he moved towards a cabinet, covered with a black velvet drape, in one of the darker corners of the room. With a rather melodramatic flick of his wrist he removed the drape, then bestowed an unctuous smile upon me.

"Solomon does enjoy his theatrics," said Madame Crowley, beaming like an indulgent parent.

I struggled in the dim light to see the blackened object through the smeared glass of the cabinet. It had been up-ended on its stump, on top of a black velvet cushion, and the wax of a guttered long-extinguished black candle had melted into the tip of each finger, so that the scorched wicks seemed to take the place of fingernails.

In front of the cushion an ornately hand-written sign read "The Hand of Glory".

"This, Mr Purslane, is a particularly interesting specimen of the phenomenon, and has other unique properties which might interest you. Fetch the quill, the parchment and the ink pot, Solomon."

Silence did as he was bid and I watched as he set the requested items down on a small table between us.

"This hand," she continued, languidly waving me to sit down upon the chair on the other side of the table to her, "belonged to the banker and convicted fraudster Henry Fauntleroy, sentenced to hang, about a century ago, for forging the signatures of his clients on letters allowing access to their funds. It's a talent that outlived him. Your signature please, Mr Purslane…"

'When I still hesitated she leaned towards me and laid the long fingers of her right hand on my arm, and used the other to turn my cheek until I was looking at the cabinet, an uncomfortably intimate gesture, her fingertips cold and dry. Inside the cabinet I could see movement, fragments of congealed wax raining from twitching fingers like flakes of dried skin. Perhaps it was dried skin but I preferred to think it was wax.

"It wants to write, Mr Purslane," she hissed. "But it can only imitate. It needs something to copy. Your signature, perhaps?"

I obliged, thinking it best to humour her harmless fancy,

though as I signed my name I couldn't dispel the uneasy feeling that I was sealing some devilish pact. I wondered if another of her minions hid underneath the cabinet, pushing a tar-blackened hand through a hole in the cushion and wriggling it about. What happened next dispelled this notion. Professor Silence produced a silver key and unlocked the cabinet, removing the still-writhing thing from its cushion with the wary professionalism of a zoologist handling a rare but deadly snake. At this point I could see why he wore gloves.

Then he placed it on the piece of parchment and took the quill from the ink pot. The mummified fingers grabbed the quill and began to write.

~~~

Oh, poor Nathaniel, was that why you hanged yourself? When you placed your signature down on paper did you sign away your genius?

~~~

"Genius?" hissed Bertie. "I read one of Nathaniel's grimoires in *Weird Tales* years ago and it was all right, but I wouldn't go that far!"

He glanced at Wilfred expecting a wordless reproof but Purslane was in a world of his own, gazing at the notebook, his memento of his brother.

"Me too," agreed Jenkins, *sotto voce*. "Mind you, if this is a hoax, Wilfred's done a good job of mimicking his brother's rather overwrought style…"

"Oh, I don't know," said Bertie. "Nathaniel Purslane was always one for the purple prose. This seems positively understated by comparison!"

Freddie Miles motioned them to silence but Wilfred seemed oblivious to their brief bout of literary criticism.

~~~

A renewed bout of scuffling from the cat basket caused me to lose my page. Instead, I turned to a later entry.

It appears the Thing is only capable of the most rudimentary form of imitation (it lacks a brain and operates by muscular memory alone), but this mimicry, once mastered, becomes compulsive. However, I need It to be able to recreate a play or poem that I have written, in the style of one of the great masters of English literature but in the hand *of that genius. How did Henry Fauntleroy develop his talent for imitating handwriting, again? Before Madame Crowley showed me his papers, I wondered if she'd discovered his life story by reading his mummified palm. His talent was something to do with the harsh disciplinary methods of his calligraphy master at school. The dark leathery skin on the palm of this five-fingered relic is scored in certain places. It doesn't take a Chiromancer like Madame Crowley to see that these are not just the scars and marks of age, but contusions from the blows of a switch or cane.*

A subsequent passage further developed this theme.

At last I feel as if I am making some progress with my little Pet, though the training has been arduous for both of us. After a few days of it I began to feel as if I was hurting myself as much or even more than the creature. After all, Its former owner had something in common with me: Henry Fauntleroy too was left-handed. And his strange memoir suggested that the pain of the discipline helped him to develop his proficiency for counterfeiting signatures. I wondered at first if the same treatment would have a similar effect on the creature, for can such a Thing feel pain, indeed merit the name of "creature", so divorced from the whole It was once part of? Certainly It reacts to the hard strokes, but aren't they just neurotic animal reflexes, without a brain to invest them with meaning? Still, I feel a terrible remorse every time I subject It to the training, as if it were my own palm I was beating. But now that It has begun rendering "Christopher Marlowe's True Histories of the Crusades*", with my verses written in Kit's own hand, I believe these measures have paid off.*

~~~

Freddie and Bertie couldn't restrain a snicker between themselves at image conjured up by phrase "my own palm I was beating", but again Wilfred seemed blissfully unaware of their mirth and went on with his narrative.

~~~

That afternoon, I found myself standing outside Madame Crowley's Emporium – with a cat basket. I hoped to return the thing, though it was as they say "damaged goods". On the dark blue sign above the shop's front window was the white-painted representation of a hand, advertising Madame Crowley's palm-reading service. The palm was divided into segments, as if it were some kind of mechanical device, with straight white lines connecting words and phrases to the different sections, which appeared to allocate occult functions to them.

The slick-haired creature Nathaniel had mentioned ushered me in.

"You must be Professor Silence," I said, not expecting an answer. I was not disappointed.

In the velvet darkness two berry eyes glimmered in the dim light. A slender hand pointed at the basket I was carrying. Muffled sounds hinted at what was inside.

"I had hoped never to see that again." A woman's voice rasped from the shadows. "Did it not give Nathaniel what he wanted?"

I said, "It rather depends on what it was he wanted, I would have thought."

"Oh, not much. Fame, recognition, glory, your approval… You are his twin brother, are you not?"

I wasn't going to rise to that bait so I repaid her question in kind. "And you are Madame Crowley, née Alice Smithers, I take it?" She nodded, so I said, rather primly, "I do beg your pardon, dear lady, but I have just read his private journal and I don't recall reading anything there about wishing for his dear brother's approval. Still, I'm sure you have your own means of divining other people's inmost desires."

The frail-looking figure stirred within the embrace of the chair's wings, and a faint smile of amusement radiated from the darkness. "Ah, you're a sceptic." She practically purred. "But I'll wager you're a little less so after encountering our little friend in the basket there."

"It is rather difficult to explain, I must admit." Remembering her less than enthusiastic response to its return, I added, "So a refund is out if the question, I suppose."

"A refund?" She repeated, dripping scorn. "My dear man, it didn't cost him a *sou*. I could see he was somewhat lacking in means. Besides, I was only too happy to get rid of the beastly object. It's a reminder of my shortcomings. Yes, Mr Purslane, no doubt you think me a charlatan. It doesn't take a clairvoyant to see that! Most people do, apart from the poor souls that gain comfort from my ministrations. But *they're* only too happy to believe. And you're right, of course. I *am* a fake. I have long since given up believing that I have some kind of gift, daring to hope that if I read the right books, followed the right teachings... But enough of this!"

She broke off suddenly, a manicured hand leaping to her eyes to massage the point where the bridge of her aquiline nose met her ornate eyebrows. I noticed that her companion had moved soundlessly to her side and laid a hand gently on her shoulder. After a spell she shook his hand off, took a deep sigh, and continued.

"When I acquired the Hand of Glory I thought perhaps it might help me but I soon found that the reverse was true. You see, Mr Purslane, in order to come to terms with my lack of any psychic abilities I had become a sceptic like you. And now with every palm, every tarot pack I read, with every séance I conduct, a little part of me dies. It was easier to bear when I'd managed to convince myself the invisible world was a fiction and I was simply going through the motions. But *here* is a phenomenon that no one can explain..."

The thing in the cat basket began scratching at the walls of its prison, as if it knew it was the subject of the discussion.

"Why didn't you sell it," I asked, "or incorporate it into your..." I struggled to find the right words.

She stepped in with suggestions. "Act? Routine? I did once try using it to perform automatic writing at one of my séances, but the results were not to the poor widow's liking. That's one client I'll never get back... Your brother was the first person to show any interest in Henry Fauntleroy's hand. No, Mr Purslane, I'm afraid I don't want it back. It looks like you're stuck with it!

"But by way of compensation, I can offer you a palm reading. On the house, as it were..."

I indulged her fancy. I didn't see what harm it could do. Her findings have since caused a joyless little laugh to flicker over my dry lips whenever I think of it.

And the image of the Regency banker, left-handed like my brother and facing a similar end, albeit of a public and wholly involuntary kind, haunts me still. As I sat in her dusty shop, her fingers creeping over my palm, her thin lips muttering her nonsense, I thought how rum it was that they punished him for forgery with the rope, and that my brother punished himself in the same way for his own forgery. When she'd finished her chiromancy, a comfort to her more than to me, I mumbled my thanks, and left her to her meditations on her failures. She seemed noticeably still and quiet when I left. She didn't even return my muttered farewell. Perhaps she was asleep.

Ah, Nathaniel, remember how you laughed when I suggested that what you needed was a good agent, and that I was just the fellow to do it! A "philistine" you called me, a "mere scrivener". It seems you have no choice now. It would probably amuse you too to see how the critics and pulp magazine aficionados have suddenly discovered your work since your untimely death. What they wouldn't give to discover a posthumous manuscript in your own hand! Well, they can, with a little helping hand. Henry Fauntleroy's helping hand. Besides, the macabre circumstances around your suicide have already helped to create a furore that will merely add to the publicity attending the release of such documents.

Surely this is what you would have wanted. I often used to ask you why you wrote, if not for money. And your answer was invariably for some kind of legacy that would transcend this brief span. And I am providing that! At present the new converts to Nathaniel Purslane's vision of cosmic terror have so little to go on, just a few pitiful scraps. With my help, and Henry Fauntleroy's, you can extend that legacy.

Yes, I know it sounds ridiculous but that was the kind of monologue that went through my head in the days and weeks following my brother's death, his benefactor saddling me with his macabre legacy.

So why did the bloodless hand refuse to oblige me? It just sat there, the waxen image of a hand. There must be something else I had to do to encourage the thing. I would have to strike it with a switch or rod, like my brother did, in imitation of the vicious calligraphy master? I was loathe to do this, yet it was the only way to make amends between us, to secure your legacy.

Perhaps, Nathaniel, your skill at literary mimicry was such that in death you could plagiarise yourself! That was your true legacy…

So Nathaniel was dead but I was able to become his executor, in a literary sense, of course. I was very much alive and likely to remain so for the foreseeable future. When Madame Crowley read my palm she saw a long life and prosperity in the dry crevices there.

~~~

"You mean all those new Nathaniel Purslane manuscripts that have surfaced over the years…?" asked Freddie Miles.

"Ah, the penny's dropped," muttered Bertie, rather unkindly. Despite his hard-nosed profession there was a certain naïve unsophisticated quality to Freddy, sometimes. It had been a long night. He sauntered over to the window, at peered out of a gap between the curtain and the frame. Outside, a sliver of moon grinned back at him. "All clear," he went on. "Not a Black Maria in sight!"

"Faked," Wilfred replied to Freddy's unfinished question, "by me, with a little helping hand."

"Helping hand!" Jenkins repeated, his voice heavy with scorn. "What a lot of tosh. You mean to say a fraudulent banker's mummified hand is the reason why you suddenly handed in your notice at the firm, without so much as a by-your-leave?"

Wilfred gave a little shrug of his head, both confirming this unlikely story and acknowledging the incredulity it was likely to inspire.

"Well, I did wonder if you and he were related," said Freddy. "Purslane's not exactly a common surname after all!"

"And your late brother's gift for purple prose seems to have rubbed off on you in the telling of the tale," Bertie added. He smiled, trying to lighten everyone's mood. Then he suddenly stopped smiling. He was looking at Wilfred Purslane's left hand, as it put the battered notebook in the inside pocket of his immaculately pressed suit jacket. The hand was not so immaculate. Of course, he knew this already, but had always assumed the scars on it were the result of some scrape incurred in the War; perhaps even torture, the contusions looked so severe. He'd never managed to draw the story out of Wilfred. Now he began to wonder if the wounds were self-inflicted.

Slaughtered Lamb

"What was *your* first job then, Bob?"

A fog of pungent sweet-smelling smoke veiled the room as Robert Benton considered his reply.

Troy Sharp had asked the five members of the Sacred Order of the Followers of Dionysus about their first experience of gainful employment, not counting paper rounds. Or not so gainful, as the case may be.

Sackville had mentioned a spell at Smith's Crisps; Greenock, a season or two grape picking. Merrick had confessed to working in the St Ivel margarine factory in Hemyock, Devon. Sharp himself had started his working life with British Rail, when that entity still existed.

The Sacred Order of the Followers of Dionysus was the mock-reverential title for this loose affiliation of gentle- and not-so-gentlemen who met every Wednesday, to break up the tedium of the working week, indulging their taste for mild narcotics, booze, salty or sugary snacks, and agreeable discourse.

When it came to Benton, his usual diffidence delayed his reply but as the joint circulated and he refilled his glass, he warmed to his subject.

~~~

This also answers your earlier question about my first trip abroad, Troy. This was it, if you can call southern Ireland abroad, though it did seem a strange land to an English provincial boy. The first things I remember from my coach journey from Rosslare were the shrines to the Holy Virgin that appeared from time to time in little gaps in the hedge beside the winding road, pale and ghostly amid the green leaves.

It's also the story of why I became a vegetarian. I often ask myself why, and when people ask me why, I can't answer in any thought-out way. I don't really buy into all the conventional ethical or ecological wisdom that's supposed to motivate me, though I might have believed it at one time. Now my continued attachment to this diet seems a hollowed-out shell of what it was – until I remember some of the events I'm about to tell you, that is. Usually I try to forget it, but not tonight.

In fact, it was my *not* being a vegetarian that got me the job in the first place. I was working for a theatre company I had met at the Edinburgh Festival. Their agitprop show about the Birmingham pub bombings and their aftermath had been playing at the Richard Demarco Gallery Theatre, where I had a summer job as Assistant Stage Manager. One of my duties as part of getting out the previous show and getting in their one was to help them hang their main prop from the rafters – the actual torso of a lamb, with meat hooks inserted into the flesh and attached to chains secured to the ceiling. The actors dramatised the carnage of the pub bombings by driving nails into the pale meat of the dead animal, amid pyrotechnics and furiously strobing lights.

I was very wet behind the ears back then. I didn't question Demarco's employing me as what would now be called an intern. I came onto his staff as a "volunteer", after all. I was there for the experience. And what an experience!

Besides, Richard Demarco wasn't the sort of man you questioned, a short intense Scottish-Italian with a shock of white hair and dark eyes.

By no means the least of my duties was dealing with the increasingly manky carcass. You see, they couldn't afford to replace it with a fresh one. So, for three weeks, during a very hot August, I carried the thing up and down the stairs to and from its resting place in the cellar, as it grew progressively more ragged from its puncture wounds, and more rancid from exposure to the hot lights of the theatre space. Its flesh turned from pale pink to a sickly yellow shot through with green, rather like Stilton. And did it stink! Perhaps more so when I discovered it was alive with maggots and threw it in a tin bath full of bleach, the sharp tang of the detergent masking but also highlighting the pungent nauseating reek of putrefaction.

Chris Mulligan's eyes laughed behind the NHS spectacles that added an air of studiousness to his butch masculinity, as he helped me stow the carcass in the bath. Chris was one of the Birmingham-Irish brothers who'd founded the Dole Players, as the company was called, funded as it then was entirely by its members' social security cheques. Watching me trying not to gag, he said he was used to the smell, having grown up in a household surviving on knocked-off meat – but without a fridge or freezer. There was something pointed about his reminiscence, which gave me the impression that he could smell my bourgeois background, rather as Hoederer in Sartre's *Les Mains Sales* could smell that of his secretary and would-be assassin Hugo, saying class is *"une question depeau"*, a matter of skin, or perhaps flesh.

But the Dole Players weren't staging Sartre, and there was nothing metaphysical or philosophical about the vile odour that assailed the nostrils of the audience. Existential maybe. It existed all right, and certainly inspired Nausea. On the other hand, it seemed to add to the play's confrontational impact. One critic wrote in *The Scotsman*, much to Kev's derision as he read the review aloud to general hilarity from the rest of the cast:

"As the story of the Birmingham Six unfolds on stage, the sacrificial lamb hangs there as a metaphor, not just for the innocent victims of the bombing, but also for the scapegoating of the hapless Irishmen with vaguely Republican sympathies, fitted up for being in the wrong place at the wrong time; its putrefying flesh symbolises the corruption of the judicial system that cynically framed them to appease a public thirst for vengeance. The festering wounds from the nails and meat hooks appear like stigmata, expressing sympathy for the suffering of these contemporary martyrs."

Well, it seemed as if someone liked it.

As the festival drew to a close, Kev Mulligan, the writer-director, told me they'd landed a fully funded tour of Ireland with their play, and invited me to ASM for the tour. The stage manager they'd taken on was a vegetarian, so couldn't be expected to handle the prop, so would I like to do it? I asked if we'd be taking the same carcass.

"Not likely," he said. "Tour don't start till late September!"

Not only that: their funding allowed them to budget for a fresh carcass for each performance!

So that's how I came to be sitting on a coach, trundling through Wexford and Waterford on my way to Limerick, the first date on the Dole Players' tour.

The initial problem for me was sourcing the meat. The budget hadn't taken account of the prices charged by the local butchers. Running a hand through his dirty blonde hair, scraped back from his doughy-white face into a ponytail, Kev Mulligan offered a solution. "Just go round the local pubs, Bob. In every pub there's always some bloke who can sort you out some knock-off meat, mate, at very reasonable prices..."

He dug in his leather jacket pocket, produced a wad of cash. His eyes stared outwards in different directions, a feature that together with his thick West Midlands accent gave him the air of a rougher stockier version of Kevin Turvey, as he grinned amiably at his own largesse.

"Off you go then, Bob." He shooed me away.

Despite some initial misgivings I soon found many a sympathetic ear among the drinkers in the Rising of the Moon Tavern when I told them what the carcass was for. One man I spoke to remembered being in England at the time of the bombings and having to avoid speaking for fear of reprisals if someone heard his brogue. With that fabled Irish *failte* hospitality, compounded by my assumed sympathy for the Republican cause, he plied me with stout before introducing me to a guy he knew who could help me out. The only trouble was, I'd drunk too much to drive so I had to do the whole thing on foot, leaving the hired car parked near the pub. My memory of the long walk to the lockup is a little hazy. My memory of the walk back with the carcass slung over my shoulder is even hazier. I hadn't eaten and I'd never really drunk that much before. The thick black ooze roiled in my gut as the ripe smell of raw meat in late summer heat filtered through my nostrils to my queasy insides. I must have vomited a couple of times on the way and only arrived back just in time for the get-in, to a bollocking from Kev, his powerfully built brother looming behind him, while Charlotte, the vegetarian stage manager, looked on through her piercing blue eyes. As I recall, she always had an amused look on her face. Her diet hadn't improved her health, for her skin was pale, almost translucent, under her ash-blonde eighties-bouffant hair.

Thus it was, every day, through Limerick, Sligo and Dublin, though the further north we went, and with an Indian summer cooling into autumn, it no longer seemed necessary to fetch a fresh carcass every day. In fact, Kev Mulligan seemed inclined to keep the lamb longer in Dublin, where the response of the Abbey Theatre audience seemed decidedly lukewarm. Maybe theatre goers used to more refined dramatic fare found the play's angry invective, shouted by six burly blokes in rhyming couplets, more than they could stomach. Maybe its message, which had seemed so urgent and impossible to ignore in the more claustrophobic Demarco theatre, was lost on the Dublin intelligentsia, swallowed up by the larger auditorium. Mind you, it hadn't seemed to set the other provincial repertory theatres alight, either, despite all the pyrotechnics.

For Kev, the answer was simple. Hang onto the carcass for longer. If he couldn't shout them into submission, maybe the stench of putrefaction would make the chattering classes of Dublin sit up and take notice, a measure that would also save cash. So, my daily visits to various pubs and lockups became less frequent. In Sligo, I even found I had enough leisure time between shows to chat up a girl named Sinead, who worked in the local art gallery. She had chestnut hair and skin like buttermilk. I say "chat up" – I was too awkward to say much, and we weren't in town that long. I left without even saying goodbye, miserably assuming I'd never see her again.

Things changed as we drew closer to the border. After a week off in Donegal we hit Clones, County Monaghan, hometown of Barry McGuigan. All the local shops sold tea towels, beer tankards, coasters and other souvenirs depicting the "Clones Cyclone" in a typically pugilistic pose.

The show that night played to rapturous applause, nothing like the polite clapping of the audiences in Limerick and Dublin. Or for that matter, Sligo. Now, I was looking at a map of Ireland the other day, and I realised that Sligo's as far north as Monaghan, indeed further north than Clones, both about the same distance from the border between the Irish Republic and Northern Ireland.

And yet in my recollections of this time, I've always come to think of it as further south. This may have something to do with the more muted response the Dole Players' show received in Sligo, compared with the whooping, floor-stamping standing ovation it inspired in Clones. But I'm getting side-tracked by the vagaries of my memory, although it does throw light on some aspects of later events and my perception of them in retrospect.

As the applause died down, Kev said, "Must be the Provos in tonight, lads!"

There was a nervousness to the jest and the laughter it provoked from the rest of the cast, derived from the knowledge that tomorrow we were to play Belfast.

This is where my cheerful little travelogue takes a more macabre turn.

Our gig at Queen's University was the final leg of our tour, and the only one in Northern Ireland. Possibly one date too many. It's easy to forget now that these were the days before the Good Friday Agreement, before the successful appeals by the Birmingham Six and the Guildford Four, before *In the Name of the Father*, before power-sharing at Stormont. The injustices the play was exposing weren't the *cause celebre* they later became. I'd go so far as to say that Kev Mulligan was something of a pioneer.

But pioneering comes at a price. We were now venturing into territory where the Catholics who made up our potential audience were the minority, in a land of army checkpoints and steel-shuttered barbed wire-clad RUC stations that looked like above-ground fall-out shelters, of vast dour murals commemorating past victories and past atrocities. We were no longer in the Land of a Thousand Welcomes.

Hanging onto the slaughtered lamb for this final date was out of the question, I suppose, though why I went on my own to fetch the carcass for that night's show I'll never know. Maybe I wanted to prove myself to the Mulligan brothers, though why they let me is beyond me. They can't have realised quite how clueless I was about the whole situation over there. I've read up on it since but back then I had no idea.

And of course, you think you're invincible at that age, don't you? That's what people say anyway.

I look back on my eighteen-year-old self with a sense of wonder at my complete obliviousness to the changes in the murals as I drove through town, as well as to the implications of the tailback at the army checkpoint. Perhaps it doesn't seem so totally stupid, I suppose. After all, one large painting of armed men wearing balaclavas looks much the same as another to the uninitiated! In hindsight, of course, it's obvious: I should have noticed when the flags the painted paramilitaries were standing under changed from the Irish tricolour to the Red Hand of Ulster, when Shamrocks gave way to Orange Order regalia.

I should have noticed that the pub I'd entered was called the Battle of the Boyne.

It might as well have been the Slaughtered Lamb.

I think I sensed something was wrong as soon as I walked in. Maybe it was the portrait of the Queen hanging in pride of place behind the bar. Maybe it was the dead-eyed stares of the three men sitting in front of it. But before the penny had a chance to drop I'd gone into my spiel about the play and its need for a fresh lamb carcass, before I knew what I was doing.

The oldest of the three men looked at me for a moment. Something about that look made me stop in mid-sentence. The older man took a sip of his pint. My throat suddenly felt terribly, terribly dry. Somehow I knew I wouldn't be offered a drink here though.

At last, he spoke. "So you're English, right enough." His voice was a low burr with a Belfast twang.

I nodded, wanting to leave, but transfixed, rooted to the spot.

"D'you love your Queen and Country, then?"

I moved my head again, not so much a nod, more a tremble. He peered at me, his eyes squinting. There were angry mutterings from the two younger men. There was a Union flag tattooed on the thick pink roll of flesh around his neck.

"Well do ya or don't ya? Maybe you prefer Reds and Provos, is that it?"

"I—" I began.

"Aye?" he repeated.

"No."

"Uh?" His face was close to mine now. I could see pink rims around his yellow eyes. I could smell his sweat and tobacco.

"Wee cunt," I heard one of the others spit.

A meaty hand reached out and cupped the side of my face. "I'm gonna show you something," he whispered. "What's your name, son?"

"Robert."

"Well, Robert. Bob? Can I call you Bob? You all right with that? Good. Come with us…"

Refusal was not an option, though none of the men offered me any actual violence. They didn't need to. Several more men suddenly appeared as if from nowhere, surrounding me in that smoky sawdust-wreathed room.

"You're looking for some meat, are you, wee man? Well, me and the lads here happen to know a butcher works round the corner from here, don't we, boys?"

There were grunts of assent, some low mean chuckles. The men corralled me and escorted me out onto the street.

"Where are you taking me?" My voice squeaked shamefully. There was an awful lump in my throat, and tears were prickling. Hot urine trickled down my trouser leg. No one seemed to notice this. It was as if it was all in a day's work.

"Just for a little walk," he replied, his voice curt. "Not far."

One of the younger men who'd been there when I first walked in the pub said something about "Murphy's". At first I hung onto this word, persuading myself it was all a joke and they were going to take me for a pint of stout or something.

I soon realised that what he actually said was: "We taking him to Murphy's place, Da'?"

It wasn't a long walk, shorter than others I'd taken between pubs and meat lockers, but it seemed longer, either because of the piss-soaked trousers chafing against my legs or because of the dreadful prospect that this was strictly a one-way journey. Somehow the worst thing was the way the men exchanged small talk as if I wasn't there, some of it, I guessed, about what was in store for me, such as discussions about the price of a jerry can of petrol, or about where the Lagan Canal was deepest.

They led me to a rusting garage door, warped so that it wouldn't shut properly. The older man, the one who'd done most of the talking, told me to kneel, and don't move or he'd make me choke on my own piss-stained Fenian cock. This he said in the same low soft voice, as he stood behind me with the others sniggering at his side. He told me to shut my eyes, keep them tight shut or he'd stab the fuckers out, to shut my fucking mouth, and keep still until the Butcher came.

I stayed like that for a while, just listening to the broken door flapping in the wind.

At some point, I realized they'd just gone and left me there. The loose stones from the concrete surface near the garage dug into my knees. Though I was alone, I still found it hard to bring myself to open my tightly screwed-shut eyes. It was like when you wake from a nightmare, yet still don't dare open your eyes until your heart has stopped hammering in your chest.

I say I was alone. At least, that's what I thought.

When my eyes finally opened there was someone there. I hadn't heard his footsteps but out of the corner of my eye I could see his right hand holding something, a long something that glinted in the sunlight. There was a livid scar on his left palm. There was a red hand tattooed on the forearm, not much redder than the figure's actual hands, which were ingrained with dark rust-coloured stains, similar to how a motor mechanic's hands are permanently grimed with engine grease. I was still kneeling so I didn't see his face. I didn't dare look up.

I heard his voice, though, a kind of rusty drawl so close it seemed to echo inside my head. "Poor Tommy… Begged me to kill him in the end. I did, mind, but only after I'd peeled him like a banana. Know what I'd like more than anything right now, Bobby-boy?"

I realised he was addressing me, but I still couldn't bring myself to look up into his face.

"A nice wee Catholic girl… Toasted chestnuts… Nice bit of buttermilk…"

I shut my eyes again, screwed them tight for a long time, but it didn't stop the scalding hot tears from rolling down my sorry young cheeks.

When I came to myself he was gone.

Somehow I found my way back to the hired car and to the sanctuary of the university, expecting a bollocking from Kev for my failure to bring back a carcass for the show. He seemed surprisingly indifferent to my empty-handed abjectness. In fact, he hardly seemed to notice that I'd come in. I stood there for a while, saying nothing. I was in shock, I suppose.

Eventually, his nostrils wrinkled. One of his beady eyes regarded me with amusement. "You wanna change those strides, mate. You had an accident or summat?"

I might have been embarrassed had it not been for my numbness. But apart from Kev there was no one else to be embarrassed in front of. Where were the rest of the cast and crew? Even Chris wasn't around to right-hand-man his brother. Kev explained they'd all gone back to their digs.

"Vice-chancellor only went and pulled the show… Death threats, he said. A fookin' lackey of British imperialism!"

So that was the end of the Dole Players' tour of Ireland. They went back to England the following day and that was the last I saw of them until the following summer when they revived the play in Edinburgh.

But I had unfinished business. I took the next bus back to Sligo, my heart pounding with the memory of Sinead's smile and her buttermilk skin, but also with the memory of the words of the man with the nine-inch blade. To my intense relief and joy she was there, though I've since inflated the romance of my return to Sligo in my memory, thinking it was further south than Monaghan.

"You're alive," I said.

"Of course I am," she laughed. "Why shouldn't I be?

What a thing to say!"

And I'm alive, too, I thought to myself as I took her hand in mine. And before anyone says anything, yes, she was *that* Sinead, the same one you all know, the girl I married!

I later read up on some Irish history, found out about Lenny Murphy, the chief Shankill Butcher, the Red Right Hand of Ulster, with a scar on his left hand and a nine-inch double-bladed knife in his right, the one he used to carve strips of skin off Tom Madden as he dangled from the ceiling of a lockup garage. It said in the book that there were 147 stab wounds on Madden's body, though the cause of death was slow strangulation with a ligature. Reading about the tattoos on his arms and the scar on his left palm, I realised he must have been the man I met at the garage, the one who seemed to see Sinead in my mind.

And yet after reading on, I knew my memory must be playing some kind of trick on me about this, too, for the book said that Murphy was killed in 1982, about five years before the Dole Players toured Ireland with their play. That didn't stop me having nightmares about a flayed human torso suspended on chains and meat hooks, rotting but still moving, squirming with agony – or maggots.

It wasn't until quite some time after I became a vegetarian that the nightmares stopped.

Creeping Forth Upon Their Hands

Sir Edmund was an Undertaker when he first encountered the creatures.

Not literally, of course. "Undertaker" was the curious name given to the settler-colonial administrators installed in the Munster province of Ireland in the reign of Queen Elizabeth I. The word may refer to the tasks these dignitaries had to "undertake" in order to discipline the population. It is axiomatic that the imperatives of their role would have entailed the services of the other sort of undertaker.

~~~

About four centuries or so later, Dora Boyle takes the N7 from Dublin, merging into the M7 and M8 down to Cork, turning off onto the N72 to reach Mallow. As she drives southwest, her PhD supervisor's mellifluous scorn rings in her ears.

"You mean to tell me you haven't even read *The View of the Present State of Ireland* yet?"

She has to admit she hasn't. Hardly the worst crime in history, but since her thesis is supposed to be on "*The Faerie Queene* and Elizabethan Polity in the Munster Plantation" she can see why he thought this was a bit of an oversight. Still, he didn't need to be so supercilious about it. She'll show him! That's why she's brought it with her to read as close as possible to Spenser's country pile, or what's left of it.

In any case, Professor Keenan had no reason to be smug after what passed between them.

"You're twice my age," she reminded him. "And what would your wife think?"

"She needn't know," was his reply. "And as for the age

gap, it never bothered Spenser..."

"This is the twenty-first century not the sixteenth," she said then left before he could start reciting *The Epithalamion* at her, or something.

Maybe that was one of the reasons she's made this trip, mobile phone switched off. It might also be one of the reasons he's become a bit sniffy about her work lately. A break from the hothouse atmosphere of Trinity is just what she needs, even without his unwanted attention. She drives along the narrow country roads through flat open countryside. She frequently has to slow down for horses. Sometimes a white woman shape huddles demurely among the leaves, a roadside shrine to the Blessed Virgin.

The sky is leaden and fat raindrops soon begin spattering the windscreen, but she doesn't mind. The rhythmic whine of the windscreen wipers is soothing, if a little plaintive. *Help us! Help us!* it seems to say.

~~~

A wretched land, damp and boggy. After spending what felt like half a lifetime in Munster, that was Sir Edmund's abiding impression of the place. But for someone who had to work his passage through Merchant Taylors, a castle of one's own wasn't something to sniff at. It was just that trotting along the roads at night could be somewhat hazardous, even with an armed escort to protect you. One never knew when an ambush might burst from the quiet trees whispering in the wind. Cut them down. Raze them to the ground. Sow it with salt. That would flush out the damn bandits!

Talking of damnation, the whole place was riddled with popery and idolatry, too. They might say they venerated the Mother of Christ but make no mistake, they meant the Magner Mater, *with all the licentiousness and degeneracy that implied. Might as well worship Circe! He wished he might call up Talos. Now there was a man who could flail some sense into them.*

There was a rumour going around that some of the Papist forces wore helmets and breastplates that already bore the marks of a previous user. It was said an old woman dwelled in the bogs and wandered them in search of food and firewood. When she came upon a dead English soldier she would remove his armour and sell it to her compatriots. Sir Edmund imagined her clad in blackened rags with an evilly pointed nose. He thought of the old ballad about the two crows dining upon the new-slain knight.

"Ye'll sit on his white hause-bane,
And I'll pike oot his bonny blue een;
Wi ae lock o his gowden hair
We'll theek oor nest when it grows bare!"

He drove the Scotch gibberish out of his head. That was why it was essential to spread the English language as well as English ways. Ireland was a good example. No wonder the local population was so impudent and impious, when they still clung stubbornly to their native tongue. When you speak Irish, you think Irish.

As the darkness pressed in upon his convoy, like the mantles some of these bandits wore to hide their faces, he couldn't help remembering the final stanza of the border ballad:

"Mony a one for him makes mane,
but none sall ken whar he has gane;
Oer his white banes when they are bare,
The wind sall blaw for evermair."

~~~

Dora stops off in Doneraile to pick up the keys to the Airbnb from a giftshop on the high street. Smelling of scented candles, the shop is the only concession to tourists, and features tea towels and other trinkets, some decorated with the ruins of Kilcolman Castle, others with something obscurer than this local landmark: handprints dotted around a patch of ashen ground.

"Good old-fashioned name," remarks the shopkeeper as she signs for the keys.

"It's short for Eudora."

"Grand," the shopkeeper says drily.

"What's with the handprints?"

"Oh, that's just the hand-walkers' marks," the woman says with a laugh, as if it's a silly question.

When Dora looks at her quizzically, her only reply is to point to another tea towel design. On it, there's a reproduction of an old woodcut showing what appears to be a man doing a handstand, but with a face that's the right way up and positioned between legs that point skywards.

~~~

Sir Edmund woke with a start and lay there, sweating in his vast bed. Just another nightmare in which the things were crawling towards him through the woods about the castle, moaning and gibbering. They were slow and weak with famine, but that did not matter. In dreams, one's own limbs were fashioned from lead. Besides, that wasn't the point. It was that these base creatures, dragging themselves like serpents through the mire, had human faces.

At times like these, he cursed his poetic sensibilities. He and Sidney had often discussed this problem. If only it were possible to instruct a gentleman in virtuous living without the need to wrap it up in a pretty story rendered in verse. Then it were possible for them to live untroubled by their imaginations. He wondered if these human beasts would haunt him thus if he were not a poet. But he was an Undertaker, too. Perhaps it was part of his job to bury the past, or at least put it behind him.

He smiled as he turned to his sleeping wife in the bed beside him, her sweet face child-like in slumber. Perhaps he should waken her and enjoy her favours, to put the terrors of the night from his mind. No, let her sleep. Such thoughts were put there by the Devil. He often wondered if the wily Earl of Cork had given him his daughter as a distraction, to tempt him into the ways of Popish licentiousness. But she was also a reminder, as the Queen's namesake, of his holy poetic purpose, a fit muse for him. Such was the duality of life.

Later, the steward took him on a tour of the grounds, showing him the strange markings in the dirt. "Footprints, my lord," the man said. "Should I redouble the patrols?"

"Not footprints, sirrah," Sir Edmund corrected him, pointing to the way the fingers splayed out, the thumbprints, too. But the steward stared at them stupidly, struggling to understand his meaning. Could the fool not see that they were the prints of

hands? *"Your patrols will find nothing. Here's what you will do…"*

~~~

It's not hard to find the cottage. There aren't many houses near Kilcolman. She finds some provisions and a note left by the Airbnb host, a Mrs Fitzgerald. It's full of the kinds of instructions and admonitions she'd expect, about the heating and the cooker and the recycling.

But there's one rather unusual request: "You may find small animal corpses outside in the yard. Please don't touch them or throw them away! They'll be gone before you know it, so don't pay them any mind. All the best and have a wonderful holiday, Irene Fitzgerald."

What an extraordinary thing to request! She certainly has no intention of touching any dead animals, apart from the bacon Mrs Fitzgerald has considerately left for her in the fridge along with some other fresh produce. Looking out of the window at the drizzle misting the panes and shrouding the land around the place, she won't be going outside today, in any case. This seems like the perfect opportunity to sit down and read *The View of the Present State of Ireland* at last.

It's a good thing she's a captive audience here in the sticks. It isn't exactly a page-turner, just a tract about two blokes with Latin-sounding names discussing the cattle grazing customs of the Irish peasantry. Eudoxus argues they're practical and sensible, making maximum use of the land available. But *Ah!* says Irenaeus, it encourages rebellion, criminality and insubordination. If it weren't for your backward Irish grazing practices, he argues, we could starve the outlaws out.

Still, it's pretty dull stuff. In some ways she can see why Professor Keenan wanted her to read it. When all his other advances failed, perhaps he was hoping to bore her into submission. Inside the copy he lent her, probably as an excuse to gaze at her with his pathetic old puppy-dog eyes, he left a note inside the flyleaf, saying "FAO Dora

Britomart." Hah! The token female knight in *The Faerie Queene*, who represents chastity. Funny how of all the virtues on offer there's only one a woman can aspire to in Spenser's philosophy. She sees his game...

The professor's that is, the dirty old dog.

And she can see Spenser's, too, with *The View*.

Irenaeus moves onto the wearing of mantles, another filthy habit according to him. He's doing most of the talking by now. Poor old Eudoxus can hardly get a word in edgeways! It provides a disguise for your rebels, Irenaeus says, a hiding place for weapons and can even act as a makeshift shelter for a miscreant on the run in a storm. It would have to be a pretty sturdy mantle, Dora thinks, looking out at the rain sweeping more persistently now past the window, to protect you against the Irish weather. But she sees a pattern emerging from this. It's what would now be called a Culture War, quite literally. For Spenser, Irish culture, whether it's the language, the clothes, the agrarian practices, even the bloody weather! – it's all a cloak for sedition. Basically, if you can't get them to bend the knee you have to starve them into submission.

"Out of every corner of the woods and glens they came creeping forth upon their hands," he writes of those starving after the Desmond Rebellion, "for their legs would not bear them; they looked anatomies of death, they spoke like ghosts crying out of their graves; they did eat of the carrions, happy where they could find them, yea, and one another soon after, in so much as the very carcasses they spared not to scrape out of their graves."

Spenser (or rather his author proxy Irenaeus) sounds as if he pities them but his conclusion, calling the famine self-inflicted, makes it seem more like contempt.

The drumbeat of the rain the howling wind hurls at the panes isn't quite enough to cover the sound of something dragging itself along the ground outside the front door of the cottage. Probably an animal, but a large one that sounds like it's at death's door. Perhaps she should investigate but it's dark now and horrible outside. She doesn't like the thought of any poor creature suffering but she has no intention of going out there to look for it and nurse it back to health. She'll have a look in the morning.

~~~

After a few days of the things being nailed to posts outside the castle gates in the dog days, Elisabeth began to complain of the stench and the flies and the piteous sight of their grimacing rodent faces. He laughed at her beguiling soft-heartedness but reminded himself this was part of God's plan to test him. He should not be deceived by her name echoing that of his Gloriana. She was her father's daughter, after all. He was a knight errant and she the woman sent to tempt him with her wiles.

"But poor Peregrine…" she pleaded. "The nurse tells me he was a-weeping to wake the dead with the night terrors all this last night, my lord. Methinks it must be these monsters you've mounted hereabouts, these gargoyles of flesh and blood as might be in the shambles!"

"Tush!" he scoffed, recalling his own evil dreams. "I pray no son of mine will be a whey-faced milksop to cringe at shadows. Unless it be that he hath more of your woman's blood than he hath of my manly sap. I hope the latter be the case, for the beasts I have displayed outside are as nothing compared to what he'll doubtless see and smell in battle."

They were after all just rats, when all were said and done, and dead rats to boot. But he wished the unseen creatures he kept hearing outside the walls would make haste and take what he'd left for them. The corpses were now so far gone one could no longer see them for the glittering carapaces of the flies that swarmed upon them! Perhaps that was the problem. The things turned up their noses at such rank carrion now, did they? So this was what happened when you appeased them. They demanded choicer fare!

Then he saw his mistake, remembering those wretches he saw crawling from the woods and glens when the English forces humbled the treacherous Desmonds some fifteen years before. They lacked the strength to raise themselves from the dirt. He could hardly expect them to be able to reach rats atop posts.

~~~

The rain has cleared enough by morning for her to consider a trudge to the castle. But first she has to take a look outside to check for any mortally wounded or dead animal that might account for the dragging noises she heard the previous night. Her search reveals nothing but some odd prints that remind her of the designs on the tea towels and other trinkets she saw in the gift shop in Doneraile, in that they look more like hands than feet. Mrs Fitzgerald won't be happy with the damage to the grass, which the prints have churned to mud. Whatever made the prints has also flattened the grass with its weight, consistent with the sounds of the previous evening.

But what she sees next distracts her from fully digesting the implications of the markings. A half-eaten rat lies in the middle of the garden path, blocking her route. She could step over it but she is so affronted by the sight and smell of the vile object that she grabs herself a shovel from the porch, scrapes it up and hurls it, gagging, into the yew hedge bordering the cottage garden. It's only afterwards that she remembers Mrs Fitzgerald's warning against doing this. She shrugs. She's damned if she's going to retrieve it and put it back where it was. It's probably an old Cork superstition, and she heard enough of those from her grandmother back in the day. She's not going to live by them now, when she's paying good money to stay here in some minimal degree of comfort.

The castle's a bit of a disappointment. Maybe it doesn't help that it's raining again by the time she gets there, soaking through her hiking boots and inadequate raincoat, so she can barely see what's left of the place. She turns back before she can take a closer look and after she nearly falls into one of the many holes that honeycomb the land around it. Stumbling around in the mist with them around is probably a bad idea, she concludes, especially given the big red sign saying, basically, "Enter at your own risk!"

Glancing back, she glimpses a large dark-coloured

animal disappear down one of them, as if swallowed up by a vast wet mouth. Something about it makes her shudder. She doesn't know why. Maybe it's the way it moves and the unexpectedness of its appearance; or it could be its resemblance, despite its crawling motion, to a man wearing a kind of voluminous hooded cloak, one that covers all its limbs, if it has any.

No, not the most appealing castle in Ireland, she thinks as she hurries back towards the car. But hardly surprising since the rebels burnt it to the ground back in 1596, leading to Spenser's precipitate return to the more civilised world of Elizabethan London, where he died two years later.

~~~

"Where is my babe, Edmund? Prithee tell me!"

He laid his hands upon her shoulders but her grief would not be assuaged.

"Fie, Elisabeth. Weep not for him. He took his fate like a man at the end…"

How much worse would her lamentations be if he told her the truth of what happened to the infant! For there were bite marks upon his dismembered remains. Aye! And the teeth were those of men. It was his belief that what took him was no mere rebel, not the mortal men that sacked Kilcolman, but some other fiend.

This confirmed his suspicions regarding the reasons for the creatures' refusal to dine on the rats he left, even when he took them down from the posts and left them on the ground where they might devour them with ease. They preferred finer meat – that of his issue and perhaps his descendants, too.

~~~

When she gets back to the cottage, feeling the want of human contact rather keenly, Dora reanimates her phone. There are half-a-dozen messages from Professor Keenan.

BEEP: "Hi, Dora. Look, sorry about how we left things. I was out of order. Hope you got there okay and the traffic was… Just take care, okay? Bob."

Well, nice he cares – not just after one thing, but "Bob"! He always wanted to be on first name terms.

She sees why now…

BEEP: "Dora, I get that you're not my number one fan right now but if you wouldn't mind letting me know you're okay, that'd be grand… Just grand."

Sounds really worried. Or he could just be the controlling sort. That would raise red flags even if he *weren't* married and old enough to be her father!

BEEP: "Listen, I did a bit of digging about the local legends. Well, you know how we were saying it was funny how you were called Boyle, Elizabeth Spenser's maiden name. Look, I don't want to alarm you or anything, but—"

She cuts him off, deleting the remaining messages. He's worse than her gran! She wouldn't be surprised if this were a ploy to frighten her into ringing him up so he could come riding down on his metaphorical white charger. Fortunately, he doesn't know where she's staying.

Something drags itself up the path and hurls itself at the front door. After the initial shock at the noise, she tells herself to think rationally. Even superstitions have their own infantile logic! The dead rat must be what they leave out for … whatever this is. It's just a matter of getting past it and retrieving it. Lovely!

She rushes out of the back door as the front door warps under further blows, then she circles around to where she threw it. The yew's bristles scratch her bare arm as she rummages around feverishly, hearing the dragging again, nearer now. It's almost dark but she can just make out the grey fur in the gloaming. She reaches out and grasps the dead rat, feeling queasy at its soft yielding limpness, but she'd rather touch that than the creature at her back whose rank breath she can smell. She throws the rat over her shoulder to draw it off but it's like a cat that turns its nose up at what's offered and hunts wrens and sparrows instead. The pressure of its teeth on her neck and the rasp of the sacking covering the arms that enfold her in a bearhug vice tells her carrion will not suffice this time, not when there's a Boyle to be had.

A Heart of Stone

Dear Roisin,

It was grand to see you in March and catch up with the old gang from school. Thanks for your address, and for putting me in touch with Sister Dolores. Sorry to hear she hasn't been too well. If only there'd been time, maybe I could have taken her with me and dropped her off at Lourdes on the way! I'll just have to pay her a visit when I get back. Shame you couldn't help me with Father Brennan, the elusive old devil. Another one I'll have to catch up with when I return from my trip. There just wasn't time for tying up all these old loose ends, what with sorting out air tickets, passports, deciding which sites to visit, etc.

As you can see from the picture, my first port of call is an obvious one – Notre Dame with all its gargoyles, the ones Quasimodo liked hanging out with. Remember the time the sisters let us watch the Disney version of that story? Until Dolores marched in and switched it off. *Blasphemous*, she said. I think she didn't like the way it showed the lecherous old priest condemning Esmeralda as a witch because he couldn't have her.

But there I go again, dwelling on the past! That's something you gave me a talking to about when we met up, so *mea culpa, ave maria* X10, etc., etc.

Lots of love from Gay Paree!

Maddie

~~~

Dear Roisin,

How the devil are you? Told you I was going to write you a postcard from every stop on my pilgrimage around the holy sites of Europe and beyond. If you're wondering who your man is in the picture, it's the architect of the

Basilica di Santa Croce here in Lecce. Cheery-looking fellow, so he is. So would you be if you managed to get yourself immortalised in stone. I know I would. He hid his features in the frills and flourishes around the main figures. Cheeky, eh?

Maybe when I graduate and get my first commission designing some high-profile project, say a hospital or government building or something (knowing my luck it'll like as not be a housing estate – like the sort developers left half built back in the Noughties), I'll sneak a wee engraving of my ugly mug somewhere no one notices, eh?

I got a train from Bari, where there's a chapel on the platform. Maybe Sister Dolores should have come! She'd feel right at home. The good Father too...

I certainly feel that way. All this sun and ancient art. I could get used to this. Not sure if they'd approve of all the sculptures though, that pinched-faced pair. Every street corner in this town seems to have an effigy of the Holy Mother with her tits out – to give suck to Our Lord, of course, so no funny business. But it's not something you'd see back home. Coy roadside shrines, maybe, but not that sort of thing. Those two might prefer a nice blood-splattered Christ on the cross, like you get a lot of over here. He's even hanging in one of the corner shops, bleeding all over the salami. Can't be very hygienic.

But I'm running out of space now. Talk again soon.
Maddie.

~~~

Dear Roisin,

No postcard this time, partly because I wanted to send you one from each of the stopping off points on the Grand Tour, and this ain't one of them. I'm at the seaside! I decided I needed to get away from the town, get some sea air. Hardly what I expected though. It's not exactly sunbathing weather. Chucked it down when the woman dropped me off at the Airbnb. The road outside the apartment block was flooded from the shower even though it only lasted a few minutes. She explained the Italian drainage system wasn't designed to cope with heavy rain. They don't usually get it, not like back home, eh? It added to the air of an off-season holiday resort, along with the empty amusement park with giant staring yellow Simpsons figures daubed on the sign, and the dead dog lying behind the fence, fizzing with flies.

The other reason for this letter was to talk about things I'd rather not on a postcard. Personal stuff, you know? Stuff I wouldn't want the postie to read. It's also stuff you'd probably rather not hear about, things you pretty much told me to stop harping on about. Well, tough titty, Roisin. You're probably the only person I know from back then so you've got some inkling of what happened to me. Not "what happened to me" – what they did to me. It wasn't an act of God. I know we were never that great friends even back then, but you're all I've got, Rosh! I know you wouldn't write back, even if you could. I'll probably be somewhere else by the time you read this, anyway. The only other option would be exchanging emails. I prefer corresponding the old-fashioned way. Partly fears of unseen eyes reading it, partly, well... The act of physically writing it down, putting pen to paper, seems more personal somehow. In any case getting a reply isn't uppermost in my mind. The main thing is to get it off my chest.

I can imagine you hardening your heart against me as you read this, the way you seemed to at the reunion. I could tell you were switching off. So I moved onto other more congenial subjects.

The Airbnb's an apartment with sea views. Well, a view of the car park that overlooks the harbour. This morning there was the Italian version of a car boot sale there. Their voices woke me, chanting their wares, so I had a look around. It was all there. Fennel bulbs and olives, bricks of Parmesan and torpedoes of spiced meats. A craft stall sold little blank-eyed effigies of Demeter, made of Puglia's red clay. The sea air made me hungry for seafood so I went up to an old man and what looked like his son selling sea urchins and mackerel out of the back of the van with a snake-haired woman painted on the side. The sea urchins looked a bit hairy but the mackerel looked like it would hit the spot.

I smiled at the young man. Why not? He was quite good looking. But instead of smiling back, he just stared at me, muttered something to the old fellow, something about *la versiera*, or maybe *l'avversiera*. I'm not sure which. Anyway, after a painful attempt at trying to make myself understood in Italian I came away with a wonderfully oily piece of mackerel, which I devoured for breakfast after walking away from their sullen looks. I thought their eyes were still following me and their voices still discussing me all the way back, but it was just Homer Simpson's bulging stare outside the disused fairground and the buzz of the flies nesting in the dead dog.

But, God, it's lonely being somewhere where you don't speak the language!

Maybe that's why I've been thinking about what went on back at school. Being in unfamiliar surroundings makes you look inwards – and backwards, I find. Maybe that's why all those backpackers go to exotic locations "to find themselves". I've never had any patience with such folk, but maybe it's happening to me whether I like it or not.

The weather's been dreadful so I've been spending a lot of time in the Airbnb apartment. So much for my couple of days by the seaside! First thing, I lay in bed listening to the shouts from the market outside and staring at the ceiling fan. No need to use it – it would make the place colder than it is already. It just hung there like a crucifix, pressing me down onto the bed. When I got up it was almost as if I was rolling out from under the weight of a man with designs on my virtue. Not that I've got any.

I certainly didn't as far as Dolores was concerned, as she chastised me for my "sordid little affair". And I don't mean just verbal chastisement either. She clobbered me to beat the band with those rosary beads of hers. Do you remember you always suspected she had a thing for Father Brennan? Well, maybe that's why she took on so when she walked in on us. So much for "our little secret".

But to call it an "affair", to act like I was some sort of scarlet woman, like I was a willing partner here, when I was barely thirteen... Jesus, Rosh! That takes some doing.

But here I go again, dwelling on the past. It was the picture on the van that did it, I think – the lady with the snakes for hair. I read up a bit on the Greek mythology. Thought I'd better since I'm going there next. I already knew about Medusa, of course, but I didn't know the full story, that when Poseidon raped her in Athena's temple the goddess punished her by turning her hair into serpents and her face into instant stony death for those who looked upon her. Yes, you did read that right. Athena punished *her*, not Poseidon, for this desecration. I can see some interesting parallels here...

Not that it happened in the chapel, you might say to the contrary. But then being a convent school, the whole place is technically a place of worship, isn't it? The whole thing was a lot more banal than Greek mythology.

I remember the dried-up old bitch dropping the tea she'd brought him as if she were that housekeeper in *Father Ted*. I don't remember her name. I can't sit through an episode personally, these days, just can't buy into the idea of cosy bumbling bachelor priests, and the old drunk one in the chair gives me nightmares, and the only person saying *go on, go on, go on, go on,* and *you will, you will, you will, YOU WILL* in this situation was the dirty old man in the dog collar.

Sorry, I hope I'm not making you feel uncomfortable, Roisin dear. I know your salad days in the convent were the best ones of your life. Or something. All right. I'm not being fair. There might be things about that time *you'd* rather forget, and maybe that's why you don't like me bringing this up, eh? Thing is, I can't. Not now. Something to do with being out here on the edge of Europe, on the tip of the Italian boot's stiletto heel.

I'm going to Otranto tomorrow, where you can see across the Adriatic to Albania on a clear day. As if you'd want to! I'll see the cathedral walls lined with the skulls of martyrs who refused to renounce their faith when the Turks invaded. I think I'd have dumped Christianity and kept my head if it was me, but hey ho. What would you have done, Roisin? I think I know what Dolores would have done, the fecking doormat.

Maybe your man sensed that when he was having the *craic* with his son, after they'd been eyeing me up in that strange way they did. When I was reading up on the old Medusa stuff it suddenly struck me where I'd heard that word before – whichever one it was. *Versiera* means a turning circle, a term used in Latin sailing jargon, apparently. Yes, it's more likely that was what he meant, a salty old sea dog like him, though why he'd be speaking Latin these days is beyond me. I'm a ship now, so I am! *God bless her – and all who sail in her!* as my uncle used to say in his cups.

Then again, it might be the old Italian word *l'avversiera* – meaning witch, she-devil, enemy or *adversary* of God.

Well, it wouldn't be the first time someone's mixed up those words. It happens to the best of us! Take Maria Agnesi. When she wrote her 1748 mathematical treatise she didn't expect some Cambridge boffin to start calling her most famous theory the "Witch of Agnesi". How do I know this stuff? Well, we architecture folk use it in topography, don't you know…

I've been prattling on for long enough. I'm going to have to love you and leave you now, my dear.

TTFN!

Maddie

~~~

112

Dear Roisin,

Back to picture postcards now – and this one's a belter, don't you think?

Here she is, the Blessed Virgin! Quite an image, isn't it?

She looks at home among the skulls, not phased at all. Gotta love the way she's more concerned with praying than with holding the baby on her lap. No one thinks *she's* defiling the temple because a god interfered with her! But then the immaculate conception took place in more humdrum surroundings, and besides, she's different, isn't she? *Virgo Intacta.*

In reality, a woman like her could easily have busted her hymen from riding a camel or something. And these days a lady can repair the damage with a discreet bit of surgery. So it's meaningless anyway.

Sorry. I know you're still wedded to the Roman Church – though not a fully fledged Bride of Christ, like Dolores. I hope I haven't upset you.

It's the child I feel sorry for. If he starts wriggling about he could roll off her lap and crack his head open on that marble floor. Maybe he's too serene to do that. Well, the Mother of God doesn't seem too worried, and judging by the look in her eyes her mind's on higher things. Still, I'd have thought His Highness might be on her mind under the circumstances…

But who am I to judge – a slut, a witch, who managed to bewitch a saintly old man of the cloth and defile his vows of celibacy at a mere thirteen years of age?

Apologies again for talking out of turn.

Mea culpa, mea culpa. Ave Maria. Ave Maria ave maria avemariaavemariaavemariaavemariaavemariaavemaria!

Off to Brindisi tomorrow. Next stop Greece – Akropolis Now! Will write again then…

Your pal,
Maddie.

~~~

Dear Roisin,

The weather's a bit better here in Athens, but as you'll see from the pic, Medusa doesn't look too happy about it. Well, neither would you be if someone had chopped off your head and stuck it on the breastplate of the woman who'd stolen your good looks and replaced them with a face that could kill men with a look. That Athena really had it in for her, didn't she? Not content with punishing the victim, she had to wear poor old Meddie's head as a trophy. You know, some representations make her look pretty hot, under all the snake hair. Once you see past that and the generally hacked-off expression (justifiable, in my view) she doesn't look any worse than I do with a hangover. I can't say the same for this one – all lolling tongue, fangs and mono-brow. And the snakes go right the way round her face giving her a scaly beard. This one's in bronze too, which somehow adds to the effect, don't you agree?

Well, this Medusa may be no oil painting but I'm kind of growing fond of her. Maybe it's because of, not despite, her ugliness. I'd even go further and say this piece spoke to me. I know I should have been looking around the ruins of the Akropolis, admiring the structure, the architecture, etc. But I hardly even noticed it. I just stared at the bronze head of Meddie for hours.

For so long, in fact, I literally began to hear her speaking to me!

The voice was low, cavernous. Given that the words were in Greek I couldn't understand it. Actually, it was probably just the museum PA system warning it was closing in five minutes or something, because when I looked around all the other visitors had left.

The funny thing was, I felt disappointed rather than relieved when I realised what the voice actually was.

All the best,
Maddie.

~~~

Dear Roisin,

Sorry, it's been a while. Actually, maybe you're relieved! Anyway, here's another Medusa-themed postcard. She seems to follow me everywhere! This one's from Didyma. This gigantic face of everyone's favourite Gorgon looks less like a monster and more like a moping Romantic poet, complete with pouting lips and cleft chin and curls that barely look like snakes at all. Only the bigger cleft right across the face hints at the inner scars...

Deep, huh?

Funny place to build a temple to Apollo, you might think, here in Southern Turkey. But this was a centre of the Ionian civilisation, and the Didymaion (cracks me up every time – keeps making me think of the Diddy Men) was here way before Greek colonisation, according to Pausanias. So there are plenty of Ionic columns to keep the architect in me happy. Not that I care that much for them. Seen one column, you've seen them all.

I should feel lonelier the further away from home I get but somehow I don't. Maybe that's the reason I haven't written for a while. I haven't been short of company. Meddie's been speaking to me again. I know it sounds crazy but it can't be a museum announcement if I hear it when I'm not in a museum, can it?

I should work out what the voice is saying. Trouble is, I don't think it's Greek – even ancient Greek. It's more ancient than that still...

The other weird thing is, I've started avoiding mirrors. It's like I feel as if someone might use them to creep up on me.

Your old pal,
Maddie.

~~~

Dear Roisin,

Final port of call on my wee pilgrimage is Chorazin. I'm really in the Holy Land now. I feel like an undercover Crusader, or would do if I were still a true believer. See

Medusa on the other side. Funny how she gets into all the pre-Christian places of worship. This one's a synagogue, by the way, in Galilee, quite near the Lebanese border. The presence of such a creature, sculpted sometime after the death of Christ, suggests Our Lord's teachings weren't enough to wean the locals off their filthy heathen ways. She looks cute, don't you think? Not like a monster at all, with her serpentine curls a discreet and elegant halo around her face, surrounded by what looks like the rays of the sun. Maybe it's her dazzling loveliness that turns all the men to stone, it seems to say, not her hideousness. And her expression is deceptively innocent for someone as vile as she's made out to be. I remember Sister Dolores saying something like that about me as she dragged me away from Father Brennan, who sat there like a little boy caught messing his pants.

"Little Miss Madeleine Devlin, would you look at you. And with a face like butter wouldn't melt…"

I did look a bit dishevelled at the time. I've been letting myself go a bit lately too. I still shower from time to time but have to get in there quickly when I do so I don't see the mirror in the bathroom, and everywhere you stay's slightly different, making it harder to anticipate where it'll be. My personal hygiene's gone a bit awry, a far cry from the obsessive scrubbing I used to do back in the day, till my skin was raw and bleeding. Maybe that's why folk are giving me a wide berth, or maybe it's just the sense of paranoia around here. All the older teenagers carry rifles here the way they carry mobile phones back home. You see them hitching rides with them slung over their shoulders. But then they're all in the army for part of the year.

I don't know if it's the tension in the air from the constant state of war but will *nobody* around here look at me directly? Caught this lad ogling me by way of my reflection in a shop window. It's not as if he was being bashful about it. He had this sort of smirk on his face, somewhere between lust and disgust.

Reminded me of Father Brennan.

That reminds me, I'm heading back tomorrow. All this introspection has got me thinking of some unfinished business back home.

I'll be in touch when I get home.

Maddie

~~~

Dear Roisin,

Home again!

It's so disorientating, the way you board a plane amid blazing sunshine and cacti then when you get off it's pissing down.

I said I had some loose ends to tie up, one or two house calls to make, and I wasn't lying. First there was Sister Dolores. As it turned out, she didn't have much time left to make her peace. Not that she recognised me. Gently cupping her face so she couldn't look away I said, "Remember me?"

Of course she didn't. I must have changed a lot from the girl she knew. There was a flicker of recognition just before her eyes dimmed, those eyes that used to be able to suck the air out of a room, now softened by dementia, and those cheekbones that I used to think could cut you if you got too close, sagging and wrinkled.

"Are you an angel of mercy?" she asked.

I suppose I must have been because her heart stopped instantly. You'll have heard about it in the papers. A sudden, unexpected case of fibrodysplasia ossificans progressiva, a very rare condition. You might call it a miracle. By the strangest of coincidences you might also have heard about a certain Catholic priest coming down with the same affliction. Unfortunately for him it's spreading slowly through the body. The first place it affected was a particularly intimate one, leaving him reliant on a stoma to piss. He could live for years like this, gradually ossifying until he can only move his lips, like Harry Eastlack, whose skeleton now rests in the Mutter

Museum in Philadelphia. Eastlack eventually succumbed to pneumonia in 1973. Instant death by pulmonary ossification is probably unheard of, so maybe they should put Dolores's heart in a glass case somewhere. But as far as I'm concerned, hers was always made of stone, though I think I understand why she was like that. For years I've wondered why she couldn't have shown me a little compassion. Didn't Our Lord wash the feet of my almost namesake? She wasn't Him of course, and yet she might have felt solidarity as a fellow female. I know now that wasn't possible for her. Sometimes women in her position can only keep their place by punching downwards.

May she rest in peace, and may he live a long, long time.

Yours truly,

Maddie.

Mum and Dad and the Girl from the Flats over the Road and the Man in the Black Suit

I think Mum's cross with Dad.

It's not because he made friends with Alison from the flats across the road. That's what often makes mums upset with dads in films and books and things.

My mum's not like other mums.

Last time I saw Alison, she looked so sad. She stopped outside the window while Dad pretended not to see her. Then she walked back to the removal van.

Now she's gone and she's taken her little girl Suzie with her, the one I made friends with. When I first met Suzie I asked her about her braids. Her hair was all done up in stiff ropes down the back of her head. Some people call them cornrows, she said. It took a long time to do, she told me.

Dad was chatting to Alison as we walked up the grey steps to their flat. He was asking her about the light that kept flashing on the landing outside their door. Couldn't the council fix it for you? He was asking. It must drive you mad!

She just laughed and told him how it always took ages for anything to get sorted.

Suzie said it was the Man in the Black Suit that made it do that.

Her mum shushed her and told her off for making stuff up. Changing the subject, Alison asked Dad what he did. She laughed when he said architect. She laughed again when he said he hadn't designed these flats. She stopped laughing suddenly when she opened the door to the flat and saw the letter inside. It was in a white envelope, with little slanting green stripes around the edge.

Dad asked if it was bad news.

She laughed again. Her laugh was different this time, sort of shaky.

We went to Suzie's room. She laughed when she saw me looking for the stairs, then I remembered it was all on one floor. We were upstairs already!

Have you never been in a block of flats before? She asked.

Well, yeah, but... Is this your room? I asked.

No, that was my brother's room, she said.

Oh, I said.

Walking past the door with the name Ben on it, we went in the next room. We played for a bit. I asked her who the Man in the Black Suit was.

She laughed and said, Didn't you know about him? All the kids in the flats do.

Suzie carried on about the Man in the Black Suit until I started to wish I hadn't asked her. Whenever the lights went all funny like the one outside Suzie's flat, you knew he'd been past your door. That meant he was going to come and take you away soon.

Why would he do that? I asked.

I don't know, she said. I think it's cos he's dead inside.

One night she couldn't sleep and she heard slow footsteps outside the flat. They were so slow she thought her brother had come back. She peed on the floor and her mum woke up and cleaned her up, cleaned the floor, took her back to bed. But through the door frame she could see the light flickering on and off. It had been like that ever since.

Afterwards, other kids in the flats said it must have been the Man in the Black Suit.

I asked her if that was why the flat next door to hers had the picture in the window of an angel or saint or something spearing a demon. Had her neighbours put it there to ward off evil spirits like this Man in the Black Suit? She gave a bitter little laugh and said, He wouldn't be stopped by no angel or saint, Betty.

I must have looked scared or something because she looked at me and smiled. Don't worry, Betty, she said, he won't come for you. You live on the other side of the road, the side with the *big* houses.

I'd never thought of myself as rich before, or my house as big, but it was true. We do live in a house, not a block of flats. Dad doesn't pay rent to a landlord or the council. He pays something called a mortgage. He says you can still lose your house if you don't pay, but if you rent that's called *eviction*, whereas if you own it's called *repossession*. Possession is nine tenths of the law, he says. You can't move into a house without vacant possession, he says. He talks a lot about this sort of thing. Sometimes I think it's all he ever talks about.

Let's play SingStar, Suzie said. D'you like One Direction?

When I went to the toilet I heard Alison in the kitchen talking to Dad in a hard voice.

Can't afford a shrine anymore, she said. My boy died so the flat's too big for us, they're saying. What do they want me to do, rent out his room to a foreign student? Only I forgot, we're not allowed to sublet, are we?

I didn't hear what Dad said in reply. When it was time to go home she was all smiles. She looked pretty, then, but not as nice as Mum. She looked pretty because her eyes were shining.

We got on really well, Suzie and me. One weekend she wasn't there, though. I went over the road to ask for her. Alison said she was at her dad's for the weekend. I turned around, disappointed, saw Dad waving at her from our front garden. Alison was waving back, smiling. Mum was watching from the upstairs window, blowing smoke rings like she always used to. She didn't wave. She did smile though. She always smiled. I sat around in my room for a bit.

Later I went for a sleepover at Daisy's.

I woke up screaming from a dream about a man in a black suit who'd trapped me and Suzie in a big wood-panelled room full of green-leather benches. He was under a bright spotlight, making a speech in a high piping voice. The glare of the spotlight meant I could see him clearly, though not the others on the benches listening to him who were not lit but sounded like him, too. He had boiled white jelly eyes like the ones on the salmon we'd had for tea last night, and baked soft pink salmon skin too, and no teeth, just gums that sucked at you like a baby drinking from its mummy. I could tell he was dead inside. I was relieved though, when I woke up and found myself screaming. Because in the dream I couldn't. It was like I'd lost my voice. It was like I had that thing Mum said she had, Larry-something.

Daisy's mum tried to ring Dad. He wouldn't answer. She drove me back. We sat in the car in the dark outside our house. She sighed and rang his phone and sighed again and rang his phone again. Finally he answered. She told him what had happened, then told me he'd come out and get me. I looked towards our house. No lights came on. Suddenly he appeared, out of breath and buttoning up his shirt, from the other side of the road. I couldn't understand it. He looked like he'd just come from the flats where Alison lived. Daisy's mum looked puzzled about it too. She didn't say anything. Dad thanked her and said sorry for not answering his phone. He took me inside.

I had trouble sleeping that night. I was worried the dream might carry on when I went back to sleep. And I was trying to figure out why Dad had been over at the flats. After a while I hugged Beatrice until Mum came and soothed me to sleep. Before she did I asked her about it. She just said Dad needed to move on now. If he was happy and he made this other lady happy, they both had her blessing. I know it sounds weird that she didn't mind them being together. Like I said, she's not like other mums. I didn't tell her about the Man in the Black Suit. I didn't want to worry her. With her watching over me he didn't come back that night, anyway. I didn't tell Dad about him either. I can't really talk to him about feelings and things like that. I don't really want to. Like I said, he's so cut off. He's *not there* somehow. I just talk to Mum about stuff like that, instead.

Mum really wanted him to be happy. She wanted them both to be happy.

But then Dad decided he didn't want to be friends with Alison anymore. Mum sort of changed after that.

Alison came over once with Suzie, the weekend after that time I'd come back early from the sleep over. Dad said Suzie was welcome to come in and play. Alison stood there like she was waiting to be invited in.

He said, You kids'll have to amuse yourselves, *I've got a lot of work on at the moment*. He looked at Alison as he said the last bit, with a funny heavy voice, like he was spelling something out.

Oh, she said, sort of surprised, and left.

She came round another weekend when Suzie was at her dad's. When I said I'd go to my room, he got me making cups of tea for them and finding other chores for me to do downstairs so he wouldn't be alone with her. When she'd gone he looked at me and sighed and said, You look so much like your mother, you know. Then he said, Without her I feel sort of … dead inside.

I asked if I should go to Daisy's for a sleepover again even though I knew that they probably wouldn't invite me after the last time. He just shook his head. The truth is, I was a bit frightened of him when he got like that, sort of not there. He got so angry sometimes, ever since Mum went away.

Like I said, if I want to talk about feelings and stuff, I don't talk to him, I talk to Mum.

At least, that's what I used to do. Until she suddenly stopped coming when I hugged Beatrice, which had always worked before.

That's how I knew she was cross. Really cross.

It was what Dad used to call her giving him the silent treatment, when she was still around. Now she wouldn't even come and see me at night anymore. It seemed like she was giving *me* the silent treatment. I think it's because he made Alison sad when Mum had given them her blessing, which must have been sort of tough for her.

When she went, Dad didn't really say where she'd gone, what had happened to her. One day she just wasn't there anymore. *Really* not there, not the way Dad often isn't there. I remember they were fighting quite hard the day before, Dad shouting. So hard I heard something break in the kitchen. I was too scared to go down and look, too scared to come out of my room, even.

She still visited me at night after that, though, spoke to me through my rag doll Beatrice. The doll has big blue eyes and bright yellow hair and she always smiles. Now she's as silent as the grave. I tried shaking her, throwing her at the wall, stamping on her until the stuffing came out. Then I said, Sorry Mum, please forgive me.

The doll just stared and smiled. What was left of her did anyway.

Thanks, Dad. It was like he made Mum go, all over again.

Was it him that made her go the first time?

When she was still speaking through Beatrice, Mum said she forgave him. I couldn't understand what for then.

Now I do.

Since she's stopped visiting me at night and talking through Beatrice, I've been lying awake in bed, thinking more and more about that time I heard something break in the kitchen, then everything went silent. I wasn't sure if it was a plate or a cup or something else. But it couldn't have been part of Mum that had broken, could it? Because I didn't hear her scream. The only voice I'd heard in the fight was Dad's angry one. Was she giving him the silent treatment? Then I remembered: Mum couldn't have screamed. For days before that she'd been talking to me in this strange whisper, because she had Larry-whatever it is, she said. Until I kept thinking I could hear her voice in my head. It was after the fight that I began to hear it that way, all the time through my doll.

Laryngitis. That's what it is. I just looked it up in a dictionary.

Will she forgive me for doing what I did to Beatrice? When I asked where Mum had gone, Dad just said she'd turned into an angel. What kind of answer is that? Eventually, when I asked him again and kept on asking him until he couldn't ignore me anymore, he said it hadn't been Laryngitis after all but something more serious. Cancer. From the cigarettes, cancer sticks he called them. He'd been trying to get her to stop smoking them. It was one of the reasons for their fights. The last time I saw her was when he took me to visit her in the hospital and she had a machine to help her breathe. After that, she went away.

And now Suzie and her mum have gone away too, not the same way as Mum did, though. They left in a taxi, not a box. I saw them packing everything into a van. I don't think they wanted to leave. I think they had to. Something to do with the letter with the green stripes around the edge. I wanted to go out and say goodbye to them. Dad told me not to. He said it would only upset them. They looked pretty upset anyway, to me. I don't see how me saying goodbye to them would have made things worse. I wonder who'll move in now the Council's got vacant possession, Dad said. I cried when he told me they weren't just leaving the street, they were leaving town altogether, going somewhere up North. I never got Suzie's address. He said, I don't know why you're so upset, Betty. You should be happy for them. Not many people manage to escape this town. Maybe he was making a joke, trying to cheer me up, but it didn't make me laugh.

The light doesn't flash outside their flat at night, anymore.

From my bedroom window I can see other lights flickering on and off in the stairwells of the flats. I wonder who the Man in the Black Suit's coming for next.

When they'd gone, Dad switched on the TV news. He had to switch it off again because I screamed when I saw a man in a black suit making a speech in front of rows and rows of others in black suits on green leather benches in a big wooden room. The man making the speech had a pink salmon face. He was laughing, taunting the man standing opposite him on the other side of the big room.

After that I had the dream again, worse this time. In this one, the Man's baby gums stopped sucking when he got to me. His lips puckered like I didn't taste nice. I knew that that was the only reason why he'd spared me. He would have screwed his boiled fisheyes up tight if they had any lids. Suzie was lying on one of the green benches in the big wooden room like on the TV. At first she looked like a pile of clothes. They were the ones I'd seen her wearing once before.

Then I saw braids sticking out of her collar, the ones people sometimes call cornrows. I could see her braids but not much else.

I couldn't scream. It was like I had Laryngitis. Like Mum did when she and Dad had the fight in the kitchen.

Suzie's clothes and skin and face were all fallen in and saggy, as if someone had taken all the bones out of her. She must have tasted nicer than I did. This time when I woke up I didn't scream. I hardly even dared to breathe. I wasn't doing the silent treatment and I didn't have Laryngitis. I just didn't want the Man in the Black Suit to hear me.

But then a little voice started whispering to me about the dream. Maybe that's why Mum doesn't come any more, like she used to, and speak to me through Beatrice.

She doesn't need to use her. Maybe Dad's right and I am too old for rag dolls now, anyway. Maybe Mum lives *inside* me now. Because the little voice I sometimes hear now sounds like her voice when she had Laryngitis, a sort of smoky whisper. The voice that tells me things, explains things that Dad can't or won't explain.

Like the Man in the Black Suit, for example. He said, Don't be silly, the man on the TV isn't a monster. He can't be. He's in the government. He's the Prime Minister.

He wouldn't explain who the Man in the Black Suit really was, just like he wouldn't explain what really happened to Mum.

I know now.

The little voice said he could have helped them so they didn't have to go away. He looked the other way. He *made* them go away with his not being there, the voice told me.

I really wanted Alison and him to be happy, the little voice whispered to me. (Well, it didn't talk *to* me exactly, more *in* me.) *He was always so unhappy with me*, the little voice went on. *Maybe if I'd made him happier he wouldn't have done what he did to me.*

So I was right. He was lying about the throat cancer. I think the machine had been to help her breathe because he broke something in her, and that made her go away. Not go away. Die. There I've said it. I did wonder why the police hadn't come to take him away if he'd killed her. But I soon worked that one out. He's a good liar and has friends in the police. I won't fall for his lies anymore.

Like the one about her turning into an angel. As if I'm still young and stupid enough to believe that kind of nonsense. I am ten years old now!

I remember what he said, after sending Alison away. That he felt *dead inside*, just like Suzie had said the Man in the Black Suit was.

I know what he is now.

It's up to me to help others like Alison and Suzie now. The Man in the Black Suit made them go away. After what

I saw on television I think the prime minister must be one of the same creatures. Maybe it was him that sent the letter with the green lines on the edge. Either there are lots of these monsters or there's one who can pretend to be lots of different people. I can stop him sending other children away. I'll be like the angel in the picture, spearing the demon. It's easiest for him to pretend to be people who sort of aren't there anyway. Like, on television. In your home but distant.

Like Dad.

I've stopped trying to breathe really quietly now. I'm not afraid anymore. I went into Dad's room and saw him sleeping. He was snoring. That helped. How can I be afraid of someone snoring?

But I know now what he wears at night when no one's watching, to go over to the flats.

A black suit. I saw it in his wardrobe. He said it was for Mum's funeral but I know different.

He asked Alison why the council couldn't fix the light for her.

But I know it's him that goes over there at night and fixes it so they go wrong in the first place!

I wondered why his eyes were closed, when the Man in the Black Suit I'd seen in my dreams had no eyelids.

I know why now.

It's not his real face. The air was whistling between his teeth, so I knew they must be false ones to cover his sucking baby gums. I couldn't see where the Dad face joined onto the pink salmon fish-eye face underneath. He's not my dad anymore, hasn't been for a long time. He went away from himself, left himself in vacant possession, so something else sneaked under his skin while he wasn't there, like those squatters they warn about on the news. That's why he made Mum go away. That's why he got away with it, too. If he's also pretending to be the Prime Minister he's in charge of the police, isn't he?

I'm going to find where the mask joins the face. I'm

going downstairs to the kitchen to get one of the sharp knives, so I can use it to cut the Dad face off the fish face. I'll make the Man in the Black Suit tell me what he's done with Dad. I'll slice off the mask even though it looks like real skin. If he screams I'll know he's just a clever fake and he's putting it on, like he put the Dad mask on.

I'm not afraid anymore.

He's still snoring. How can you be afraid of someone who's snoring?

Face Down in the Earth

Sunlight bouncing off wet tarmac dazzles him as he drives along the hair-raising hair-pinned single-track road. It is a blazing gold-white ribbon stretching into the distance amidst mountains garlanded with foaming burns, flanked by banks of dripping green ferns and tough violet heather arching above rocky outcrops on one side, and a drop down to a silver loch on the other.

All very picturesque, reflects Ramsay sourly, wishing he was back in Edinburgh with Fiona. Ah, Auld Reekie, where two vehicles can get past each other on the road without having to rely on passing places.

Lucky for him one of these turns up when the sudden intense burst of sunlight plays the trick on his vision.

For that's what it was, his mind insists as he sits in the passing place trying to calm down after skidding to a halt there, nearly aquaplaning the car through splashing rainwater to avoid the shape he thought he saw in the way.

One of the sheep perhaps? They're always wandering out and playing with the traffic. The stupid creatures think they own the roads as well as the hillsides they inhabit.

Still, he shouldn't be too hard on them. After all, he wouldn't be where he is today without them! Not that he's a sheep farmer or shepherd, though one of his illustrious forefathers was a major factor in their introduction to these rugged hills and glens, admittedly at the expense of the rural human population.

A major Factor.

He smiles at this play on words, breathing a little easier. He doesn't like to dwell too much on the past though. It's here and now that matters.

It can't have been an errant sheep. Too dark. And too tall, though squat compared to him.

And sheep don't stand on two legs.

Spots, motes of light, dance before his eyes as he squints through the windscreen. There's no sign of the figure he almost collided with. He rubs his eyes until the backs of his eyelids turn into a congeries of fuzzy grey polygons and splotches of light. Then he looks out towards the loch. In the distance, white blobs of sheep graze near the ruins of an ancient crofter's hut – just four squat dry-stone walls without a roof. The blinding evening sun chases away the tatters of cloud that loomed dark and wet over the glen only moments before.

He should have known it was a mistake to drive west at this time of day. But Dougie was insistent that Mr Ramsay should come and look at the shower block in person. Why can't the man deal with a simple problem like this himself? That's what Ramsay pays him for, after all.

He needs to make up some time if he's going to catch the last ferry across the Sound. The light dies very late in these parts at this time of year, yet he knows that it'll be fading fast by the time he makes the crossing. Of course, he'll be permitted to take his car across. A far cry from the days when the islanders used to have to swim their horses across the Sound, tethered to their fishing boats. He's not an islander, not really, as far as anyone who lives there is concerned, and only islanders are permitted to take their cars across, just a few at a time, on the wee rust-bucket Caledonian MacBrayne ferry.

But they let him on just the same, though as usual he senses the granite disdain in the cobalt eyes of Shona, the hard-hatted high-viz-jacketed ferrywoman, full of that mixture of hostility and deference he's come to know from his previous visits. He doesn't actually live there; he owns a small croft with a campsite on his land, which makes him an islander on paper.

He's trying to avoid that cobalt stare by gazing out over

the choppy waters when the thing appears bobbing between the waves. He sees a luminous silver shape keeping pace with the lumbering Cal Mac hulk, hears snatches of a crooning chant in an unfamiliar tongue. Or not so unfamiliar. Gaelic. He doesn't know any, of course, but he recognises its sounds, its lilts and cadences. He remembers the legends of the water-horses he read about at a more impressionable age. But the creature's too small for that. A woman? He can't quite make out the face, which seems to be immersed in the black turbulence of the sea. The spray must be blinding his eyes to give him such a daft idea. His heart quickens pleasantly at the undulating feminine shape with its silver sheen, less pleasantly when the face rises up. The blank black eyes. The head grey and shiny, tapering to a white-whiskered snout.

He laughs at himself for getting spooked by a seal. And the Gaelic incantation? Just the pre-recorded piped safety announcement, read first in Gaelic then in English. *For the Sassenachs like him*, he can imagine some of the islanders thinking, the ones like Shona, at any rate. Not that they mind taking the money spent by the Sassenachs his campsite attracts, he reminds himself. And anyway, he's no Sassenach any more than the countless other Scots that no longer speak a language that's all but dead, despite official attempts to revive it.

Though the crossing only takes about ten minutes it seems like an age before the ferry lowers its creaking metal tongue to disgorge its passengers. His car's facing the wrong way now. He suspects Shona of arranging this deliberately with the pilot, to force him to reverse onto the narrow concrete jetty, and to carry out an agonising five-point turn that threatens to plunge him and his Range Rover into the dark lapping waters.

When he's completed this under her amused gaze he edges the car slowly up the concrete ramp, past a huddle of huge men muttering and smirking over their lobster creels. The blood rushing through his skull seems to whisper at him in the dead tongue: *Mortair.*

The wind's dropped now. The weather turns on a sixpence out here. While flecks of mackerel cloud charcoal the darkening sky, he drives past the shop selling everything from wellies and waterproofs to midge repellent and the kinds of books on Scottish folklore he remembers from his youth. He follows the narrow road along the shoreline, which bends round to the West, taking him to a crossroads. His property is just beyond.

As he climbs out of the Range Rover, his feet crunching on the gravel, the sheep on the nearby hills bleat their greeting to him. Dougie's there too, standing expectantly. So are the midges, out in force in the suddenly oppressive stillness of the air. Not even a breeze stirs the sea, which lies as flat as a millpond. He can feel a faint but insistent tattoo on his scalp. He claps his hand onto the clammy skin of his forehead. His palm comes away dotted with swatted insects too hungry for his flesh to get away in time.

"Damn things," he mutters.

"Have ye no tried that Avon Skin So Soft, Mr Ramsay? It's just the thing for—"

"You've not dragged me all the way up here to discuss beauty products, Dougie…"

"No, Mr Ramsay. Right enough."

Crestfallen, Dougie ushers his boss-cum-landlord inside the croft's modest pebble-dashed bungalow, away from the insects' relentless gnawing. Dougie's ma stands in the kitchen, her arthritic hands clasped together. It's hard to imagine her frail miniscule frame giving birth to her stocky broad-shouldered son.

"Ah, there ye are, Mr Ramsay," she smiles. "Ye'll be tired after all that travelling, eh?"

"Oh, it wasn't too bad. Mind you, that Shona gave me the evil eye, as usual…"

"Och, ye shouldna pay her no mind," she says. "You sit yersel' down, Mr Ramsay. I'll put the kettle on."

"Have you been on Facebook, Mrs MacPherson?"

Ramsay asks in a teasing tone he knows amuses her, glancing at the laptop on the spotless kitchen worktop. Despite himself, he likes being mothered by the tiny neat old woman. She laughs.

"Oh-ho, no, Mr Ramsay! Ancestry Dot Com… It's awfie interestin'! Eh, Dougie?"

Dougie, who has remained silent in the corner mutters his agreement.

"Well, son," she says, eyeing the gloaming outside the window pointedly. "Go ben and get yer bits."

Dougie frowns uncertainly.

"Mr Ramsay'll have to stop here the night and we canna expect him to go in the caravan. So you'll have to do that."

"Aw … aye, right enough."

"Sorry about this, Dougie," puts in Ramsay. "It won't be for long, probably just one night. Then, you can show me what the … er, problem is in the morning."

There's a slight edge to Ramsay's voice. Dougie lowers his eyes – in embarrassment?

"Wi' the dunny…? Aw, aye, right enough, Mr Ramsay. I'll go ben then." He goes through the door to the back bedrooms.

"He's a good lad, Mr Ramsay," Mrs MacPherson says.

"That he is, Mrs MacPherson."

He wouldn't like to say that Dougie's "slow", certainly wouldn't dream of saying it aloud in the old woman's presence. The way he'd put it is that Dougie is phlegmatic where his mother is quicksilver spry.

"I just canna understand why he needs ye to come all the way out here for a wee plumbin' problem!"

"I dare say he has his reasons. And it's nice to feel wanted, I suppose."

He's being diplomatic, for her sake.

Changing the subject, somewhat to his relief, she moves onto the ritual of showing him to Dougie's small, spartan room, checking he's comfortable there, asking if there's anything else he needs, etcetera.

She must have slipped a wee nip of something in his tea because before too long he's lying exhausted on the bed, fully clothed, staring at the corrugated metal of the ceiling, where the heads of two rusted nails might be eyes. Closer scrutiny shows him their pupils' odd shape, with the dip in the middle of each suggesting a rounded hourglass. Curled horns crown the woolly face from which they stare at him, though the head sits on the hempen-smocked shoulders of a man.

"Thought ye might like the new heid, Mr Sellar," the head's voice bleats. *"I've heard ye prefer sheep tae folk…"*

He rolls over in bed, away from the creature's face. But in the small grave-like gap between bed and wall a naked wrinkled body lies on its stomach. "Face down" would be the right expression, except that the hag's face grins up at him as if her head were twisted right round one hundred-and-eighty degrees, crooning softly and horribly in a dead tongue. With a dead tongue.

Mortair.

Her spindly arms reach out to wind themselves around him.

Gasping awake, he struggles free from the tangled sweat-soaked sheet.

He lies there for a while, breathing hard.

Why did the sheep-thing call him Sellar?

His great grandmother's maiden name.

~~~

"Sorry for turfing you out last night, Dougie."

"Aw, it's nae bother, Mr Ramsay."

They're crossing the field, their galoshes squelching through the flat expanse of water-logged grass, which is broken up by a handful of bedraggled-looking tents, and hillocks bristling with grey rocks and coarse grass, as if the cropped sward of the campsite were breaking out in defiant warts or boils of the surrounding wilderness.

As the sodden ground sucks at his boots, Ramsay feels the full Scottish breakfast of square sausages, potato pancakes, pikelets, coddled eggs, beans and white pudding, lovingly cooked for him by Mrs MacPherson, sloshing around in his stomach.

"Of course," adds Ramsay, "I wouldn't have had to do it if you'd been able to... Did you not try digging some kind of drainage ditch around the block?"

"Aye, I did that. It's just... Well, as I was digging I found something."

Ramsay sees the narrow trench like a miniature moat around the breeze-block shower-and-toilet block to help drain off the excess wastewater that Dougie's told him has been building up in there. It branches off into a wider trench that extends into the neighbouring field, a boggy no man's land where heather bristles from soft spongy yellowish clumps of marshy ground. Ramsay notices the rusty darkness of the ditch water and reminds himself that the black peat-rich soil stains the water that colour.

The trench comes to an abrupt halt. Four iron posts have been driven into the surrounding area, festooned with red-and-white hazard tape. As they approach it Dougie begins to speak with a manic fluency Ramsay has never heard in him before.

"Ma doesna ken aboot it, Mr Ramsay. If she got wind of this... With all her Ancestry Dot Com blether she'd have a field day! Didna want the happy campers gettin' wind of this either, by the way. There's enough of them clearin' oot as it is, what wi' the dunny floodin'..."

Ramsay peers back at the campsite. The tents do indeed look a little thin on the ground over there. In fact, the campsite's almost deserted.

"You said you dug something up," he prompts Dougie.

"Dug? What d'ye call a man wi' a spade in his heid? Doug. What d'ye call a man wi' no spade in his heid? Douglas...!"

Dougie grins in the expectation of mirth from Ramsay, which never comes.

"You dug something up?"

136

"What…? Oh, aye."

Dougie lifts the hazard tape, ushers him into the red-and-white striped enclosure. Ramsay stares down at the long yellow-brown tapering shapes just visible in the dark water. He can just make out the triangle of a scapula, the featureless dome of the back of a cranium…

The back of a head.

"Did you not call the police?"

"Well, even if I had, it'd take them half a day to get here fae the mainland, Mr Ramsay."

Why is Dougie grinning at this? And why are the midges out already at this time of day? Ramsay slaps his hand against the back of his head as their relentless gnawing begins.

"Aye, the wee beasties come oot earlier and earlier," says Dougie, though he seems unaffected by them, and his eyes have a disconcerting glint in them. "They just love these marshy conditions. But you shouldna worry aboot the polis. She's no a victim o' crime. Well, no in the normal way. See the way she's lying? Face doon. That's the way I found her, by the way…"

Her? How does he know the sex of the skeleton? And what's the significance of her being laid to rest face down?

"Face doon in the earth," another voice calls, a female one from the direction the two men have come from. "The way they buried the Gaelic Bards during the Clearances, to make 'em haud their wheesht when they were deid. Mary MacPherson was one of them, Mary Mhor nan Oran. Oh, aye, ye can learn a lot fae Ancestry Dot Com."

Ramsay spins round and sees Mrs MacPherson's tiny frame through a blur of frantic midges, which seems to take on a vaguely female shape in front of her. Somewhere in their humming drone he can hear the skirl of a mournful Gaelic lament, a dead tongue singing the song of the dead. She seems such a fragile figure in that vast ancient landscape. Yet her voice rings out, and her laughter too. When he sees the ancient blades she and her son are holding he suddenly wishes he'd rung Fiona last night before he dropped off to sleep. Will he never hear her smoky voice again? He looks desperately over to the campsite, thinking to call for help.

Empty.

Have Dougie and his ma used the flooded shower block as a pretext to evacuate the campsite, to isolate him in this lonely place, this deserted, depopulated place? And he's come here willingly, like a lamb to the slaughter. He could fight off the doll-like old woman but her huge granite-muscled son…? Not likely. He could run but the weight of history is dragging him down, along with his condemned man's hearty breakfast.

The female-shaped cloud of midges dance towards him, buzzing arms locking him in a toxic embrace, lips composed of hovering black dots locking with his in a kiss that itches and burns, driving all thoughts of fight, flight or for that matter anything else from his maddened brain.

He retreats into the ditch as much to escape the midges as the MacPhersons' blades. All this does is enable the diminutive old woman and her squat son to tower over him.

"Ancestry Dot Com," continues the old woman, almost dwarfed by the huge blade. "That's where I found out about Mary. It's where I found out about yer great granny's maiden name too. Sellar. Descended fae Patrick Sellar, the Duke of Sutherland's Factor, who burnt folk fae their homes so he could graze the Cheviot sheep on their land. That song ye can hear… It's about the Factor. Ye can see why he wanted to shut her up! Didna work though, eh? Look, all this haverin' on about the Factor is makin' her turn in her grave…"

Well, part of her anyway. The skull is no longer facing down. Ramsay's jumping in there must have stirred the peaty water, so that the skull grins up at him like the face of the hag in his dream. Is it this turbulence that's making its jaw wag as though miming the singing?

Sellar. The dream hag called him that.

But he remembers his history, family history too, on his mother's side. "Factor Sellar was arrested," he blurts out, dodging the blade, "charged with murder—"

Mortair, the breeze seems to echo.

"Aye, and he got off wi' a skelpt wrist," Mrs MacPherson mutters.

A flick of the blade in the old woman's bird-like wrist slashes his cheek but the midges' onslaught is such that he barely feels it. They even get in his eyes, nibbling at his eyelids when he tries to blink them away.

He tries to speak, to plead, but his mouth feels as if it's crammed with wool and the words come out as a bleat.

"But I'm... I'm not the Duke of Sutherland," he splutters, with midges invading his mouth, peppering his tongue with tiny bites. "I'm not even Patrick Sellar—"

"Aye, but ye'll have to do," she says. "Ye're the closest thing we've got."

"It was nearly two hundred years ago!" he chokes out.

"Not to her," she hisses, pointing her blade towards the singing skull at his feet. "To her, it's like yesterday..."

The Fall Guy

When I was little, like many small boys of my generation, I watched a hell of a lot of action shows on television. It never occurred to me at the time that the actor who played the rugged hero wasn't the one actually slugging it out with the villain, jumping off tall buildings, and so on. I hadn't fully taken in that what was happening wasn't real at that point, anyway. Not really. And yet I somehow knew, deep down, that no one got hurt.

Apart from the stunt doubles.

The risk of injury is part of the job. They're trained in how to take the falls with minimal risk so the A-listers don't have to, but that doesn't mean there's no danger. It wasn't until I was a little older that I became aware of this profession. One of my favourite childhood television shows was *The Six Million Dollar Man*. It starred Lee Majors, so naturally I tuned into *The Fall Guy*, a later show in which he starred as a stunt artist who got into all sorts of scrapes both on- and off-set. I was a bit older by then, a bit more sophisticated, enough that it tickled me, the irony of him playing a stunt man when he probably didn't even do his own stunts himself. That was when I started watching more closely during the action sequences, to see if I could spot the blurred anonymous face in the Lee Majors wig, wearing Lee Majors' clothes, fleetingly visible for a few seconds, deceiving the viewer with a conjuror's misdirection and sleight of hand. When the network showed re-runs of *The Six Million Dollar Man* I'd amuse myself by trying to see the face above the collar of the iconic red tracksuit. It got better when home video came in and you could slow it down and freeze-frame it.

Even then, however, the faces of the stuntmen were elusive. Sometimes you could make them out briefly but mostly the directors took care to make sure the doubles were only visible from the back. Sloppy editing occasionally allowed you to glimpse a comically mismatched face, but only briefly, in long shot, and the primitive nature of the analogue technology meant the features were indistinct, shot through with the fuzz of interrupted tape.

By the time DVD came in I'd grown out of this obsession, anyway, and it seemed a little morbid looking for the faces of the dead or maimed.

All right, that's perhaps a little melodramatic, but when I said you couldn't eliminate danger I wasn't exaggerating. As I grew older I began to look closer into the behind-the-scenes histories of the television shows I'd loved as a child. I discovered the hidden casualties of slip-shod safety standards among those unsung heroes of the industry, stunt doubles killed or horribly injured in accidents on set, like Roman convicts killed for real on stage, their exemplary punishments serving the audience's bloodlust. Of course, you hear about these things when a leading actor dies performing his own stunts. I'm thinking of *The Crow* of course.

At the time, learning about these lives sacrificed to entertain me affected me profoundly. It was something of a loss of innocence.

~~~

Like my father and uncle, I was born in January and have often wondered if there was some significance to this. The month is of course named after the two-faced Roman god Janus. Maybe that's why I became fascinated at a young age by the tale of Edward Mordake in the 1896 encyclopaedia *Anomalies and Curiosities of Medicine*. I first read about it in one of those books of "true mysteries of the unexplained" that were all the rage when I was growing up, though I've since discovered the story was apocryphal.

According to Gould and Pyle, the authors of this tome, Mordake was born with a rare condition, a secondary face on the back of his head.

Of course, such things are not unheard of in medical science: Craniopagus Parasiticus, Diprosus, Polycephaly. Most specimens are stillborn. There's little chance of reaching adulthood with such conditions. Mordake, we are told, survived into his twenties and took his own life and presumably that of his "devil twin".

This brings me to the more lurid aspects of the tale.

According to the *Anomalies*, Mordake is said to have begged his physicians Manvers and Treadwell to "crush it out of human semblance", so tormented was he by the second face's nightly gibberings and mutterings. He even took the trouble, before he poisoned himself, to request its posthumous destruction, fearing its "dreadful whisperings" might pursue him beyond the grave.

One other notable feature of the case was the sex of the reverse head. In keeping with its general demeanour – that of opposing every action and expression of Mordake, smiling and sneering when he wept – the parasitic twin-face's sex was the opposite of his, that of a woman "lovely as a dream, hideous as the devil". In one of the more lurid accounts I read in my "true mystery" books there was another twist of the knife. Towards the end of his life (it claimed) Mordake was further plagued by nocturnal visitations, knocks on the door and windows of his country house by an intruder in the grounds. He was unable to make out the face of his tormentor because it wore a cloak, a cowl hiding its features.

But after his death the bobbies found a corpse in the woods nearby, a woman, naked under her cloak, her face a featureless blank, her hand clutching a scalpel.

~~~

Despite my birth month there was, I hasten to add, no secondary face on the back of my head. Yet I did wonder at times if there was someone watching over me. During my childhood I had a habit of wandering off on my own when we were on our long summer holidays in the Hebrides. I'd get myself lost in the glens, get stuck in peat bogs, climb vertiginous cliffs, and almost fall into crevasses hidden by banks of ferns, oblivious to any danger around me. The scents of heather and seaweed filled my nostrils; the far-off bleating of sheep and screech of gulls the only sounds to reach my ears.

On one occasion I lost my nerve while climbing, my eyes gazing first down the sheer drop below, then above at the seemingly insurmountable climb ahead of me. I became paralysed with terror. I thought of the dead sheep one of the local crofters had shown me, dried blood tangled in its porridge-like wool. The animal had panicked, he explained, and hurtled off the edge of cliffs like these. My own panic hung over me like a great black cloud, smothering me, stopping my breath. As consciousness started to fade I felt a strange dislocation, a disbelief that this could be happening to me, a feeling that I was watching the event from outside myself.

I came to myself at the top of the cliff, my face wet with tears as if I'd woken from a dream awash with over-whelming grief. I must have blacked out. But how had I completed my ascent? There was no one about in this wilderness to ask. All I could do was try and find my way back to the cottage my parents rented, which was owned by the aforementioned crofter. As I stumbled through bogs and over rocks I wondered at the perversity in my nature that made me seek out these dangerous situations in lonely places. It was the first time I became aware of this quality in myself, and indeed of the charmed life that allowed me to indulge it without repercussions.

When I returned to the cottage just before dark there was little drama about my disappearance. Father was out fishing with his brother. Mother was in the cottage meditating. This setting allowed them both to pursue their separate interests and, increasingly, separate lives. Perhaps

Mother's transcendental state was so total she had been oblivious to my absence. Yet she seemed convinced I had been around, or at least surprised that I hadn't been.

~~~

The blackout on the cliff was not the last of such episodes, but later ones had a different cause.

As I grew older and approached manhood it was universally assumed I would follow in my father's footsteps into the surgical profession. But I went off the rails, developing an excessive and precocious attachment to alcohol that led to lost hours and alarming lapses of memory. This threatened the "bright future" my father had mapped out for me.

In the most frightening of these incidents I found myself dancing on the track at a tube station in front of horrified onlookers. I could see rats scurrying about under the platform. By some miracle I managed to climb back up without touching the live rail before the train hit. As it screamed into view I briefly thought I glimpsed a charred smoking thing disappear under its wheels. A rat perhaps, but it looked far too large for that. Another time, I lay down in the middle of the street near my parents' West London home. I might have been crushed by an unsuspecting motorist had a neighbour not spotted me and dragged me to the house. I only know about this because my mother told me of it afterwards. I was fifteen at the time. Whatever death-wish spurred me to these self-destructive acts, it remained unfulfilled.

~~~

It was during a later visit to the cottage that one of these shameful incidents revealed the true nature of my situation, in all its putrid and gilded blue-bottle glory. It so happened that my sixteenth birthday fell during this particular vacation and my parents in their wisdom organised a party for me. The guests consisted of my uncle, my mother and father, me, and our landlord and his family.

The crofter, Willie MacKinnon, filled the kitchen with his presence, his ever-present smile of polite contempt for us widening the square face under his tweed cap. He leaned proprietorially against the sink, as well he might. He'd built the place after all, and I mean with his own bare hands, not in the sense the phrase is often used, to mean so-and-so paid someone else to build such-and-such place. His nose was hawk-like, his lips fleshy and carnal, his blue eyes watchful behind his glasses, his feet spaced wide apart where he stood.

"Ah, the birthday boy," he said as I shambled in, his voice sardonic. But then his voice always sounded sardonic.

My father and his brother stood there like Tweedle Dum and Tweedle Dee in their matching tweed jackets, muttered something to each other in French, something that's puzzled me ever since, something like "Doigt du Seigneur". At least that's what I thought it was at first – "finger of the lord", especially since my uncle was waggling his plump index finger suggestively. Then I remembered the stock phrase was "Droit du Seigneur", a feudal lord's right to enjoy the favours of his tenant's bride, which could have been a bitter joke at my mother's expense. As I listened to their sibling chuckles over their jest I did wonder if their laughter might be a kind of whistling in a graveyard. MacKinnon made them uneasy. They'd always communicated in one kind of secret language or another and French was as good as any in this situation, allowing them to flaunt their supposed educational advantages in front of their host, even as my father hosted him.

But their view of him as a pig-shit thick man of the soil was seriously misguided. When I'd visited the croft's main building, sent on errands to fetch jugs of sour milk from the herd or exchange notes for bags of fifty pence pieces for the electricity meter, I'd seen shelves groaning with books including a copy of my mother's pop-feminist best-seller,

Apes versus Angels: A Brief History of the Sex War.

"That's the wife's," he said when he'd come in with the coins or jug or whatever it was this time and caught me staring at it. "I'm more of an Ed McBain man myself," he added. But though there were plenty of well-thumbed paperback thrillers there were numerous other weightier tomes on subjects as varied as economics and animal husbandry – even three large volumes of Marx's *Capital*.

"What he wrote about the Highland Clearances was a real eye-opener," MacKinnon said, enjoying my shocked expression. "You thought I just had it for show, didn't you? It's the wife who's got the degree and all, but I've done a fair bit of studying in my own time. You've got to pass the time somehow during the long winters here. There's only so much drinking and fucking and playing cards a man can stand…" Again, he grinned at the look on my face.

I'd heard my mother talk of Morag MacKinnon as some sort of suffering martyr. Maybe it was she who'd given Morag the book as a gift, some sort of spur to domestic rebellion perhaps. Morag now stood with her husband in the kitchen my parents rented from them. Actually, she stood some distance away from him, chatting to her daughter Sarah while he exchanged guttural words with his two sons, both at least as heavily built as their father, the older one, Donald, at his right hand, the younger Billy at his left. Morag was a wiry fox-like woman with a dry wit to match her husband's constant air of scorn. Anyone less like a martyr you couldn't imagine. The way my mother told it, she'd abandoned a promising academic career in favour of a life stoically battling the peaty soil and the dour elements, turning a blind eye to Willie's infidelities. But I do wonder if there was an element of guilt to the manner in which the author of *Apes versus Angels* viewed their relationship. Well, perhaps not guilt exactly. She was a believer in free love, a creed my father was only too happy to honour in his way, but which sometimes came into conflict with her advocacy of the mystical Sisterhood.

Finally, there was Sarah, a vision in stone-washed jeans and mousey perm. She was tanned and freckled like her mother, but not so weather-beaten, in a faded maroon and white-striped rugby shirt ballooning to accommodate her burgeoning womanhood. She'd inherited her father's mocking blue eyes and sensual lips. I remembered my father's briefing earlier that day when he'd caught me gazing out of the window at her as she traversed the smallholding on some errand. He'd decided to impart some of his Experience of the Fairer Sex.

"I've seen the way you look at her, old sport. There's no fooling this old dog! But there's no point being bashful, the way you usually are. Take it from me, faint heart ne'er won fair lady. You have to show her who wears the trousers – you understand?"

I nodded wearily.

"And don't forget, you're quite a catch, you know!"

"Yes, such a handsome young man he's grown into," my mother agreed. She'd just floated into the middle of our father-son chat, in her kaftan. "Just be yourself, darling, and she'll be putty in your hands," she purred. I groaned inwardly. If there was one thing I hated more than anything, it was both of them fussing over me.

"I don't mean that, Gloria, though it's true of course. But he's not just a handsome young man. He's a handsome young man with a bright future. Young Sandra would be a fool not to want to land this one!"

"Miles!" Mother protested. "Her name's Sarah."

"Well, whatever her name is, don't be fooled into putting all your eggs in one basket, old sport."

I looked back at him blankly. My mother huffed out of the room.

"Look, just make sure your old man's covered up," he said, ruffling my hair and handing me a foil packet containing something I'd never seen before. Through the crackling material it felt like a ring with a piece of skin stretched taut over it. As I examined it, turning the mysterious object over and over in my hands, I could hear my parents arguing in the next room.

It had all sounded so easy when he'd said all that. But now, standing there with an expanse of granite floor between me and her, the room felt simultaneously a vast intimidating cavern and a tiny cramped cupboard. I felt my father and uncle's identical pairs of beady eyes boring into my back, wordlessly egging me on. Something in me balked at the "droit du seigneur" he'd urged me to exercise.

On the other side of the divide, the presence of Willie and his sons added to my anxiety. They pretended disinterest, discussing the price of sheep dip and the like, but the occasional shrewd glance in my direction told me otherwise. Morag had gone over to chat with my mother leaving me painfully aware of Sarah standing alone. My mouth felt parched. My father was on hand with a whisky tumbler.

"Bit of Dutch courage, old sport," he whispered.

"Are you no going to top *us* up too, Miles?" MacKinnon called over.

Finally, feeling a little light-headed, I found myself at her side, exchanging mumbled pleasantries about the weather as she smiled shyly back at me. Was there genuine warmth that might have translated into something deeper and sweeter, or was it the polite attentiveness required of her in her role as the daughter of the croft? Now I'll never know, but it's fair to say the McKinnons weren't known for making a big song and dance about the social niceties of making their guests feel welcome beyond providing basic amenities. Perhaps Sarah was the exception.

"Sorry the weather's not been better for you, David," she said, her voice soft as milk, but not the sour sort I'd often fetched from the croft.

"Oh, I don't mind," I said magnanimously. "It's not like we come here expecting the Costa Del Sol." Her laughter was like music. "Now you're going to say if we'd come a month ago it would have been blazing sunshine, right?" I added.

"Well, it's funny you should say that…"

We both laughed then. It sounded too loud for the stony room where our respective families stood expectantly, making half-hearted small talk amongst themselves. I felt a deadly silence spring up between us, heavier and more impenetrable than lead. My skin felt prickly, itchy, simultaneously dry and sweaty.

"Quite a party," I remarked drily.

"Better than *my* sixteenth," she replied.

"That bad, eh?"

She didn't seem to want to go into details so I didn't press the point. She quickly changed the subject. "I'm surprised your uncle stops so far away – what with the two of them being twins."

I muttered something about my relief the cottage he rented was on the other side of the island.

"Aye, I could see how it can be a bit much sometimes – both of them together and all…" Then she asked, "Do you ever get them mixed up?" This in a low voice that seemed to draw me closer. I could see the golden down on the side of her face, smell her hair.

"No, but I think my mother does sometimes," I whispered.

She let out a shriek of what could have been laughter, so piercing it shook me away from her.

My mouth felt horribly dry, the silence unbearable.

"What are you two whispering about?" my uncle brayed. "Something improper I hope!"

I made a beeline for the Macallan bottle, my father muttering, "Well all right, but don't blow it by getting plastered, old sport."

When I turned back to my quarry, I saw her father had moved towards her, saying something I couldn't quite hear. Once he'd left her alone again I lifted my glass to my lips only to see it was empty. Before refilling it I went back over to her, offering to get her one too.

"Not for me, Miles. Actually, I'd best be going soon. Some of us have got work in the morning."

"Cows to milk?"

"Aye, those heifers won't milk themselves."

"Are you sure? Not just one for the road?"

"Well, it's no but a short distance, David."

Things begin to grow hazy around this point. I remember babbling about everything and nothing for a while – anything to ward off that terrible leaden silence, pretending not to notice Sarah's increasing surreptitious interest in her watch. At some point I grabbed the almost-empty Macallan bottle from under my father's nose and tried to fill her empty glass but her hand quickly covered it. "All the more for me", I observed gallantly, as I poured the last of it into my own glass, oblivious to her eyes flashing a look of dismay towards her mother standing nearby. I remember nothing else after that.

~~~

I woke up to a knock on my bedroom door, then my father stepping smartly in bearing a tray laden with a full English breakfast. The smells of it made my stomach church with nausea.

"Eggs frae Oor Wullie's ain hens," he began in a mock Scots accent. "Not as curdled as the milk, I trust," he went on in his own voice, "but I imagine you'll be needing a bit of a pick-me-up, old sport. How are you feeling, by the way?"

"Oh, a bit hung over," I said, my head beginning to pound. Then I remembered. "Look Dad, I'm sorry about the Macallan…"

"Not me you need to apologise to, old sport. Shame about the whisky. Still, if you can't down a bottle of Macallan on your sixteenth, when can you? But you need to learn to hold your drink before you pull a stunt like *that* again…"

I struggled to digest his words as I contemplated the

glistening food arrayed before me. My head swam in grease along with the fried bread and bacon and square sausage.

"Stunt?" I repeated. "What … stunt?"

"Ah, you don't remember… Thought as much. Never mind. Still, least said soonest mended…"

I had no appetite whatsoever but my fork slipped from my fingers puncturing the runny yoke, saturating everything in a daffodil-yellow avalanche.

"Dad, what happened?"

"I'm rather afraid you over-bounded your step, David."

Despite the facetious jumbling up of the words, the way he used my name instead of "old sport" alerted me to the seriousness of the situation.

"What do you mean?"

"Well, when I told you to be forceful, I didn't mean… Well, *that*."

My stomach lurched in much the same way it had when I'd got stuck climbing that cliff and stared back down the way I'd come. The black pudding on my plate resembled an abyss.

"Well, what?" I asked. "What did I do? I don't remember what happened!"

"Right. I see. Perhaps that's just as well."

No it bloody well wasn't. A picture of me was emerging from my father's dark hints, a portrait he'd only let me glance at sideways on, one I didn't recognise, or didn't want to, though it looked and spoke like me. My evil twin perhaps? But I had to know what I'd done, look at my other self squarely in the eye.

Suddenly, maddened by his evasions, I reached out and grabbed him by the wrist, over-turning the breakfast tray and scattering its contents all over the quilt, demanding that he tell me what outrage I'd committed.

"All right! All right!" he said, freeing himself from my grip. He wiped a splatter of egg yolk from his tweed jacket with the handkerchief he kept in its top left-hand pocket.

I sat there propped up on the bed listening to the sound of my hard, laboured breathing roaring in my ears, the steady *drip-drip-drip* of the over-turned coffee cup lying on its side. I was dimly aware of the scalding heat of its spilt contents soaking through the counterpane.

Eventually he spoke.

"Got to watch that temper of yours, old sport. Might be your downfall one day, though what poor young Sharon had done to provoke you is beyond me. Mind you, she can give as good as she gets. Kick like a mule, that one. Hope you're not too sore down there…"

I shook my aching head. I couldn't feel a thing "down there".

"Well, it was the only way she could get you off her, once you'd … wrestled her to the ground like that. In front of everyone in the room too! You're lucky her old man and his brothers were outside at the time or you'd have got worse than a pair of sore sacks…"

Again I checked my groin. Nothing. Numb. Everything felt numb apart from my head and my gut.

"Well, when they heard her cries and rushed back in, saw you like that, I just said you must have lost your balance – as we all do in our cups. They just laughed and nodded. Probably think I've sired a son who can't hold his drink. And they'd be right, I suppose…"

He let out a bitter little laugh and began rubbing at the egg yolk stain again. I wanted to slap his hand away.

Still, it didn't sound so bad now he'd told me what had happened. Did it…? From what I could make out, all I'd done was fall over drunk. It was just that the landlord's daughter had been underneath me at the time. But I was less than convinced by this spin on it. Thinking of her trapped underneath me like that, the "sex war" suddenly seemed a very asymmetrical one.

And my father's face still looked grave.

"They seemed happy enough with this explanation at the time but I don't know what she's said to them since…

"Of course, she'd be a fool to start blabbing about a schoolboy error like this to the authorities, risk ruining the life of a young man with such a bright future ahead of him over a bit of clumsy boorish behaviour brought on by one too many, eh? But who knows what the fairer sex is capable of once they get a bee in their bonnets!

"Anyway, let's not worry about that just yet. The police are a ferry-journey away. Not that she'll press charges if she knows what's good for her. Let's clean this mess up and go downstairs to face your mother."

She was sitting at the kitchen table smoking a cigarette. At first she refused to meet my eyes with hers much less speak to me. I suppose you could say this had hit her quite hard. For her, I'd always been the exception to the rule, the angel embedded behind enemy lines with the apes.

Though I tried to put the tray down on the sideboard quietly, a slight clatter of crockery caused her eye to jerk my way. "Well, that's a waste of a dead pig." She blew smoke out to drive the point home.

"Look Mum, I'm sorry about what happened."

"What *happened*?" she repeated, her voice shaking with cold fury.

"What I did."

"It's not so much what you did but what you said." Another puff of smoke. "Those obscene degrading things you spat out at that poor girl as she lay there helpless…"

Not entirely so, according to my father, but he hadn't mentioned any verbal abuse.

"What … things?" I asked.

"Do you need me to spell it out? Do you think I can bear to sully my mouth by repeating them?"

She turned her face away and took long drags from her diminishing cigarette as if to mask herself in its haze. I fiddled aimlessly with the cutlery on the tray.

I opened my mouth to speak, to tell her it all felt like a forgotten dream that had happened to someone else, not me, but the words stuck in my mouth like the sickening remnants of half-digested food. *What was I going to say?* I reproached myself in an internal spasm of self-loathing. *It wasn't me, Mum, it was my evil twin? He poured those foul thoughts into my mind and put those vile words into my mouth. What a convenient conceit! What a wonderful cosmic get-out-of-jail-free card!*

But in spite of her anger, which with characteristic entitlement I knew would abate in the end, probably already was doing, Mother was already on hand with a get-out clause of her own.

"And you didn't help, Miles, plying the boy with booze."

"Boy? He's a man now, my dear." He addressed me, desperately. "Anyway, it wasn't me doling out most of it, old sport, it was your Uncle Matthew." He turned back to my mother with a sneer on his face, which he pressed close to hers. "I sometimes wonder if you can tell us apart, my dear…"

I stared at the breakfast debris so I only heard the slap followed by, "Don't you dare make this about me, you prick! You set this up with him to get at me. I heard what you two were saying about the *Droit du Seigneur*. I suppose you thought he was doing her a favour, asserting his ancient rights, spewing his noblesse oblige all over her! What were you saying to him when I walked in on your little pep-talk – something about how all the nice girls love a bad boy, was it?"

"Well, you'd know all about that, wouldn't you, darling."

"Just what are you…? You bastard."

Her voice was dangerously quiet, followed by the kind of silence that heralds a thunderstorm. His eyes gleamed as he stroked his reddened cheek as if caressing a badge of honour, tilting his head as if daring her to strike him again on the other side. I don't imagine it was what the Bible had meant by turning the other cheek.

But I'd heard enough. I listened to their voices as if

through a fog of tobacco smoke and lies, continuing the increasingly bitter recriminations. I crept out of the kitchen and stood in the porch staring at the mist-shrouded farmyard where rocks crouched like shapeless beasts.

After a while they finally became aware I'd left the room and followed me. They began calling me back, warning me not to go outside as I stumbled out of the cottage to breathe in the cool damp air. Their voices, growing fainter as I walked on, sounded almost fearful. I couldn't understand why they were so worried since they'd been more interested in tearing strips off each other than addressing me. Far from making anything about my memory lapse clearer, they'd left me with more questions than answers. Thinking of my father's insinuation about his twin brother – and the way Sarah had shrieked with laughter at what I'd said about my mother confusing the two, as if she'd heard some whispered rumour I hadn't – I was beginning to wonder who I was. Who my father was, at any rate.

I don't know if I was hoping to see Sarah, to apologise to her. Whether or not that was advisable, she was nowhere to be seen. When I did see her eventually she seemed to bear me no ill will, was even friendly if a little distant, so I said nothing about that lost evening. We passed the time of day, nothing more. *Least said, soonest mended*, as my father might have put it.

I wandered on, into the mist. Beyond me I could see the croft house looming in the mist, sat atop its rocky perch. Nearby stood a wooden post supporting one end of a washing line. It had always reminded me of a stake for a witch, or a whipping post. Now it seemed it was just such a thing.

Three large men stood around it, a smaller figure lashed to it, sagging beneath repeated blows from each as if they were taking in turns to land a punch on the face, or sometimes a kick in the groin for variety. It was difficult to make out the features in the fog but I could see it was dressed in my clothes, or rather replicas of the ones I was wearing. The face might have been mine too at one point, but as I moved closer I saw that any resemblance to me, or indeed to any human being, had long since disappeared beneath a mass of bruises, contusions, scar tissue, the limbs twisted, broken, set, rebroken...

One of the men broke away from the punishment beating. Willie MacKinnon's grim face emerged from the mist, leaving his sons to continue their bloody work in his absence. "Off you go, David. You don't want to see this, son."

And for once there was no trace of sarcasm or contempt in the way he addressed me. There was even a little kindness there but none left to spare for the wretched creature wearing my clothes. I heard the wet sound of flesh splitting under another heavy blow.

As I walked away the truth struck me. This was my stunt double, the one who took all the falls for the harm I did to myself, the punishment for what I did to others. I thought of those youthful brushes with death, getting stuck halfway up cliffs, then blacking out and coming to at the top. Though I'd made the mistake of looking down when I was climbing, I hadn't once I was out of danger. I might have seen a broken body lying at the bottom in my own clothes, shattered limbs writhing like a crushed but still-living insect.

Then there were the later escapades, often linked to alcohol, as I sought to prove my father wrong and build up my tolerance for drink. The time I danced on the tube track and yet managed not to touch the live rail. The time I wrote off my father's Bentley yet emerged unscathed.

I began to wonder if my walking, suffering Dorian Gray portrait made me invulnerable. Was there any risk I couldn't take? Was there any crime I couldn't get away with?

~~~

At the age of twenty-one I resolved to put this to the test.

By this point I'd managed to restrain my more self-destructive tendencies enough to get most of the way through a medical degree. I overcame my penchant for self-flagellation, put that all behind me and learned to be at ease with myself, even the more unsavoury aspects of my personality. Instead of feeling guilty about them I embraced them. I learned to listen politely to my father's hearty nostrums. *Be discreet. If you can't be good, be careful. Always keep your old man covered up. And whatever you do, don't get caught.* I even took some of his advice on board. Stopped being such a wet blanket, as he might have put it. I was, after all, following in his footsteps, professionally speaking. Perhaps in other ways too. There were rumours of his conquests, sexual and otherwise, occasional bleatings of worse, from the inevitable grudge-bearing casualties left by a respectable man on the road to success. After all, the profile of such a man, according to popular wisdom, often corresponds with that of a psychopath. I even found time to extend my studies into my leisure time, managing to combine recreational activities with professional development.

Fortuitously, the MacKinnons had fallen on hard times and had to sell the croft to my father. I imagine he relished the class revenge. He let me use it as a little hideaway, using the romance of an island love nest to my advantage, as well as my own status as a top paediatric surgeon. I built a surgery there for my own private research projects. I don't remember much about what happened there. It all seemed to happen at one remove.

I do sometimes wonder, though, if part of me wanted to get caught, just to see how much abuse my other self would take, to see whether he might become mutinous if I pushed him too far. It was the same sort of perversity that made me tamper with the straps on my own parachute when I went skydiving recently for a charity in aid of the children's hospital where I now work – a desire to test the forces that charmed my life. Maybe it was that spirit which made me slap-dash about packing the right maps and climbing gear when I went mountaineering alone in the Cairngorms. Of course, in the end the instinct for self-preservation kicked in. I remembered how to release the emergency parachute. I managed to let off flares and mountain rescue got me down with only mild exposure.

The carelessness that allowed the young woman, a journalist investigating medical malpractice, to escape from the surgery I've kept secret for five years now is one I may live to regret, but not for much longer, I think. Somehow she made it to the mainland before I could stop her. The police are a ferry journey away but there has been no news that he has handed himself in, in my place. It's only a matter of time before they come with a warrant for my arrest and there will be no way out then. I cannot face the prospect of a trial, not after what they're likely to find buried near the *Viburnum davidii* I planted when I took possession of the croft. I'm going to find that cliff where I got stuck all those years ago. If I throw myself off it, I wonder if he'll take my place at the bottom this time.

In the Hold, It Waits

I

As I lie here on this cot and wait for darkness to enfold me, I see patterns in the shadows on the wall of my cabin: faces I have known, forms of things unknown, shapes and things without shape. My body is cold as a corpse now, as if all the warmth I brought with me from the land of my birth has departed its mortal temple.

Outside, tiny white spectres tap on the windowpane: snow, as deathly pale as the skin of the Englishman who gave me that accursed casket – of which more I shall relate – this frozen rain that is a stranger to my native land. 'Tis said that when such as he first came to the shores of our great continent we thought them phantoms. Perhaps that was why we submitted so readily to the irons they clapped us in. We thought them too insubstantial to confine us and enslave us – mere things of spirit! Yet, like the Adzor that dwell in the forests of my homeland, and can paralyse a man with their tiny fists, our captors were solid enough.

And what of us? How did they see us? Not as things of spirit. No! No spirit at all resided within our frames, according to their lights. We were "black gold", precious bane from Africa's soil.

Not me though. They did not harvest me.

I was born in 17–, and though of my parents I recall but little, I remember enough to know that they placed me with a kindly Dutch mariner before the slave traders took them. I have often wondered what it must have been like for them to send forth their infant daughter into the world thus. But I cannot think of these matters for I have hardened my heart to them, as they must have had to do so, knowing what lay in store for them and what would have done so for me, had I remained with them.

Though he was a white man, my guardian did not share the view of many of his fellows that Africans are but chattels to be used and discarded like the toys of wanton children. For him, the vast ocean was a Republic where all might live free and equal, ungoverned as it was by Man's laws. Yet he was all too aware that the obverse of this Liberty was the harshness of the sea, where one is free from the land's protections as well as from its restrictions. This he taught me, and much more besides.

Rudolf Van Leyden was a resident of Cape Town, although his abode was less fixed, it being his vessel. A disloyal employee of the Dutch East India Company, the finest man I ever knew, my father aside, and him I never knew, not truly. He was killed in 17— by a gang of his countrymen who hated him for associating with such as me and treating me as his peer. They reduced his body to mangled carrion, much as a lion in the Veldt might do, save where a beast would use tooth and claw, they employed fists and boots and clubs and knives. I was lucky to escape with my life. Yet such is my history, a series of "hair-breadth 'scapes i' th' imminent deadly breach", as the Moor of Venice might have put it – for as well as instructing me in the marine arts, and his own native tongue, Van Leyden taught me the English one, reading to me from Shakespeare, Milton, Spenser and others of their ilk.

I still wonder that they did not turn their attention upon me when they had finished spilling the old man's blood. Perhaps they had exhausted their bloodlust upon him. I flatter myself that they feared a lusty young mariner might put up a stouter resistance than someone more advanced in years. (Under Van Leyden's tutelage, and on his counsel, I had kept my hair short and my breasts bound, to give casual and ignorant onlookers the impression of manhood.) Or perhaps they hated him more for betraying his kind, according to their drab bedimmed lights, than they did me for my accident of birth in being the creature they so despised.

After he perished in this terrible manner I vowed my revenge upon those that so brutally slew my guardian and cast him into the Veldt to feed the jackals. Yet how should I do this when their faces were covered with scarves? One was bolder than the rest and wore none. His coarse ugly aspect I shall never forget, as well as his actions. He it was that delivered the *coup de grace*, though I think it possible that my wretched guardian had already quit this sphere. Then he added insult to injury by emptying the foulness of his bladder upon Van Leyden's corpse, which still shook with the spasms of his departing spirit. Tears of rage and grief blinded my eyes, but only for a few moments. Though the others might escape my wrath this crude lout would pay the tithe for his fellows. With the back of a sweat-stained hand I wiped the womanly brine away from my eyes before those jackals in the forms of men had finished cheering and whooping over their fiendish handiwork. I was gone before they began to disperse. But I would be back.

I felt sure that his murderers would be watching for me if not searching for me, so I fled. Van Leyden, already fearing for his life, had bequeathed me his ship, though belonging to the Dutch East India Company it was not his to give. Nevertheless, glancing about me nervously as I made for the harbour, I purloined it. Thus was my inheritance the means of my deliverance. If the harbour master noticed the nocturnal flight of the vessel I new-Christened the Van Leyden, he was too dull-witted to give chase before I was out in the open sea.

Before I breathe my last though, let me say this: I was not a monster before I watched this horror from my hiding place behind a blasted hibiscus. There are things I have done that would freeze the marrow of a pampered pink-faced merchant in London or Bristol, who grows fat on the proceeds of sugar cane harvested by such as my mother and father, wheresoever they might be, if their weary battered frames still walk the parched earth. Such deeds as might stamp me as a creature deserving of the contempt of the brutes that slaughtered my guardian, I say to them: if I be such a creature you made me so!

II

I had not had leisure to make provision for my voyage. As Van Leyden's apprentice I had learned to survive on the open sea. I knew I could not exist on the dry biscuits and brackish water in barrels that I had inherited along with the vessel that contained them. I caught and preserved fish in pails of brine. Each day brought a new challenge as I set sail around the Cape of Good Hope, the horn of Africa. The days were so crammed with labour and hardships that they sailed by as swiftly as my vessel, and before too long, I had sailed northeast, with Mozambique port and Madagascar starboard, and I soon tethered the ship I had now made my own in Zanzibar.

It was there that I set about assembling a crew for the journey back. It was there also that I met the man who gave me that accursed casket.

Why did I do it?

I needed gold to hire a crew, to feed them and keep them loyal.

I do not recall this man's name. But I remember his eyes, pale grey yet ablaze with a kind of cold fire. This sounds like a paradox, a contradiction, yet does not Milton speak of "Darkness Visible" when he paints his vision of Hell? Those eyes sat under a brow crowned by lank hair of a similar colour – iron-grey, as the chains that my mother and father must have worn. And the complexion? I have never seen a white man so pale of skin! The Dutchmen that stabbed and bludgeoned my beloved guardian unto his untimely end were all burnt lobster-raw by the sun's blazing orb. Not this Englishman (for such he was). He was a man who clearly avoided the heat of Heaven's orb, and its light. All such men's noses lack the generous breadth of the natives of these lands, but his was particularly thin and pointed, resembling an arrow or a knife that stabbed down as he nodded his head to answer my questions as to the safety of the mission he proposed. As for his frame, it seemed wasted, his arms like thin brittle branches ill-covered by his crow-like black coat sleeves, his chest queerly concave-looking.

You may wonder how a man of such unappealing aspect managed, without even giving me his name, to persuade me to go with him to his lodgings – a mean dwelling for an Englishman, I thought, his chamber all hung with staring-eyed marionettes uncanny in character. I have often asked myself this, too. The casket was wooden and intricate of ornamentation, large enough to hold a cat; not a big cat but the smaller more domestic variety. I did wonder what manner of object it contained. An animal? I will not say that I heard movement, exactly, but when I picked it up to load it onto the ship I could swear it beat and pulsed with a strange force that made the nerves in my fingertips tingle and throb, as if seared by the same icy blaze as its owner's eyes. Before I had touched it I'd imagined that perhaps the box contained some kind of treasure that the Englishman wanted stowed abroad for safe keeping, for he seemed rich enough, judging by how handsomely he remunerated me for my trouble, though it seemed curious that he spent so little of his fortune on his living quarters. And what kind of baubles shudder and pound with a terrible vitality? What manner of treasure chest freezes the fingers such that one fears they might wither and drop off like grapes dying on the vine in a frost? As I hugged my frozen digits to my bound chest, I burned with curiosity as to its contents. But in the terms of our contract the Englishman had expressly forbidden me to open it on pain of forfeiting payment. He must have known this was an empty threat as this payment was already in my hand as a condition of service, for he had furnished the box with a stout padlock that only a key held by its recipient might open. I had to content myself with speculating upon its contents (or inhabitant) by way of examining its exterior, an intricately carved arrangement of mystifying shapes.

Shakespeare's Moor boasts of the "anthropophagi, the cannibals that do each other eat, and men whose heads do grow beneath their shoulders", and the tales of my own country speak of wondrous beasts, spirits and homunculi. At my guardian's knee I even heard the Legend of the Flying Dutchman that haunts the Cape of Good Hope. None of these tales are as strange as the myriad monstrous beasts that swarmed around the lid of the chest, animated horribly by the vibrations from within. I have heard tell of creatures with many heads or limbs, but these here had eyes that could not be counted, or that stared from limbs that protruded hideously, hard by others that ended in crab-like claws. As I looked closer I began to suspect that some of the smaller shapes were in fact the letters of some strange alphabet, spelling words of a language that was neither English nor Dutch nor my own Tiv native tongue, nor any other I knew of. Blinking to expel these fancies from my overcharged brain, I stowed the chest in the cargo hold, dismissing the impression that the shadows of the things thus set forth in those obscene sculptures writhed in the crepuscular light.

It is easy to be wise retrospectively, yet experience should have told me to shun his gold and refuse this cargo. Van Leyden aside, naught but trouble had come from the ghostly strangers who had come to this land as visitors and then remained to become its masters. And there was something uncanny about this man, his vagueness about the provenance of the box and the purpose of its transportation unto the Tierra del Fuego.

The crew I assembled in Zanzibar were loyal and would have followed me to the ends of the Earth, though I knew not then that I would indeed go there! All were former slaves who had lacked the means to purchase their freedom, so had escaped from their captors and now skulked in the shadows in fear of discovery. They flocked to my cause and would likely have crewed my ship for no monetary reward beyond their immediate means of subsistence. Even had I deemed it just to offer them bed and board alone, I yet wanted the means to furnish them even with that. But I did not judge it so. They were not my slaves and I wished to pay them for their labours, and pay them generously, if not handsomely.

Thus I took the Englishman's eighty bags of gold.

III

The gold still sits in a strongbox in my chamber. My crew were trusting enough not to demand payment ahead of their labours but suffered me to keep it as security against their premature desertion. Now I think them foolishly trusting. This voyage was to be their passage to a better life in the New World, so they thought, the bags of gold the means of starting them on their way. I remember how joyously they laboured for me. We were well-provisioned then. I had fifty men under my command. Now there is but me.

We travelled to Ranter's Bay on the isle of Madagascar, there to use some of the remaining gold to purchase several barrels of *boucane*, the dried meat whence the Buccaneers there do derive their name. This would be our provender on our voyage. At first, the inhabitants did seem like to attack us, seeing the flag of the Dutch East India Company, for our sails were yet white. It was only when they spied our rag-tag sable-skinned crew that they relented and counselled us to fly the Black Flag in their waters in future. I replied that not only the flag but the sails also would be black ere long! They laughed heartily at this, but suggested we keep them white to dupe other Dutch merchant vessels into suffering us to approach them, close enough for us to board and plunder them.

After their earlier hard looks they now welcomed us with open arms, for many of them too were slaves that had escaped or purchased their liberty. Others were mariners from the lands north of the Mediterranean that had quit the near-slavery of service in the merchant navy. At Ranter's Bay, I heard tell of a farm labourer born in England who became the Admiral of a fleet of ships, for in the Pirate Republic a humble cook can a governor be. Their law is that the longer one survives the hardships of their way of life, the further one can ascend to the commanding heights of martial glory. Not that rank is all for them. Nor is it unassailable. Each captain is subject to recall by his crew. If he be found wanting a new one is elected. We adopted this equitable system when we quit Ranter's Bay, along with a brace of stout cutlasses which we did purchase from those bucks! Their manner of governance applies equally to the female sex, which they do not regard as the weaker one. Never did I feel the need to disguise my sex to earn their respect.

The same was the case with my crew. I decided to test their loyalty by putting my captaincy to the vote, partly in jest as we were in our cups during our revels on the shore. Unanimously, they again proclaimed me their sovereign, heaping new honours upon my head. The first mate Julius, a native of Zanzibar, took up a length of seaweed and garlanded it about my brow as if it were Caesar's laurels, or more aptly Barbarossa's plumed turban! The whole ship's company and our island hosts cheered his act, in the name of God, Allah, or whomsoever they worshipped. Many simply did so in the name of Liberty. I wonder what my crew would say, if they could vote now upon my fitness for office.

After a few days in the company of the Buccaneers, we set off once more into the Indian Ocean. It was there that we came in sight of a Dutch caravel laden with spices from the Orient. We had little need of its cargo though some seasoning might serve our *viandes* well. It was one of their crew I required. I spied him through my glass. I wondered if he would recognise me, this Dutchman I had seen passing water upon my dying guardian, the steam of his rank feculence rising from the old man's twitching corpse.

As we drew closer the mariners on deck began to apprehend that our vessel was not as they had at first thought amicable, populated they now saw, not by their pasty-faced compatriots, but by a duskier-skinned rabble in particoloured garments of threads and patches. There was panic in the white man's eyes as he beheld me and the manner in which I gazed at him. I know not if he yet recognised me, but if not he could see that I recognised him and that was enough. I had no shortage of time to remind him who I was.

Our port hard-kissed their starboard, and the hue and cry went up among us. The battle was short having caught the occupants of the caravel all unawares. We left with one prisoner, who looked as if he envied his comrades lying hacked and bloodied on the deck. Well might he. There were not many of them. Those that raised a hand to defend him were but few. Most cowered in the wheel room while my crew slaughtered the ones that remained abroad. This was well. The fewer lives lost in the capture of that bloody dog the better. I had no quarrel with them, and every drop of blood shed to save his skin was a drop wasted, according to my lights.

IV

Not long after we had taken our leave of the caravel the Heavens went black, as if night had fallen in an instant. At first it seemed as if a storm was upon us, though there had been no warning of its approach. If tempest it was, it came suddenly, descending upon us from a hitherto cloudless sky. Though I am no follower of the white man's Jesus cult I have since wondered if their God was signalling his

Divine Retribution for the massacre we had wrought upon the crew of the Dutch caravel. We had not been tyrannical with our cutlasses, only slaying the few that offered resistance. Yet, as I lie here shivering in my cot I wonder if we might have avoided what came after had we held back from even this minimal carnage and striven harder to take the bloody dog without shedding a single drop of any of his shipmates' blood.

But no! We gave them fair warning. They had ample opportunity to surrender and yield their undeserving comrade to us. They chose to stand and fight, and they lost.

In any case this was no tempest. I stared Heavenwards and saw the oscillation of thousands of black wings. The noise I heard was their awful beating, not the rumble of thunder. This was a terrible murmuration! Yet the wings were leathery, not feathery, more like those of black bats than those of birds. Their bodies were blasphemous spindly parodies of men, with over-sized heads like black eggs, each with vast pointed ears, a mouth crammed with savagely pointed teeth, and a single lidless eye in the centre of the brow, the size of a platter on which one might serve a hearty meal.

Julius began raving. "Popo Bawa!" he screamed, pointing northwards. Following his thin calloused finger, I could just make out the island of Pemba. There, I could see the source of the black swarm, swirling Heavenwards like the epicentre of a tornado. He then bade us to take cover in the wheel room, the lower deck, anywhere we could conceal ourselves from the onslaught. Most escape routes were soon cut off by the winged cyclopean-eyed daemons. The only place to go was the wheelhouse. Even if we could all have fitted therein, time's winged chariot flew by too fast.

Julius swiftly grabbed me by the forearm and hauled me inside. I glanced back once but did not a pillar of salt become, though what I saw blasted me to Hell in an instant. I caught a glimpse of an inky blur with splashes of crimson, limbs flailing, ripped asunder, before the door slammed behind us. Julius began heaving furniture before the door and bade me do the same.

"We should have tried to fight them off!" I cried, and beshrew me but my voice was thick with wrath that he had usurped my authority.

"It would be in vain," he replied. "I know these beasts. They are natives of my homeland, bats that have taken the forms of men."

He said no more then but cocked an ear to listen, as if to bid me do likewise. There were no windows giving onto the deck, which was a mercy, but I could hear the screams – and all were those of men, not daemons.

"Had we remained outside," I snarled, "we should have perished fighting alongside our comrades and slain some of those monsters into the bargain. This way they shall find us out when they have finished with them, and we shall die like cornered rats." I spat the next two words out. "Like slaves!"

He shook his head, with a terrible bitter smile. "Listen," he said. "What do you hear? The sound of brave men fighting to the last drop of blood?"

There was a horrible silence now from outside. No, not quite silence. The occasional pitiful moan and whimper shattered the dread stillness, and another thing broke it too, a wet squelching sound like something feeding, or worse. I could stand it no longer. I began pulling the lumber away from the door. Julius did not raise a hand to prevent me. His coward's way had worked, he doubtless thought, so it was safe to emerge. Opening the door, I stepped outside. It felt soft and yielding underfoot as if treading in a mire.

Then I saw why this was so.

The whole deck was carpeted with the remains of my crew, men who had stood proud and erect not two minutes before. Steam rose from coiled guts, bringing with it the miasma of soiled latrines. Here and there a dismembered arm or hideously contorted face lay on that thick red sea, as if their former owners were drowning therein. Who knows where the remainder of them lay, somewhere amidst it all, as though the monsters had made of them a jumbled-up puzzle for me to solve and reassemble.

One of the scattered arms stood nobly erect, holding up a cutlass as it might be Excalibur, mocking the martial defiance I had urged in the safety of the wheelhouse. Its blade shone immaculate, the one thing on that deck not sprinkled or stained with life's blood. Another arm directed a sword downwards, this one stained red unlike the upward-thrusted one, towards a torso dismembered but for the glassy-eyed head, piercing the heart, as though this man had elected self-slaughter in preference to the tender mercies of the Popo Bawa.

So transfixed was I by this awful spectacle, the majority of my crew torn to messes in a matter of minutes, that it took me several seconds before I became aware of the keening ululations rising along with the steam from that ocean of blood and entrails. Someone yet lived amidst this carnage. I waded into the guts, sinking deeper with each footfall. Amidst the bloody mire a body floated, still breathing but barely alive. I thought to rescue this one survivor until I heard what he said, saw why he said it.

"Finish me," he moaned, his eyes starting from his head, blood bubbling from his mouth, his breath coming in agonised gasps.

I recognised him though he seemed like to his own ghost, his eyes haunted by something they'd beheld. This youth was the most comely of all in my crew. I had often thought how pleasant it might be to take him to bed but counselled myself against it, for to do so would be to abuse the privilege of my rank.

I had read how great kings and potentates had been deposed because of ill feeling amongst their courtiers brought on by the unjust advancement of minions and favourites. I had sanctioned my crew to recall and replace me by common consent if I failed them, and my taking this lad as my paramour might trigger such a vote of no confidence. Were it not for the circumstances, I could have laughed to think that they might judge me unworthy for such a small misdemeanour, looking around now at the ruined flesh and spilt blood that surrounded me, where floated the shell of the youth I had briefly fancied my heart's desire, a husk that still breathed though robbed of its true vital force.

The delicate features I had once longed to caress were distorted by a terrible misery that aged them far beyond his years; the beardless chin now sported a red beard but not the noble one of the Moslem Corsair Prince. I looked in vain towards his throat and chest for a mortal wound whose crimson might match and justify the scarlet wound his fair mouth had become. I looked further at his torso and covered my mouth to prevent myself from adding to his indignity by expelling the contents of my own guts upon him. His nether regions were an open wound as if some devil had impaled him, for indeed some devil had, but not with sword or stake.

Then I thought of the vast cloud of the Popo Bawa. Had that entire regiment of abominations taken their pleasure of him like a swarm of ghastly incubi? Gently, I stroked his brow, or tried to, for he all but shook me off, writhing in bitter anguish as if he could not bear to be touched, even in chaste kindness. It was then that I sensed moisture upon the hand that had attempted to offer him solace, which I at first took for hectic feverish sweat. Rubbing it between my thumb and forefinger would not remove it for it resembled the loathsome residue left by a snail in its wake, which clings to the skin if you do touch it. This was not sweat. I forced myself to return my gaze to the youth's tortured countenance where I saw a film of the same hideous substance upon him; also upon the rest of his frame and the garments which had been torn to shreds and tatters by the preternatural forces that had assailed him.

"Finish me," he moaned. "End this…"

Wiping the remainder of the clinging slime from my fingers with a piece of cloth, which I then hurled into the human morass that surrounded me, I slowly felt for the cutlass at my side. I drew it reluctantly, then closed my eyes and felt hot tears scalding my cheeks, my sobs echoing the moans of the boy who lay before me, begging surcease.

"Why?" I murmured.

"When the heat is upon them," replied a whispering voice, so close it might be inside my head, "the Popo Bawa will surge forth and claim the fairest youth they can find." It was Julius. He had crept out of the wheelhouse and was now at my side. I had not heard his footfalls for he had crossed the soft corpses that covered the wooden deck boards. "It matters not to them whether it be man or woman they take, but they will slaughter all that stand between them and their quarry."

With that he took out his own cutlass and slew the poor lad, running him through and stopping his heart thus.

"Could we not have saved him from them?" I asked, still weeping freely.

Julius shook his head.

"They would still have had him and left him thus mortally wounded but without us alive to hasten his end, for we too would have suffered the same fate as these poor wretches." He turned away from the merciful slaughter he had wrought and stumbled across the corpse-strewn deck of the floating charnel house the Van Leyden had become, becalmed betwixt Madagascar and Pemba, a sitting target for any further onslaughts by the winged terrors.

In the sudden awful stillness I could feel the rhythmic vibrations from below. I knew what it was. Down in the cargo hold the box was pulsating with whatever unseen horror it held. Consumed with rage and remorse I made for the hold. It had suddenly stricken me with a terrible clarity that the thing in there was the poisoned wellspring of our troubles! It had brought us nothing but ill fortune while in our care. The Popo Bawa had homed in on us like a falcon to its master, but one that had turned Turk and, rejecting the morsels offered as reward for obedience, had instead attacked and devoured its benefactor. The casket down there was like a beacon to the monsters, or like to a runic charm hidden on a victim's person that calls unto a daemon, who rends him asunder to retrieve it. Yet take it they had not so I must remove it before they returned, or so it seemed to me at that moment.

When Julius saw the direction in which I was bent, he called to me. "Captain! Captain! Why go you down there?"

"I have work to attend to, Julius," I replied. "I must end this plague upon us."

"Have you not done enough?" he cried.

"What mean you?" I asked.

"Why, nothing!" he said, his eyes fearful.

"Then leave me to my work," I said, anger rising in me at his queer manner.

"Are you sure it is wise for you to descend to the lower depths in your grief?" he asked, placing a restraining hand upon my shoulder, which only inflamed me the more.

"Question you my judgement?" I demanded, shaking off his hand. "Perhaps you wish to put it to the vote! Why, there are no others to argue against you, so it would be politic to challenge me thus and become captain yourself unopposed. Yes! I see now that you have been planning this all along…"

It shames me to relate, but I grasped the handle of my cutlass. He lowered his eyes as if looking despondently towards the place where I was now heading. I continued in that direction, with no hand to stay me now, for he suffered me to proceed into that darkness. I took hold of the lantern that hung by the door that led below, and lighted it. With each step down the stairwell the sound increased in volume, the very planks of the ship creaking and straining with it. The lantern's light seemed to pulsate in time with the audible throbbing of the casket. Its illumination was feeble yet I did not need more light to see where the box sat squat and malevolent in the centre of the hold, its queer carvings seeming to wriggle and cavort in the lamplight, its sides to expand and contract with each horrid drumbeat.

The Englishman had forbidden me from opening the box on pain of breaching our contract, but I did not need to break its seal in order to discover what it contained! What could hammer out such a terrible rhythm so relentlessly? Something that had beaten inside the now hollow breast of that pale spindly necromancer; something that had grown bloated and diseased on his evil thoughts and deeds. This must be why he cut it out like a canker or tumour, shut it away in the box he bade me take thence. To cut such an organ from the breast of any normal person would surely end his life, but this was no ordinary man!

My mind was so fixed on the box, on taking it thence and casting it into the wide Indian Ocean, that it took me some little time to focus my eyes on the other shape that moved slowly, so horribly slowly, in the darkness. I moved the lantern the better to see it, even turned the handle to lengthen the wick. Then I swiftly shortened it again, wishing that I might unsee that which had once been a man.

Leg irons fixed him to the floor of the hold, not that such restraints were necessary to forbid escape. There was little fight or will to survive left in the wretch who lay there, grotesquely mutilated, his eyes two sightless holes, his mouth and nose a bloody pulp, his flesh tattooed with the scars of countless burns and cuts and contusions, his limbs hanging shattered and useless. And yet he lived.

"Who has used you so ill?" I asked. But at the sound of my voice he began to whimper like to a whipped dog. "Tell me what man did this," I again entreated, "that I may punish him!"

Then I remembered there was but one left, save myself. If it were one of the others, their sentence had already been served. Nevertheless, I asked again: "Which one of my men used you thus?"

As the wretch screamed and begged for mercy, I heard the voice of Julius, who had appeared at my side. I barely heard him as he spoke. "Not a man. A woman."

When I understood his meaning I almost turned my cutlass upon him, but something in his strange manner gave me pause. Was this the Dutch captive we had taken? If so, he had received punishment, but not at my hands for I had not yet had leisure to repay him for his part in the murder and defilement of my guardian. And this man did not seem familiar, even allowing for the disfigurement for which Julius appeared to hold me culpable.

"Why, you must be a madman to speak thus," said I in scorn. "I never used him thus."

"You did, Captain, and more besides. Shine your light yonder."

I did so. Other pale-skinned wretches lay, wounded in like manner, some yet more grotesquely. Somewhere amongst their number I spied the one we had taken captive from the caravel, as yet unblemished, though quaking with terror, huddled in his own waste. But whence came his companions in misery? I could hear the triumphant beat of the swollen occupant of the Englishman's casket.

"This is impossible," I said to Julius. "We had not long left the caravel before those monstrosities attacked us!"

"Aye, and they at least were merciful in comparison to this! But hark… Do you yet call me a madman, Captain, seeing these victims of your wrath? 'Tis true there was but little time for you to visit it upon that wretch from the caravel, but more than you have thought, for I believe your imagination has contracted the time between that first caravel and the Popo Bawa's onslaught, making it a far shorter interval than it truly was. Forgive me, Captain, but I do believe your wits have quite, quite turned. Do you not remember the others we laid siege to?"

I shook my head and put up my sword, silent at last,

bidding him with my eyes to proceed with his tale.

"Each time we spied a Dutch ship you would see him, the brute that slew your guardian and pissed upon his still-twitching corpse. The first time, we thought that would be the end of it for had you not achieved your vengeance? Then we approached a second, and you spied your quarry again, only this time saying the first had been in error! We should have stayed your hand after this, but you had gone too far in blood by now. By the third there was unease among some of the men about the soundness of your judgement. All we could do was hope your wrath might have spent itself by now. It was only the Popo Bawa that stopped you else you might have continued onto a fourth, a fifth, a sixth, a seventh, even unto infinity, though the men were growing mutinous and might have refused to carry out your commands had I not persuaded them to continue.

"There were mutterings among some that you had picked out these Dutchmen mistakenly, believing them to be he whom you sought, your fevered brain projecting the countenance of him you hated so onto these innocents. Others pointed out that these constant bloody assaults on Dutch merchant navy vessels might if they continued draw the ire of the maritime authorities upon our heads. Only the combination of your implacable determination and my gentle persuasion spurred them to further sorties to this end.

"O! Would that I had refused to take your part in this and agreed to the demands of some for a vote on your recall! But their voices were too few, for most were too timorous to challenge your authority fearing your wrath might be turned on them. Perhaps they might have lived if we had listened to this minority and resisted you, for 'tis my contention that your excess of misdirected vengeance has rained Heavenly retribution down upon us!"

V

As he concluded his tale I hung my head in sorrow at my own forgotten misdeeds, kneeling, begging forgiveness of the ones I had so grievously harmed, those that were able to listen. Now that the red fog of bloodlust's fever had lifted and I was in my own right mind, I could think and reason what to do. Julius and I would nurse these poor wretches back to health. Those that lived could be my new crew, if they so desired; those that preferred not to do so, we would grant safe passage to the destination of their choosing. The sails, which up until now had remained white on the counsel of the Buccaneers of Madagascar, we would now daub in black as I had formerly desired; not as a martial sign to terrorise our foes but as a friendly warning to bid Dutch ships keep their distance in case I again took leave of my senses!

There was much to do. We had still to clear the deck of its horrid burden. I would undertake this sad task, giving them as decent a burial at sea as time and my own strength could afford. Julius would minister to the wounded below as the sight of me still inspired them with terror, those that could see, while the wretch with both orbs snuffed out still mewled and screeched at the very sound of my voice.

As I commenced my grisly toil, I beheld a terrible sight, one that had not reached my brain before; my mind had previously been all occupied by the vista of carnage that covered the deck. The confluence of corpses lying there had screamed for my eyes' attention, drowning out the object I now beheld, or rather its new position. The barrel in which we stowed our fresh water now lay on its side, rolling a little with each gentle motion of the becalmed vessel. Those unspeakable abominations must have over-toppled it in their vicious assault. Or else one of my own crew had done so innocently, while trying to fight off the monsters. Either way, the result was the same. We had no fresh water, what little still remained pooling in the curved side of the barrel. All around the ship's sides the vast unmoving millpond ocean mocked me with its useless expanse of undrinkable brine!

I found a pail and gathered what little I could from the barrel within. I took it down to Julius and the others, who still moaned at my approach, but more weakly. Julius shook his head sorrowfully at this as his eyes met mine, for it meant not that they were less afeared of me, but that they were going into a decline.

"Here," I said. "This water might help but use it with care for..." And I could not help myself from weeping. Oh! Would I could take the salt from my tears and make them drinkable! "'Tis all there is left!"

He started at this then held his head in his hand, his other mopping the fevered brow of one of his patients; and he too wept.

I returned up to the deck to carry out my funeral duties, though it felt more like clearing refuse, and seemed to take an age in the heat with no water to sustain me. Flies hummed and cavorted around this shambles, hoping to make this meat the breeding ground for their vile progeny. Scavengers circled overhead making ready to feast on the remains of my crew. Sometimes I wondered if I should just leave the carrion for these winged vermin, who seemed like to the Popo Bawa's more lethargic cousins. I wanted to go thence to my cabin, drink my ration and collapse into a fog, returning to shovel the gleaming picked bones to the sides and fling the lightened load overboard. Yet I could not. Disposing of them with some kind of honour was the least I could do for my fallen crew, who had suffered and sacrificed so much for me.

At length I came to that most pitiful sight, the lad who had begged for death after his foul ravishment by the horde of Popo Bawa. His brow was smooth again, its peace only disturbed by a solitary fly resting there. In my fury I flattened the insect, leaving a beauty spot that would be the envy of any foppish knave that flatters and simpers in any prince or emperor's court. Then I crooned my elegy and dragged his limp body, still slender and delicate as it had been in life, unto the balustrade. There I toppled it into the ocean, its depths as salty as my tears.

VI

All the corpses thus disposed of, I descended below to see how it was with those I had so savagely maimed. There was not a murmur at my approach, which I feared did not signify that they had improved. Julius remained there still, head in hands, not even attempting to provide further solace. Casting my lantern towards them, I covered my mouth to stop a Vesuvius of nausea from erupting forth. Their flesh was leprous, their wounds blackened and gangrenous. I forced my gorge back and heard the faint sound breaking the noisome silence.

That box, with the filthy black heart inside: it was this that had poisoned them, infected their wounds!

It had slowed its hideous beat down and quietened it to a murmur, to make me forget about it while I was occupied with all the other misfortunes that had beset us withal! But I would forget no longer! This time I would take it thence and cast it into the depths, wearing the same thick gloves that had protected my fingers when I bore it hither!

Julius saw me gathering it up and looking bewildered asked why I did this. I explained that this was the source of our troubles.

"But the water…" he said faintly, his arm feebly indicating the near empty bucket. "We did not think to boil it. That might be why these men are so sore afflicted…"

Beshrew me, but I barely heard his words, and barely listened to their meaning. "Water, boiled or not, does not account for my bloody and unnatural deeds," said I, "for your failure to resist them, for the Popo Bawa's onslaught, for the becalming of this vessel. This does! Its presence engenders our ill fortune and once we are free of it they will be restored."

He made no move to stop me, his head again sunk in

deep despair. I ascended the stairwell with hectic feverish motion. Slithering over the blood and guts that still mired the deck, even after I had removed most of its provenance, I dragged it towards the balustrade. The box seemed to grow heavier with each pull, as if the monstrous organ inside were swelling in obscene tumescence to resist my jettisoning it. Yet I persevered, using the grisly slipperiness on the boards to assist its motion, as 'twere some vile dinghy. I could feel the sharp edges of the carvings cutting into my hands, even through the thick gloves, as I lifted it over the balustrade so that my fancy thought the monstrous forms thereon were snapping and clawing at my palms with tooth and talon and pincer. The splash when it finally fell into the ocean seemed louder and more terrible than any of the bodies I had likewise cast overboard.

I then began the laborious task of cleaning the remaining human debris from the deck, employing broom and shovel, mop and bucket. Time after wearisome time, I filled the wooden pail and slopped it overboard. With each sickening splash of its voidance I thought I could hear an echo as of a heartbeat muffled by water. But I refused to listen, thinking it my fancy, like the unnatural motion of the strange carvings.

When I had thus obliterated every last trace of my wretched crew I bent my efforts to blackening the sails, climbing down exhausted from the rigging when I had finished. I lay down on the scrubbed boards under the sun's pitiless orb, until it was cloaked by the black sails on its downwards path, for twilight approached. As I gazed at the darkening Heavens I again wept with bitter remorse for the errors and bloody deeds I had committed, praying that my good angel would prove the stronger now that the accursed casket was overboard.

At length, I raised myself again, berating myself for my self-pity. What of those fellows that lay down below? Had the purging of that cuckoo in the nest reversed their unhappy decline? I took myself there to see. All was still. Julius sat in a kind of daze and shook his head at the entreaty in my eyes.

"All… All are dead," said he.

To my shame, I had no tears left for these strangers I had pulled into my tragic orbit. All I could think was, with a bitter inward laugh, more corpses for me to cast overboard. In the darkness of the hold I then lapsed into the deep lethargy of sleep.

When I awoke, I could smell the dead. A thought struck me and I shook Julius from his slumbers. "But the box…" I began.

He did not reply. I thought he did not understand my meaning, but he was still shy of full wakefulness. Rubbing his eyes, he took a few laboured breaths, then spake: "If it was the source of their distemper, as well as sickening them, perhaps it was also quickening them…"

"Aye," said I, an awful thought taking shape in my brain. "They were mortally wounded. Perhaps they might have died before without its presence. We know not what properties it had."

"What properties it *yet* has," he corrected me.

And I thought of where I'd cast it, and what I'd cast in there before it.

Almost as swiftly as I'd thought it there came a knocking from the about the hull, as of men scrabbling for purchase upon it and clambering thereon, or more properly what had once been men. I took Julius by the hand and together we ascended to the deck where more horrors awaited us. I ran to the port side and peered over the balustrade. Below me I could see them. Limbs hanging from tendons, when they still remained, flesh hanging from faces, signifying that sharks or other voracious marine denizens had already begun finishing the work of the Popo Bawa.

My crew were returning to me, everyone, at least what parts of them remained, doubtless quickened by that hideous beating heart. I should have smashed that casket open with an axe and hewn that foul lump of flesh into tiny slivers! Yet I suspect each ghastly morsel might have continued throbbing with unnatural life, its vital force and fearful influence multiplied like Hydra's heads.

I ran to the starboard and the prospect was the same, with one twist of the knife for me. There was my sweet boy, the beauteous lad defiled by those abominations, his pretty curly scalp hanging from his skull like to a hood flapping free, scrambling up towards me as 'twere the grotesque parody of an ardent lover clambering a trellised wall with a rose between his pearly teeth.

Some of the bodies were little more than stripped bones, others bloated sacks of flesh garlanded with seaweed. Some were but torsos or limbs, rent asunder by the Popo Bawa, yet even these crawled or somehow hopped upwards. Many of the quickened dead still had their cutlasses about them, and from the expression in their terrible fixed glassy eyes I knew there was malice in their intent.

"Let us in," they mewled, those that still had tongues with which to do so, or heads to hold tongues.

We began casting what we could back overboard to repel the invaders. Brooms, pails, even the barrel that had lately contained our water supply – all were hurled towards our former comrades to knock them back into the ocean. We knew this would be but a temporary measure for they would return and keep returning until they had us.

We now had our cutlasses ready. Yet there were but two of us, and our resolve had been sorely tested so that ere long we might sink willingly into sweet oblivion before this new onslaught. The only spur that might encourage us to fight for our lives now was the hideous thought that, should we die, we too might turn revenant, condemned to an uncanny living death as puppets of that English necromancer and his accursed casket.

Perhaps my earlier prayers for forgiveness were answered. After we had repelled the first assault dark clouds that I thought harbingers of our final dissolution had begun to lour in the Heavens, and this in a morning sky that had been the clearest azure but moments before. Where the black sails had hung starkly limned against the blue Heavens they were now indistinguishable from clouds as midnight-hued as they.

A cutlass wagged over the balustrade signalling the beginning of the unnatural onslaught's second wave. A lightning flash illuminated the darkening sky. Julius stepped forth to engage it with his own weapon, then gasped with horror for another blast of light shewed it to be but an arm, severed at the shoulder, sinews hanging from the wound, a bony socket peeping out yet blindly thrusting its sword and slicing it hither and thither as though 'twere still joined unto the body!

Then the storm began.

We welcomed it at first. The rain lashed down washing away the tears and sweat on our begrimed faces as well as any charnel morsels remaining on deck. A sudden gust of wind dislodged the unholy disembodied intruder from the balustrade, back into the depths whence it came. Peering overboard, I spied ripples signifying the oncoming of tidal surges in the water, while overhead the blackened sails rippled and billowed. The Van Leyden was in motion once again. Some of the piecemeal revenants were still struggling to fasten their talons, or whatever they yet had with which to grip, onto the belly of the ship but to no avail. The vessel now easily outpaced their ragged attempts to swim! More lightning flashed down like Jove's thunderbolts but as I remarked half in jest to Julius, if this was the vengeance of the Almighty, I'd take it over that of the Fiend!

Yet rest upon our laurels we could not. The vigour of the tempest was soon unlike any I had yet known, either during my apprenticeship with Van Leyden or afterwards as captain of this marine heirloom he left me. Vast waves loomed about us so that at length, having repelled the attack of the revenants, we now faced a new invasion from the very ocean itself. I set myself to the wheel for I had most experience of steering this vessel through choppy waters. To Julius I assigned the laborious duty of bailing out the encroaching brine with one of the wooden pails that had not gone overboard in our defence against the quickened dead. He looked despondent at this division of labour, but what choice had I?

It took every fibre of my being to guide the Van Leyden through that storm. A bushman stretching his bowstring taut as he aims his arrow's point at the heart of a game animal, drinking placidly, unaware, at a waterhole, yet ready to canter thence unto safety at the slightest sound, leaving his predator famished: thus was each of my frayed nerves as I steered that vessel, whose timbers strained under the weight of the tempest and through those mountainous seas. From time to time, I risked a glance over my shoulder at the deck where my one remaining comrade listlessly scooped pails of brine back overboard. His apathy troubled me but I had not the time to exhort him to greater efforts, nor to reassure him that all would be well. I bent my will to maintaining as steady a course as I was able through the storm until it should abate. Glancing again towards him, I noticed a change in his attitude. He seemed to be cowering from something, his eyes starting from his head, his hands clutching the pail towards his breast as though 'twere a shield.

Then I saw why. He was not alone.

Three shapes, all black with rot and gangrene, shambled towards him, some with limbs hanging or dragging limply, as if shattered. The Dutchmen tormented by my hand! They must have turned revenant, too, and crawled up from below deck. But how, since the box that had quickened my crew lay in the depths long hence?

I had no leisure to find an answer to this question for

they were bearing down upon the unhappy Julius and would doubtless come for me once they had finished with him, seeking vengeance for the monstrous injustice I had wrought upon them when alive. Abandoning the wheel momentarily and trusting that the ship would not capsize for those few seconds when I neglected my duty, I leapt to the door of the wheelhouse and flung it open, shouting to Julius to cling fast to the balustrade on the starboard side where he crouched, cornered. Not waiting to see whether he followed my counsel, I flung myself back upon the wheel, turning it sharply to the port side, almost toppling the ship, before yanking it starboard to restore its upright position – or as upright as the tempest would permit.

At length, I awoke from a kind of trance-like slumber. All was calm. I knew I must have continued piloting the ship through the tempest for some hours, perhaps even days, though after some time I must have begun to perform my duties without conscious thought, like an automaton or marionette, not even peering over my shoulder to check on Julius. When the wind finally dropped and I needs must steer no longer, I can but think that I fell into a faint from exhaustion. Slowly and painfully I extracted my limbs from about the wheel. It had left its imprint upon my flesh as if I had been joined to it by compulsion or put to the torture on it. I felt as stiff and cold as one of those corpses I had cast hence, with the rigors of death upon it. Shuffling slowly, I turned to see what had become of Julius, the last of my crew.

VII

I spoke to him often after that, to ask how he had fared in the time between the height of the storm, when I turned the ship to cast the Dutchmen's revenants ocean-ward, and our arrival here in the frozen wastes of the Antarctic at the urging of the north wind. For many a long day, he kept his counsel. Time after time I addressed him, awaiting his reply, but answer came there none. This I attributed to his lips being frozen fast shut by the cold. I even tried breathing upon them, that the warmth from inside me might unfreeze them. I could not do this for long for I needs must go thence to my chamber lest I succumb to the bitter temperature myself. I could not take him, though it would be of benefit to me to share bodily warmth, for he was still clinging close and fast with every limb to the balustrade as I had counselled him, and let go of it he would not, though I tugged at him with all my might and main. Yet my breath upon his mouth might have had some effect for at length he began to answer my entreaties, though it were some days since I had begun. It was passing strange, but he whispered through his shut lips without them moving.

"Thank you, Captain," said he, "for breathing a little of your warmth into my lips. It was like unto a kiss from you, something I might have once desired, had you wished it, for knew you not that I did love you, even as you did love that beardless youth? 'Tis no matter. I can say this now without fear of giving you offence, for know you not that I am dead, frozen here where I clung?"

I shook my head refusing to believe that he too was dead after enduring so many hardships with me. Yet I could believe his amorous declaration. Had I had leisure to think on it before, I might have perceived his attachment to me. While the youth he mentioned would surely have spurned me had I pressed my suit upon him, thinking me a man with my bound breast and cropped curls, Julius had always seemed to me as if he might have the capacity for loving either sex, and I had something of both within me. Even in that vast frigidity, I was suddenly overwhelmed with a warm tenderness for my First Mate and last companion. Again, I blew my warm breath upon his mouth, thinking to revive him for if my crew could turn revenant, why not he?

A sound came from between those cold lips, something like a laugh. "O, sweet kiss of life, to breathe upon me in such wise, but too late I fear, captain of my heart, for so you were! Why else did I comply with your madness when you captured and ill-used those Dutch mariners? Had you not captured me as surely as you had them I had else quit your service or suffered the men to mutiny. Aye, and I endured torments of spirit as sharp as those of the body they did. In secret, I succoured their wounds with unguents, all the while fearing your wrath should you discover my treachery. How it pained me to make you face the truth of your actions and to watch you suffer the consequences thereof! Yet it gave me joy to be with you to the last. When I clung here during that storm, in my mind 'twas you I imagined I was clinging to. I died dreaming that I embraced you. Farewell, captain mine, for I leave you now, having spoken words in death I never could in life."

With that his tormented spirit departed, to a better place, I hope.

VIII

So here it ends, or should do.

Yet questions remain. Why did the Englishman have me stow that ill-starred casket knowing I would surmise its nature and discard it? Did he not guess that I might smell out its evil influence on my fortunes and cast it into the nether regions of the vast dark ocean?

Why do I endure?

As I lie here in this cot it seems I have waited an eternity for death to claim me. I know somehow that my travels are far from over. In my reveries, I sometimes see this ship, as others shall glimpse it hereafter, haunting the Cape of Good Hope, still spectrally white with the hoar frost it has gathered about it here. For I know now that my life is the very warp and woof of legend. Those travellers who spied the Flying Dutchman must have looked upon the Van Leyden, haunting them from the future not the past.

I hear a sound, a faint beating that could be the snowflakes gently patting the windowpanes of my chamber, or perhaps my own heartbeat. Yet my breast feels hollow, as though the sash I used for binding it has trained my womanly bosom to wither away. Perhaps then, if heartbeat it be, its provenance is elsewhere, further down. Down below.

But that cannot be! Did I not hurl that accursed casket into the depths? Yet it made the dead return. Who is to say that it cannot itself do the same?

Yes! That must be why that necromancer suffered me to jettison it, knowing it would come back. Is this to be my fate, to be his puppet, undying and unable to die? Perhaps that was Julius's fortune and his virtue: his capacity to die while I must live on, eternally it seems, perpetually quickened by that vile heart.

Already my restless spirit is plotting a course to the Tierra del Fuego, to transport it to whatever foul purposes he has in mind for it. I know not what that be, or indeed how it shall travel there, for the Van Leyden is again becalmed here in this frozen desert of ice. Perhaps the occupant of the box shall conjure up another mighty wind to take itself hence. Or perhaps it is merely patient, unhurried. It has all eternity.

In the hold, it waits.

The Cutty Wren

1

These days, of course, I never listen to folk music. I wasn't too keen on it to begin with. It was Jenny Underwood who overcame my resistance to the genre. She did love a good ceilidh. You wouldn't catch me near one now. Even the sound of an accordion makes me shudder.

We used to sit at the back of the local folk club, laughing at the names of some of the songs they played. How we chuckled at "Granny Hold the Candle While I Shave the Chicken's Lip"! What a strange image that title conjures up; yet somehow it echoes the rhythm of a reel or jig. "Shove the Pig's Foot a Little Closer to the Fire" was another one that occasioned a good deal of mirth. That's something we'll never do again. Those songs are no laughing matter to me now, and whatever you do, don't ever play "The Cutty Wren" in my presence.

Ceilidhs were her favourite way of letting off steam. She would press-gang me into accompanying her to the ones the folk club organised so we could both dance somewhat ineptly to what passed for music. After my initial reluctance I have to admit I rather enjoyed it, spinning Jenny round and round until she squealed with delighted terror.

But that was as far as things went.

It had been easier than usual for her to twist my arm into coming to this one as I faced another solitary Christmas. I opened the door, and there she was, tinsel in her hair, a green tartan dress, and a glint in her eye.

I knew that wasn't for me of course. Usually, before the night was through, she'd have paired off with someone, sometimes sparing a glance in my direction, one I'd invariably refuse to return; the last thing I wanted was her pity. The very nature of some country dances encourages such behaviour, I suppose, the way they force one to move from one's original partner to a succession of rivals. Sometimes I flattered myself she was trying to provoke me into making a move but she knew I found the notion of office romance unthinkable, and every time I touched on the subject with Professor Underwood she showed every sign of agreeing with me. Besides, it was clear to me that she looked elsewhere for such liaisons. My function was simply to ensure that she did not turn up at the door without a male escort. I had no illusions that she would be leaving with me.

I could always have followed her example and sought an alternative companion, I suppose, but I preferred to sit on the side lines, mesmerised by the whirling blur of dancers. From time to time I'd see Jenny in the arms of her partner or spinning with gay abandon, her dress fanning out, and I'd smile a bittersweet smile and close my eyes as if lost in a dream of what might be.

That night I opened my eyes from my reverie to see she was no longer on the dance floor. Few were as the caller had taken a break leaving the band to play "The Cutty Wren", a lilting haunting ballad in a swooping minor key. Suddenly, there she was, standing by my chair, an odd fierce look on her face, cold steel in her eyes. I saw the man with whom she'd been dancing but a few minutes before hurriedly making for the exit, his hand covering his reddened cheek.

"Come on," she said, straightening her dress, which I saw was ripped at the hem. "Let's go."

2

We walked towards the car in silence. Occasionally I glanced in her direction, noting how the green tartan dress set her grey eyes off, but also how oddly the jauntily attached scrap of tinsel sat with her angry brooding expression. Neither of us knew quite what to say. Actually, I'm speaking for myself here. My mouth kept opening but nothing came out. Possibly she felt no desire to talk anyway. It was a clear chilly windless night, a harbinger of frost no doubt. Under other circumstances the star scape might have been romantic.

"Good thing I haven't had a drink," I muttered, unlocking the car door.

We got in.

As both driver and passenger doors slammed shut with a resonance the intense silence seemed to exaggerate, she finally spoke. "You weren't doing much dancing tonight, Ian." There was a sardonic edge to her voice.

"No," I agreed. "I wasn't."

"Come on, Ian. Say what's on your mind."

"Suppose there's nothing there," I said.

"Oh, don't give me that," she said with a snort of derision.

"Well, what do *you* think, seeing as you're so sure there's something?" I asked.

"You tell me," she pressed back with what sounded like a sigh of exasperation. "It's *your* mind."

This was turning into verbal tennis, the frustratingly fractious kind that veers back and forth between deuce and advantage.

"Well…" I began.

To stretch the metaphor, my abortive mumble of a reply had weakly tapped the ball back over the net enough to place it on her side of the court. She smashed it back ferociously.

"It's obvious. *How sad*, you're thinking, *the way she puts herself about, throws herself at every man in there. How needy. How desperate.*"

"I've never said—" I began. I couldn't take my eyes off the tinsel, nodding furiously along with the head to which it was attached.

"It's written all over your face, Ian. Well, I'm not desperate. I do it because I want to. Because it's fun. *Fun.* Remember that, Ian? You should try it some time."

Game. Set. And Match.

3

Things soon thawed between Jenny and me, surprisingly quickly. Not long after, early on New Year's Day in fact, the phone rang. It was Jenny. "Do you remember that song they played at the ceilidh at Christmas, Ian?"

I stuttered, surprised that she should want to bring that event back up again, surprised that she was ringing at all after the terms on which we parted that night. I was a bit slow on the uptake, understandably at eight o'clock in the morning on the 1st January. Not that I'd been doing anything much more lively than watching *Jools Holland.* Alone. Nevertheless, she had caught me on the hop, coming straight out with it – not even so much as a "Happy New Year".

"Oh, come on, Ian, mate. You must remember. It was the one no one was dancing to, unless they were slow-dancing. Or like, goth-dancing. It was sort of a bit shoe-gazey for a folk song."

I cringed inwardly at her affectation of youthful speech patterns, a kind of verbal mutton dressed as lamb that served to remind me why it would never have worked between us anyway. I was some ten years her junior yet I didn't feel the need to babble in this fashion.

"You mean 'The Cutty Wren'," I said.

"That's the one. It didn't seem very festive, and yet it's traditionally played on Boxing Day. I got a lead on its origins, on the night of the ceilidh as it happens – and maybe something else. I'm going to follow it up. You up for it?"

"What exactly?"

"A field trip," she said. "We're going to hunt for the Cutty Wren."

4

"Try not to spill your pint on it, Ian," said Jenny.

"Are you trying to keep it in mint condition?" I asked, looking at the piece of paper already stained with dirty fingerprints. It looked as if a car mechanic had been handling it. The dark smudges could have been ink, I suppose. Yet there was something oily about them, and they were brown rather than black.

"I don't want the ink to run," she said.

If it is ink, I thought. The writing was similar in colour to the odd fingerprints. But she was right. It was already hard enough to read in the dimly lit public bar where we'd met to discuss this, even without the further hindrance of messy smudges. I struggled to focus on the writing, which looked like a stick insect had been dipped in ink then set loose on the page. Here's what it said:

> *On top of an eagle*
> *I flew to the heights*
> *So I became regal*
> *By stowed-away flight.*

"So what do you make of it?" she said at last.

I sat back and sipped my pint. The craft beer's head left a froth moustache on my upper lip. I licked my lips then wiped off the residue with a handkerchief I kept in the top pocket of my navy blazer. I glanced at Jenny. She smirked at my fastidiousness. I pretended not to notice, then replied. "It refers to the story of how the wren became king of the birds by hitching a ride on an eagle," I said.

"Oh, you're good," said Jenny with a smile. "*The Golden Bough*?"

"No, Wikipedia."

"That pint looks nice by the way. I might get one for myself."

"Let me," I said.

"No, I'll get it. Want another?"

I still had over three quarters of mine to go so declined her offer. As she went to the bar I thought of *The Golden*

Bough and how it related to the upstart wren. It certainly seemed to fit the burden of the song:

And what will you do there? says Milder to Mulder.
Oh, we may not tell you, says Festle to Fo
We'll hunt the cutty wren, says John the Red Nose!
We'll hunt the cutty wren, says John the Red Nose!

Jenny Underwood's smoky voice broke into my thoughts. "There's a theory that the wren came to represent Richard II during the peasants' revolt of 1381," she said, dumping her pint on the table.

"That notion is at best ... questionable," I said. "The Ceremony of the Cutty Wren dates back to Neolithic times."

"The sacrifice of the king," she said. "The death of the year-king in winter. Its rebirth in spring."

"Indeed," I said. "That seems to be what your scrap of paper's saying. Where did you find it?"

"It dropped through the letterbox just after I got back from the ceilidh. And that wasn't the only thing that happened..."

"Well, there was that guy who —"

"Forget him. I have.

"No, I meant when I got home. As I opened the door I could see a dark shape flapping about in the hall. It shot out of the front door, only just missing my face – a bird that must have got inside and panicked. Caused havoc in the kitchen – salt all over the work surface."

"A wren?" I wondered.

"No, I caught a glimpse of white feathers against the black – a magpie. Anyway, after I'd shut the door again – a bit shocked to be honest with you, Ian – the paper dropped through the letterbox. But it got me thinking. Magpies are well-known for nicking shiny objects ... maybe this rhyme was the first clue in some weird treasure hunt."

Remembering what she said, I can't help thinking of Rossini's opera *La Gazza Ladra*, the servant girl hanged for the crime of the thieving magpie.

"Right," I said, somewhat sceptically. "That certainly sounds … unusual."

"You think that's freaky. I haven't told you what happened the next morning. Coins under my pillow."

"First a magpie, then the tooth fairy," I said drily. "I hope you remembered to throw some of that salt over your shoulder…"

"Sneer all you like, Ian. They were farthings minted in 1951: three of them, all with a wren engraved on them."

"Probably fetch a pretty penny," I said, shivering despite myself.

"Well, I reckon there's something at the end of all this that's going to fetch a damn sight more," she said.

I should have told her to take those three farthings to the nearest antique shop, get them valued and have done with it. Instead I said, "That's as maybe but we're still no closer to finding it."

"Well, that's what I thought when it turned up," she said. "But later I looked inside my car glove compartment and found this…"

She reached into her handbag and produced another scrap of paper with similar markings. She handed it to me. It said:

But now I must pay
And must bear the crown,
On Saint Stephen's Day
To lie underground.

This situation was starting to make me feel rather uneasy. I wondered if it was having the same effect on Jenny.

"How did it get into your car?" I said, wondering why her informant couldn't have just posted it into her university pigeonhole. In the light of what later happened it would have been apt, given the pigeon's legendary homing instinct.

"I suppose I must have left it unlocked. The central

locking's faulty and I don't always check."

"All the same... You weren't even driving that night. That means..."

She nodded. "Yes, sure. It creeps me out a bit that whoever gave me the paper knows where I live, and which is my car. But I think I'm on to something interesting here, Ian. It all makes sense now. The clue to each new message is hidden in the one before. So the second message 'stowed away' in the car glove compartment. That's what made me look for it..."

"Wouldn't you have found it anyway?"

"Have you seen the state of my car?"

I hadn't, but I could guess what she was driving at.

"Receipts, post-its, parking tickets. Other random bits of paper. I could easily *not* have found it..."

"Okay," I said. "So how about the third message? Where's the clue for that one in the second? Is the third one ... 'underground' then?"

She puffed out a mouthful of air. Her breath smelled sweet. I couldn't help wondering if mine did.

"Could be anywhere if that was the clue," she said. "No, no, no. Can't imagine it's that... Something to do with the crown, maybe."

"'Bears the crown'," I said. "The wren loses the crown at that point in the story, I'd have thought..."

"Maybe it bares its head when it loses the crown," she suggested. "And bears it somewhere else to yield it up in sacrifice."

"But it loses its head as well, I think."

"Crown can mean head – think of Jack falling down and breaking his crown in the nursery rhyme. But this is getting us nowhere..."

I nodded, taking another pull on my pint. This was thirsty work. "Could it be something to do with St Stephen's Day?" I wondered.

"Of course, the Feast of Stephen. 'Good King Wenceslas'. Christmas carols!"

"Well, obviously," I muttered. "But I don't see where this is getting us!"

"Which tree bears the crown?" she asked, grabbing my wrist so tight it hurt. "Of all the trees that are in the wood?"

"Aah…" I said. "And there's one on the campus. Right outside the faculty building…"

5

Maguire and Malone –
The Northern folk bind me!
The middle of the town
Nearby you'll find me!

The previous two had been child's play compared to this.

We'd found the message in a bottle, about the size of the kind used for miniatures, tucked under the glossy but painfully prickly leaves of the large holly bush next to the door we used every day to go to work – somewhat overgrown, I might add, and Jenny made a mental note to have a word with the head of the grounds maintenance team to give it a long overdue trim when the Spring term started in a few days' time. Smarting from slight but painful injuries sustained in my efforts to extract the hidden missive, I was inclined to agree with her. On the other hand, if they had cut the bush the gardeners might have raked the insignificant-looking bottle out and thrown it away along with the rest of the litter trapped under its fibrous stems and spiky leaves.

Then again that might have been the best thing.

6

I was lying there trying to work it all out when the phone rang. It was Jenny.

"'Middle of the Town'," she said, straight away.

"What?" I mumbled, rubbing sleep from one eye. "Which town?"

"That's just it. It's not a town, it's a village."

"Which village then?"

"Middleton. It's a village near King's Lynn. They still perform the Ceremony of the Cutty Wren there every St Stephen's Day. You see, they carry the bird in a cage made of holly, and — "

"Jenny, it's still the holidays, you know."

"I know. I just thought you'd be interested, Ian."

There was a note of accusation in her voice, as if I wasn't showing the commitment she expected of me.

"I am," I protested. "It's just... Well, we're a bit late for the 26th December."

"But not for Plough Monday," she countered triumphantly. "They do that too. First Monday after the Epiphany. First day back at school, as it happens. Let's go and check it out. You don't mind driving, do you?"

7

Jenny was like a dog with a bone, waving away any objections I might put up.

"We're going to look like tourists," I grumbled as I steered the car towards Middleton. "Sticking out like a pair of sore thumbs."

"Oh, they won't mind," she said. "I'm sure they love all the attention."

I wasn't anticipating the kind of circus you get in Lewes or Ottery St Mary on Bonfire Night, or in Padstow or Minehead on May Day. All the same, I hadn't expected the place to be as dead as it appeared to be when we got there.

None of the shops were open even though it was still early. I pulled over by the local pub, called The Plough Inn appropriately enough. The sign swinging above the entrance showed the device from which it derived its name, decked in gaily coloured ribbons. It had an entourage of darkly clad men, some women too going by their clothing, their faces obscured by the shadows of their wide-ribboned hat brims. There was a disembodied head in a periwig at ground level, the plough horse's hoof

198

poised to trample it, its expression as appalled as it should be at this prospect. Earth piled around the face indicated its owner was buried up to his neck, arms trapped by the heavy soil as the horse bore down on his defenceless skull with its heavy burden, whose sharpened ploughshares gleamed in the light of a fat full moon.

The pub didn't look any more inviting than this sign suggested, the windows devoid of light. Was nothing open round here? It was cold enough to make my breath visible, and I'd set my heart on enjoying whatever local curiosity we were to see from the comfort of a warm hearth.

"What about the other bit of the rhyme?" I said, as much to make conversation as anything else. "'Maguire and Malone'. Is there an Irish presence round here perhaps…?"

"*There's* your answer," said Jenny, referring to the wheezing strains of an accordion and the rhythmic jingling of bells and clacking of sticks in the distance, growing steadily in volume, with the clopping of horses' hooves adding its own syncopated rhythm.

"Morris Dancers," I murmured.

"In these parts they call them 'Molly Dancers'."

"Oh, I see – Molly Malone," I said.

"And the Molly Maguires," Jenny added.

"And 'these parts' means Norfolk: short for 'Northern folk'," I put in, feeling quite pleased with myself.

But I went quiet as the Molly Dancers drew closer, jingling and tapping and dancing, some in collarless shirts, dark waistcoats and ribbon-decked top hats that reminded me oddly of funeral directors', some in bonnets and dresses, but all with soot-blackened faces.

"Maybe it's not such a bad thing that this doesn't draw a big crowd," Jenny remarked. "Imagine the outcry if a bunch of educated city folk came along and saw these yokels blacking up!"

I winced as the procession drew closer, hoping none of the intimidating figures had heard her refer to them as "yokels".

"It's nothing to do with race, you know," said a voice from the darkness.

Its pitch was high and female, its tone jolly but gently reproving. Its owner stepped from the shadow of the pub sign, a hand outstretched in greeting.

"Caroline Blake. Local historian. And white witch if you believe the gossip…"

She was short and plump, her face framed by a thick tartan scarf and one of those ethnic-looking knitted hats with multicoloured tasselled flaps that cover the ears, useful no doubt against the raw air, which was making me shiver miserably. Spectacles with thick tortoise-shell frames and thicker lenses made her pale blue eyes seem to fix us with an unnerving stare, but other than that she seemed harmless, the kind of eccentric at least one of whom is assigned by law to every English village.

"I'm Jenny," said Professor Underwood, going for informal first-name terms. "And this is Ian."

"I knew that," I said. "About the blacking up, I mean."

The two women exchanged a smile and a knowing look, bonding over my defensiveness. Jenny moved to accept the proffered hand, her fingers long and tapered against the short stubby ones of Caroline Blake, whose round diminutive figure, engulfed in one of those long dark-brown wax coats with shoulder wings, seemed to emphasise Jenny's tall elegance.

I continued my bluster. "But others mightn't. That's all I was saying. A lot of people aren't aware that—"

"Yes, yes, Ian," Jenny interrupted. "That poor people in the countryside used to cover their faces in soot when raiding landowners' property to make them less easy to spot and identify at night – the 'black gangs'."

My mouth gaped open. "So you knew that all along?" I said somewhat testily.

"Yes," she said. "And?"

"And yet you were talking like it was *The Black and White Minstrel Show*! I don't get you sometimes…"

I shook my head theatrically.

"*I* don't think it's like that," she said, then added with a dangerous edge to her voice, "but I know some people do, as I think you were pointing out, Ian."

"I hate to break up the domestic," hissed Caroline, "but the plough gang's here!"

The procession had drawn closer to us now, making me feel vaguely embarrassed about our near argument, though I was secretly rather glad of Caroline's choice of words. You only have that kind of friction with people you care about. But any anxieties I might have had that the Molly dancers might take offence at our discussing them so loudly and academically appeared groundless. Their white eyes stared straight ahead, standing out against their darkened faces in the light of their torches, not even acknowledging the three spectators with a sideways glance, transfixed by something beyond my understanding. At their head was a black shire horse dragging a plough bedecked in ribbons and bells, steered by a burly figure in a dress and a bonnet. I shuddered, thinking of the pub sign.

They finished up in the pub car park a little way away from us, raucous laughter signalling their return to their everyday selves. A light cast our shadows onto the road on which they'd just passed us, a steaming pile of fresh horse dung gleaming wet and assailing my nostrils with its earthy aroma.

~~~

"I wouldn't have thought there'd have been much woodland left here in the eighteenth century," I said.

Jenny had been regaling us with the story of how one of the "black gangs", led by a ruffian known only as "King John", had responded to a certain Mr Wingfield charging for off-cuts of timber that had hitherto been free of charge. Under cover of darkness, he and his merry men had crept onto the woodland and ring-barked every tree on the plantation, with a note demanding repayment for the local peasantry on pain of further destruction. Such bitter social struggles seemed a long way off, now we were sitting warming ourselves in the Plough Inn, which had opened once the ceremony was concluded. One of the celebrants had served us our craft ales, now disrobed of his vestments though traces of soot clung to his face, giving it a look of knowing contempt as he served me, at least in my imagination.

"No, this was in Surrey, I think," Professor Underwood replied. "The same 'King John' is said to have ridden in triumph through Farnham Market with half-a-dozen deer poached from the Bishop's Park. Of course, dear old Robert Walpole put paid to this sort of thing with his 'Black Act', which made it a hanging offence. But there'd have been similar resistance in these parts to the draining of the Fens, wouldn't there, Caroline?"

Jenny turned to her new best friend.

"Indeed," Ms Blake agreed. "Plough Monday is a vestige of it. On the first Monday after the Epiphany the plough gangs would dress up and go round the larger houses of the district, crying 'Penny for the Plough!' Anyone who didn't pay up would find a big gouge on their lawn – the calling card of the plough. Some wore women's clothes to defend themselves from any legal reprisals arising from such vandalism."

"Of course!" Jenny put in. "They thought we couldn't be held responsible for our actions, silly little things that we are…"

"Exactly," agreed Caroline. "That's why they call themselves 'Molly' dancers, from the traditional name for men dressed up as women. But even those who didn't do the cross-dressing thing had their faces disguised with soot when they went around demanding money with menaces in this way. Same sort of basis as Wassailing or Trick-or-Treating, really."

"And the hunting of the Cutty Wren," Jenny added.

"Ah, yes," said Caroline. "'The wren, the wren, the king

of all birds, on Stephen's Day was caught in the furze. Although he is little, his family is great – I pray you good landlord, give us a treat!'" She addressed the second couplet to the bar, raising her glass suggestively, but it didn't even raise a smile from the surly barman and no more than sour mutters from his fellow Molly dancers.

"So what's your interest in the Cutty Wren?" she asked.

"Oh, we're … researchers looking into the origins," said Jenny, with cautious vagueness. Even then I sensed there was something more to her interest in this piece of folklore.

"Why *do* they hunt the wren?" I asked.

"It's a funny old bird," Caroline replied, "with a habit of creeping into rocky crevices, caves and the like. Sometimes they nest among tombstones. So naturally they've come to be associated with the Underworld, with the dark forces abroad at this time of year."

Jenny nodded. "At one time," she said, "many people must have believed the light would never come back … unless they made a sacrifice. But why the 26th December in particular?"

"Ah, now that's another good story," Caroline said. "St Stephen's Day: when the saint hid from his persecutors it was the chirping of the wrens that revealed his hiding place. But we've rather strayed off the subject of Plough Monday, I fear…"

"Yes", I agreed. "What about the poor fellow on the pub sign? Did he owe a bit more than a penny to the plough gang?"

"Oh, much worse than that," Caroline said darkly.

"Perhaps there was a sliding scale for repeat offenders," said Jenny, breaking the air of solemnity that had suddenly descended on us.

General hilarity ensued between us, but I noticed that neither the soot-stained barman nor the group of Molly Dancers gathered near the bar joined in with our laughter though it was clear to me that they had been listening to every word.

After our mirth had subsided, Caroline Blake went on. "Nothing poor about him, my dear," Caroline said with a smile. "Far from it. And a Justice of the Peace, to boot. He was a local bigwig who named names, turned King's Evidence. It was the biggest thing in these parts since the Levelling of the Dikes back in the 1640s. Fifteen men sent to the gallows for poaching, foraging and other such heinous offences, their families left to fend for themselves, some starving to death."

8

The following weekend, Jenny stood me up.

After getting back from Middleton we'd returned to our usual routine of work, rest and play, with her dragging me along to ceilidhs at the weekend, me pretending not to care who she left with. I assumed she'd kicked our "Cutty Wren" project into the long grass for now. After all, the clues had proved fruitless and we'd come back home empty handed, scratching our heads and still none the wiser as to where the treasure hunt was leading. We'd driven back feeling tired, irritated, frustrated and vaguely guilty. It hadn't brought us closer together, as I'd secretly hoped it might. Perhaps it had just lured us there rather didactically for a lesson in the brutality of history.

She'd vaguely invited me to a ceilidh that Saturday. I hadn't had anything else on so I'd agreed to accompany her. As the time had drawn nearer she hadn't called to confirm the details so I'd tried to ring her. All through Saturday there'd been no answer from her landline and her mobile went straight to answerphone.

It wasn't a firm arrangement, so I'd shrugged and thought no more about it, toying with the idea of going out to the dance myself without her.

Just to spite her, eh? I thought sourly. *Like she'd care.*

In the end I fell asleep in front of some awful television programme, waking up bleary-eyed and stiff-necked.

~~~

I didn't hear from Jenny until Sunday evening. It was still early, but it had been dark for some time when the phone rang. Without any greeting or other preamble, she said, "I went back there."

"Really? Where?"

"To Middleton," she said. "With a spade and a metal detector. Well, not Middleton exactly. A few miles northeast of it. 'Nearby you'll find me', it said. It took me a while to work it out, but then I remembered the three coins I found under my pillow, the salt spilled by the magpie. I looked on the map and there it was: a lonely little place called Three Farthing Hill on Salt Heath. There's a Bronze Age long barrow there, surrounded by gorse bushes…"

"So?" I said.

"'The wren, the wren,' remember? 'Got caught in the furze'? Well, it was – or rather under it. Something was, anyway. It just took a bit of digging to find it. Something small and very shiny and *very* valuable."

"Great," I said, fighting my sense of grievance that she'd left me out of her endeavour. "So did you bring the Molly Dancers back with you or something?"

"Ian, what are you on about?"

"Well, it sounds like one of their accordion players is warming up."

She muttered something else in a voice suddenly shaky, almost tearful. Not like her at all, but then she hadn't seemed her usual self throughout the call. I couldn't make out quite what she was saying, just the gist, that something had come back with her all right. It was difficult to understand with all the wheezing going on in the background, as if someone was playing the squeeze box, but no notes were coming out.

"I wish you bloody well hadn't said that, Ian," she said, still sounding upset but in a brittle and irritable way.

"Sorry," I said, back-tracking hopelessly. "It's probably just the line."

"No, Ian. It's not the line. I can hear it too."

She sounded as if she was trying to keep her voice down to prevent someone there from over-hearing. Yet I knew she lived alone and rarely had visitors apart from her occasional one-night stands. And sometimes me.

"You're really frightened, aren't you? Look, why don't I come over? For that matter, why didn't you let me come with you when you went back up there?"

Conscious of the querulous tone to my voice on this last question, I might have expected her snapping rejoinder.

"Maybe because this was something I wanted to do on my own, Ian." She'd raised her voice in irritation at this point but then lowered it again, as if she'd forgotten herself but was now renewing her attempt to conceal her presence from the implied listener. Whoever it was had stopped wheezing, perhaps suspending breathing in order to hear her, because respiration seemed a more likely explanation for the sounds than a faulty accordion, when I thought about it, which I tried not to as much as possible.

"I thought I was on my own when I dug it up," she went on, speaking barely above a whisper so I struggled to hear it. "But after a while I felt sure something was watching me. Then I saw it was just a few wrens nesting among the stones. I could hear them singing. I can hear them now. I think they're going to give me away like they did St Stephen. Can you hear them, Ian?"

I listened to the dead air for a moment, straining to hear birdsong. Was that a faint churring? No, it was just the whirring you sometimes get on the line.

"Oh, God, Ian," she said, her voice high and tiny. "What if it's homing in on this thing I dug up?"

The next thing I heard was the beep of the line disconnecting.

9

I should have gone over there straight away. At first, I was too full of resentment at her snubbing me by going to Salt Heath without me, even suspecting that she'd deliberately tried to shut me out of what sounded like a lucrative find, keeping all the glory for herself after I'd helped her with the initial legwork. But I didn't let myself think that was the reason for my delay. I told myself she didn't want me to go over there. *She'd said this was something she wanted to do on her own*, I reminded myself. *Well, let her!* A small mean voice added.

I soon talked myself round but by the time I got there she was gone. Would I have been able to help her if I'd gone immediately? I'm not sure. My hesitation had been enough to avoid encountering whatever had come for her. Perhaps it was my cowardice as much as my spite that had held me back. Whatever the reason I'll never know exactly what happened to her.

The inevitable police investigation followed. It was only later that I found out what they discovered in her lonely flat. No body – not so much as a drop of blood.

For a while, I wondered if I should tell them about the conversation I had with Caroline Blake when I asked her if she had any ideas about what might have happened to Professor Underwood.

"Underwood, you say? Is that her surname? Well, bless my soul, what a small world we live in! That was the name of the chap in the wig on the pub sign, the Justice of the Peace who sent those men to the gallows."

A little genealogical research confirmed that this was no coincidence at all, but I don't think it will help the police work out why their search of Professor Underwood's flat yielded only a floor dotted with feathers and a mud-spattered gold amulet in the shape of a small, plump bird.

Zombie Economy

Sometimes you'll spy him at the crossroads among the whistling canes, with the milky pebble eyes that have seen it all. Despite their appearance of a caul of cataracts he is not blind. He could tell you a few tales if he could speak – slaves whipped or drowned or burned alive or eaten alive by dogs or boiled alive in cane syrup.

But he cannot speak; his tongue removed for its sharpness over a century ago when this lush and fertile island was still called San Domingo – before the rebel slave armies of Toussaint L'Ouverture blazed a trail across it.

Carrefour serves a new master now, but there are no longer such things as masters and slaves these days! There are not supposed to be, at any rate. The Aristocracy of the Skin still exists. It always comes back in different forms whenever the masters need it, just like Carrefour did when Baron Samedi chanted in a queer nasal sneer over his grave at the crossroads. Chains of iron can be broken and cast aside, melted down and refashioned into bayonets to use against the planters, but invisible chains can be somewhat harder to shake off. They stick to your skin like boiling cane, the sticky sweet death. Nothing burns like sugar does.

~~~

The priests call them "les maudits", the cursed: a contraction of "mauvais-dit", which reminds us of the phrase about speaking ill of the dead. Except that the living dead are the result of a Bokor speaking ill to the dead. The use of this pejorative term for these unfortunates might be considered somewhat contradictory for the priests of a religion that saw resurrection as a miracle and a blessing. But then perhaps that's only the case when their Lord does it. For a mere man to assume control over life and death is a blasphemy of course – doubly so if that man happens to be black! I wonder if they might feel differently if a white man were to appropriate the methods of the Bokor.

From *A People's History of Voodoo*, by Derek Benjamin, 1946

~~~

Carrefour's new master, in the wide-brimmed hat of a French Catholic priest above a scraggy goatee beard, has eyes somewhat different: pale as his ghost-like skin, but burning and piercing with mesmeric power. They have enabled him to enslave his rivals and further enslave those who were once slaves in life. This was their lot when the island was a French colony, and it is their lot now too in their living death. As for the ones who used to lord it over him, it gives Lemaistre an extra frisson of pleasure to turn them into senseless things at his beck and call, but after a while the joys of inflicting what would be agony for the living onto those who seemingly cannot feel wears thin. Where is the amusement in inserting a sewing needle into unresponsive flesh that will not bleed, or into the pupil of an eye constantly staring unblinking into the distance? Much better to use it on a clay or rag-doll effigy of someone still living – how tiresome that these flesh-dolls refuse to struggle or scream!

That is not why he endured the humiliation of paying the Bokor to instruct him in Voodoo, a man who joked that with his white skin and goatee beard he looked like he should be a burnt offering to the Loa. Well, that witch doctor, grinning so hard that the graveyard soil and ash mask cracked and crumbled from about his mouth, soon laughed on the other side of his face when his student turned those powers against him. Sometimes he fancies he can hear the Bokor's *gros bon ange* screaming with rage and pain from that bottle cast down the plantation well whenever Lemaistre torments his undead flesh.

Disappointingly, it's probably just his imagination.

The things cannot feel, can they?

Lemaistre isn't sure. Whenever a zombie worker stumbles, tumbles into the sugar mill, it does not struggle or cry out. Nor do its comrades intervene to save it from becoming one with the cane. Does this mean it is a senseless nerveless thing, a machine made out of flesh, muscle and bone, without soul or spirit? Or is it a locked-in consciousness, aware of every nerve shredded by the grindstone but unable to articulate its agony? He hopes the white zombies who slighted him in life at least are not numbed to the pain of their unnaturally prolonged animation.

The awareness of the black ones does not matter to him, apart from the Bokor of course, the exception to that rule. Such foolish accidents simply mean another spoiled batch of sugar, or one with a higher protein content, but a mangled zombie is easily replaceable. Moreover, the creatures' dumb acceptance of their fate, as well as their minimal food and sleep requirements, makes them an excellent source of cheap labour, literally inexhaustible. Even in life they lacked the higher sensibilities. He once read of how parents would watch with apparent indifference as their children were snatched by the slavers, knowing there was no point in resisting the armed gangs. Not until they organized themselves into a fighting force.

For most white people, zombies are a freakish abomination – monsters! But not for him. Here their living death is banal, commonplace, just a normal part of everyday life. In their failure to comprehend this his fellow Europeans reveal themselves as more superstitious than the Africans they despise as ignorant savages. He, Lemaistre, is more enlightened. Learning these ways was just a commercial transaction, one in which he admittedly cheated the other, for no doubt the Bokor hadn't bargained on being reduced to a soulless shell. This also meant Lemaistre didn't have to pay him.

But that was a bonus. Lemaistre's main objective was to establish a plantation on the most economic lines available in an age when slavery had been abolished here over a century ago. For Lemaistre, recruiting the dead was slavery by other means, a zombie economy. Yes, these menial zombies are just for business; the ones who used to push him around in life – the Bokor, the banker, the chief executioner – these are for pleasure. Making them run errands for him, when he was once in their power, gives him a thrill of satisfaction, only a small one when he has no idea of their levels of awareness, but a thrill, nonetheless. Yet the real trouble is not that they seem to feel so little, but rather that his own sensibilities are so blunted he can hardly feel enough himself to enjoy his power. Perhaps that dulling of his senses is also the reason why he barely notices the small blemishes and dis-colourations darkening the pale skin of his torso, one of them nestling in the dark wiry hair of his groin.

~~~

How the French officers used to wonder at the uncanny fortitude of the slave rebels they tortured.

Look at these peculiar creatures! they'd whisper to each other in hushed voices. *We burn them, we maim them, we destroy them, and they just smile back at us, rather like Saint Lawrence, who when seared on a griddle simply told his persecutors to turn him over and roast him on the other side. There was one we fed to the starved dogs, who tenderly caressed the hound eating him even as it bit his hand. Another milky eyed with blindness danced away on his shattered leg from the mud where we beat him to the ground. Why, they cannot be men as we are! So they do not require the same consideration.*

From *A People's History of Voodoo*, by Derek Benjamin, 1946

~~~

Whenever he grows tired of tormenting his once high-up male minions, Lemaistre looks for a woman to control. Their heightened emotional sensitivity makes their entrapment so much more piquant than these stolid patricians, who were all so thick-skinned and hidebound in life he cannot imagine them capable of suffering even after administering the herbs and incantations that transported and transformed them from life to death to living death.

The Englishwoman is a lily, pale, delicate, sensitive. Therefore her name suits her well. The Englishman would like to tend her, nurture her. *Fertilise her too*, thinks Lemaistre lewdly, with a cynical secret smile. Lilies are there to be crushed under his bootheel but he would like to enjoy this one first. As with the local dignitaries he's enslaved, the problem is that the same measures necessary to make this possible would also dull her senses, or at least any signs of it in her demeanour, such as sighs or cries or weeping. The knitting of her brow in sorrow. Even the flat lifeless indifference of despair cannot be distinguished from the effects of his sorcery. But it doesn't matter. He'll have her but he'll not keep her long, unlike the Englishman who will love her forever. That poor fool hopes Lemaistre's potions and incantations will tempt her away from Patrick, her fiancé, but he too will soon realise the emptiness of her eyes and the absence of her bottle-trapped soul will make the possession of her body a futile trophy, an empty vessel.

But she would never love either of them were she in full possession of her senses. The Englishman is a lumbering oaf, affable enough in his way but without that spark of something unusual that sets Lemaistre apart from other men. Lemaistre on the other hand makes the English-woman's skin crawl. Oh, she doesn't say so but he can tell. And yet he has a terrible light in his eyes that can make her his if he could but overcome her resistance and fear.

Lemaistre does not consider any cosmetic measures to his own person. It does not occur to him. He is not built to please a lady, lacks the social niceties to make the kind of polite conversation that might put her at her ease as a preamble to making love to her.

Yet she is also isolated from other women here,

surrounded by men competing for her attention, her only female confidante a sullen maid. Perhaps that is the reason why she is becoming catatonic, not Lemaistre's magic, after all, retreating into herself under the strain of the Englishman's blandishments, as well as her own fiancé's bullying solicitude. She is never truly alone and this has made her shut down, her eyes glassily staring, her face a china doll's blank porcelain visage, brittle and expressionless as the crude effigy he uses to try to manipulate her movements.

Lemaistre prefers to believe the triumph is his, the result of his wizardry. His exultation over this helps to distract him from the black blotches forming upon his body. They are becoming more painful by the day, too much even for his stoical nature to endure. No wonder no sentient woman could ever love him! That was always the case, but now these blemishes have spread and grown that has become even less likely. At night he stares at the pale puffy flesh of his chest and belly, and begins to wonder if either the pain or the unguents he has administered upon himself for its relief are causing him to hallucinate.

For they are beginning to resemble faces.

And when Lemaistre's startled eyes peer closer at their image in the glass he begins to fancy that they all share the same familiar features.

He wonders if he might have allowed the Bokor to stray too near the sea. Others' enslavements of the living dead have been undone by accidentally feeding the creatures biscuits laced with salt, bringing them to their senses, giving them the apple of knowledge of their deaths, restoring them to life momentarily before the shock of this revelation stops their hearts. Lemaistre has been careful to avoid this but perhaps the Bokor's will is so strong that the mere scent of the salt on the wind might be enough to free his *gros bon ange* from its glass prison down the well. He could then pretend to remain entranced while plotting his own occulted curse on Lemaistre, speaking ill to the usurping zombie master, making *him* one of *les maudits*.

As if in answer to his deepest terror, one by one the tiny blotches open a pair of miniscule eyes in faces he now sees are indeed doll-like replicas of the Bokor's, in miniature, the same size as that of the effigy he used to control the Bokor's movement – with one important difference.

Each one grins back at him from the mirror in triumph.

~~~

Carrefour is not blind of course, any more than he was back when Napoleon's men set upon him, though the silver occlusions' resemblance to cataracts added to their sense he was a soft target. He can see too well what his master is too blind to see, why Lemaistre is so unlucky in love. Not that love is exactly what he wants.

It might help if you trimmed your goatish beard and tamed your wayward single brow, thinks Carrefour, having watched Lemaistre's many failed attempts on Lily's virtue from the shadows on the edge of the plantation he motionlessly guards. He says nothing though. He's silent. Totally silent. If the crickets were to cease their whirring and the Loa-worshippers their chanting, you would hear that he doesn't even breathe. Carrefour doesn't miss the rhythmic hiss in-and-out of his own lungs working. He doesn't even know he's dead. Were he to touch or taste salt, awareness of his own mortality would return in a flood of remembering. Then he might be able to dance the way he did, away from his beating, but he is too weary to cavort around like he did then.

He still has the limp, over a hundred years later. At least the Bokor put him on light duties, guarding the crossroads. There's no trace of the makeshift grave now. Fields of tall, fibrous cane have covered it, almost as tall as he. Countless feet have trodden back the earth he clawed aside, no longer needing to breathe but desperate to move, to taste the air with his mouth if not his lungs.

~~~

Ardel watches the world of Port au Prince drift by from her table, a blur of carriages, chickens and mango-sellers, hears the clop of hooves and the shouts of the market traders, smells the sweat and dung and sugarcane. She has always enjoyed people-watching. Perhaps that's why she wanted to write. It always seemed a good way of making a virtue of shyness and the feeling it engendered of being an unseen watcher of others' affairs.

The young English couple, newly-weds possibly, or maybe engaged, certainly seem oblivious both to her presence and her surreptitious scrutiny.

"Let's get away from here, darling," the English woman says.

"But you're better now, aren't you?" her fiancé replies.

"I know but I'm worried I'll get sick again if I stay."

"All right then, Lily. Back to merry old England it is then. You can go back to catching the common cold."

The Englishwoman, or Lily, as Ardel now knows her to be, laughs at this, an edge of hysteria to her mirth. "Oh yes, darling! What I wouldn't give to catch a cold instead of whatever that nasty tropical fever was I was laid up with."

"Well, you're over it now," says her beau. "But our goatee-bearded friend seems to have caught it off you."

"That beastly man! I wouldn't let him come close enough to catch anything off me!"

"Really? I was beginning to wonder if you'd fallen under his spell, my dear, the way you wandered around in a dream during your illness."

"Don't be silly, darling! You can be quite the green-eyed monster at times, you know."

"You were sick. Now *he* is and all of a sudden you're well again. Odd that…"

"What do you mean by that, Patrick?" Her eyes narrow at something in his tone. Trouble in Paradise, perhaps? Before it can turn into a tiff, a calypso singer comes cavorting into the café crooning a deceptively cheerful yet somehow haunting little ditty about domestic scandal.

A waiter comes to collect the American woman's empty coffee cup.

"Tout va bien pour vous, Mademoiselle Wray?"

Ardel nods and smiles back at him, soothed by the melody despite the unhappy tale it tells. It may provide a solution to the writing problem with which she's struggling: how to tell the story of the love triangle without too much exposition dialogue or flashbacks. What if the younger son were to take the heroine out for a drink at a café such as this, to ingratiate himself with her and show up the older brother as the cad he is? But it backfires spectacularly because of a seemingly innocent yet pointed song about *another* domestic scandal. She wonders what Curt would make of her idea.

She notices how the couple has fallen silent, the young man, Patrick, looking sullen and his fiancée, Lily, eyeing him apprehensively. Yes, trouble in Paradise indeed…

A spoon clinks on Patrick's saucer. Ardel notices the thunderous expression upon his face. Apparently so does the singer, as he decides discretion is the better part of valour and abruptly ends the song. This is too late for Patrick, who swallows the last of his coffee and stands abruptly, his tall lean frame seeming to tower over Lily, his moustache almost bristling with irritation.

"Let's go," he says to his fiancée.

"But darling I haven't finished my coffee!" she protests.

"Very well, I'll see you back at the hotel then."

And abruptly he leaves her at the table looking shell-shocked. Ardel tries to make eye contact but Lily looks away, as if resenting her sympathetic scrutiny, staring desolately into her cooling coffee. Ardel looks away too, instead exchanging a rueful glance with the calypso singer who gives a little shrug of his shoulders, as if to say, *Well, you can't please everyone!*

Hearing the scrape of a chair she looks back towards Lily to see her rise from the table, her eyes staring. Mechanically, she counts out the coins needed to settle the bill then wanders away from the shade of the café terrace into the unforgiving Haitian sunshine without even blinking at the sun, as if unseen hands were tugging her via an invisible rope tied about her slender waist.

~~~

Lily walks with slow and measured steps back to the hotel. *Like a sleepwalker*, she thinks. Indeed, she wonders if she's sleepwalking into disaster, going ahead with this marriage. She hasn't much option now of course, but the forthcoming nuptials loom like the black clouds of one of Patrick's moods – rather like the literal black clouds gathering on the horizon. No matter how much she drags her feet she knows she'll end up in the same place, so she keeps going, her gaze fixed upon the dirt track beneath her feet. It's as if she's locked into a preordained route, rather like the one upon which her life has been fixed up to now.

Yet when she finally raises her eyes to look at her destination she sees she has arrived not at the hotel but at the plantation house. A fine mist of rain, blown in off the sea by strengthening winds, shrouds the white marble pillars and arches of the mansion, swirling around it, wafted by the surging gusts. The howling wind brings heady scents of mango and sugarcane like a lover's caress, but its keening howl reminds her of the cries of tortured slaves.

Where did that thought come from? The history of the place, no doubt. But why is she here, not back at the hotel?

Maybe her feet have a mind of their own, responding to her misgivings about her engagement to Patrick, blown off course like a ship in a storm. Or perhaps some other force has guided them, the same one that has made her a bit off lately, not quite herself. It must have caught up with her again in a moment of weakness, when Patrick's ungallant behaviour left her all alone in the café with the busy-bodying woman looking on, and a bill to pay.

The heavy wooden front door stands ajar on the raised front porch, as if beckoning her inside. She answers its summons, not fully understanding why she's doing so. The gloom hardly looks inviting. But then neither was the thought of going back to the hotel to soothe Patrick's troubled brow, try and lift his black mood, which would no doubt darken even further if he knew where she was now. He would assume she came here for some unlikely tryst with the house's owner. As if she could ever feel desire for that vile creature with his frightful goatee beard and permanent sneer! He might have used some furtive means of bewitching her into forgetting herself for a while – perhaps the same means he's used to guide her steps to this accursed place.

Nevertheless, despite her better judgement advising her to resist she follows the urge to climb the steps up the porch, towards the door. Even in the humid tropical heat she feels a chill from the darkness inside. Shafts of light reveal flickering motes of dust and there is a musty smell, suggesting the master's budget does not stretch to domestic servants.

She is about to turn away, give in to her better judgement, when from the inner recesses of the house she hears a faint mewling voice cry: *Help me… Please!*

~~~

Carrefour smells salt on the wind.

So does the Bokor, of course, but there's nothing new in that. His duties as one of Lemaistre's leg-men have often taken him close to the sea – enough to allow the scent of it to prickle his nostrils, making him breathe again and aware of himself. It usually takes more than that for a zombie to shake off his invisible chains, and the result is generally a release into death, breaking the suspended animation that has hitherto kept the untenanted corpse in shambling half-life.

But the Bokor's will was stronger than the others so he was able to break free from his enchantment with a mere sniff of the brine, smelling salts for the soul, and when it flew free from the bottle trap and reunited with its former host he clung onto life, biding his time until his own enchantment could work its magic on the one who'd usurped his powers, keeping up the pretence of stolid glassy-eyed undeath, arms and legs stiff, feet dragging as he trudged around the plantation and sometimes further afield on various errands, waiting until the moment was right to savour his revenge upon the white devil who stole his magic.

Carrefour on the other hand was not pretending. But now he breathes in the strengthening briny gusts that tickle the hairs inside his nostrils. His limbs still feel leaden, as those of a man waking from a rum-laced stupor, but this unfamiliar motion inside him, of lungs working, sucking in and blowing out air, is a pair of bellows reigniting the embers of his knowledge of life and death. Before, he was confined to the plantation by barriers he could not see but could never cross, condemned forever to stand at the crossroads and guard the cane fields, his consciousness locked inside a shell that would not obey its synaptic commands, for it danced to the beat of another's drum, lately guided by an avaricious malevolent intelligence. The wind now howling through the towering fibrous crop beckons him to cross that forbidden boundary for the first time in centuries – free at last.

~~~

The cry for help draws Lily inside the door even though something about its timbre makes her reluctant to go any further. It sounds muffled, as if the voice is struggling to make itself heard through cotton. As she hesitates it renews its pleas.

Help me please! I cannot see.

Or breathe, she surmises from the way it seems to wheeze between each plaintive appeal. Tentatively she edges along the corridor towards the source of the whining voice and the laboured breathing, leaving the door open as if to secure her escape route. But a sudden gust of wind slams it shut, darkening the place. Unnerved, she wonders if Patrick has noticed her absence and is coming to look for her. She doesn't know whether to be relieved or disappointed by the prospect that he hasn't. Despite her terror at this situation there is a kind of fierce joy within her at facing it herself, without having to defer to her fiancé, who would no doubt take control both of the situation and her.

The sound, or sounds, for she now hears others too, come from upstairs.

Slowly, hesitantly she ascends them, her curiosity and concern for the plight of the person issuing the plea overcoming her fear. Once she has reached the top a long corridor awaits her with a door at the end. It appears the pleading voice emanates from behind this door. Or rather, voices. For it isn't just one voice she hears – there is a host of others too, laughing, their voices shrill with mirth though muffled by fabric too.

They sound like children, so nothing to fear there. But how many are in there? It does sound crowded! Maybe the poor little things are trapped.

But why are they laughing?

She stares at the door. Something about the contrast between the hilarity of the squeaky voices and the misery of the one pleading for help makes her reluctant to open it. It sounds as if a gang of sadistic small children are tormenting one of their playfellows. Yet she cannot leave the poor little mite to their tender mercies.

So gingerly she turns the handle.

The man whose summons brought her here is inside but his power over her has waned now. She moves of her own volition, pity for him mingling with her loathing. He no longer stands so still and imperious, but lies sprawled upon a bed whose sheets are so twisted and sweat-soaked they have become a thick wet rope.

He turns his face towards her, if you can call it a face.

Her breath comes hard in terrified gasps at what she sees.

His eyes have lost their lustre. Indeed, they are no longer visible. In the dim light the whole head appears veiled by a second skin, rendering the face a featureless blur. Sensing her presence though he cannot see her, he rises from his supine position, his arms outstretched, pleading, and again the voice issues its plaintive cry for help.

She backs away.

His voice still sounds muffled. No wonder, given the film of skin covering the place where the mouth should be, but that doesn't explain why it sounds as if it's coming from somewhere lower down than the face. She can see the lumps that so torment him tenting his stained nightshirt and feels as if she ought to give him succour, but somehow horror and loathing of his blank facelessness and writhing diseased body overcome compassion for the wretch, and she recoils from his arms. They must be weeping sores, or else he must be sweating, for there are damp patches where the cotton bulges.

The children she thought she heard laughing are nowhere to be seen.

But there is another person in the room, standing by Lemaistre's sickbed. She wonders if he is the plantation owner's doctor.

It is this other figure who prevents him from scratching by grasping his arms in a half-Nelson. Lily has to admit she's rather glad this man is restraining Lemaistre from coming closer to her. The two men are locked in a bitter struggle, the zombie-master bucking and squirming for release. The face of this other appears white in the dim light but the hands are darker. The pallor covering the features is ingrained ash-like chalk, Lily realises, her dark-adapting eyes eventually recognising one of Lemaistre's praetorian guard of zombies. Except his eyes are no longer glassily staring.

The expression is no longer blank either.

Were it not for the fierce grin on the face of the man

restraining his former master, whom she only knows by his clothes, the ones he hasn't ripped in his torment, Lily might have believed the arms pinioning the struggling figure were motivated by mercy – that he wanted to stop Lemaistre from tearing his skin open in his frenzy. But the ash-faced man's words contradict this interpretation of his actions.

"No, tyrant, usurper, you will not harm my little ones! You tried to steal my magic and make me your toy. Now I repay you … many times over."

Until now, neither man has noticed the new arrival. Not that Lemaistre would be able to see her with his eyes cauled thus. At length the ash-faced one spies her, his head turning towards her. She flinches back in terror at his crazed expression but she is frozen in his sights, like a rabbit before a cobra. This was the effect Lemaistre's eyes used to exert upon her when they were still there. He begins to laugh and his laughter seems to echo shrilly around the dusty chamber. It is the laughter of children, perhaps the little ones he mentioned.

His attention focussed momentarily on Lily, he loses control of his patient or victim – she still can't tell which! Lemaistre breaks free from the other man's grip and begins scratching and clawing at his body, under his nightshirt so it rides up higher, enough for her to see his thighs, groin and torso.

She covers her mouth, averts her eyes, and not just because she has just seen a part of him even Patrick hasn't yet revealed to her, but rather because what she saw there is far from what she expected to see, even with her somewhat limited knowledge of masculine anatomy.

As she turns to flee, the Bokor, the witchdoctor, calls after her. "Yes, that's right, run! Save yourself before the storm hits. It's coming and will spare no one. *Run!*"

And as she runs, what she just saw and heard comes back to her in flashes as stark as the lightning now shivering and blasting the sugarcane fields she crosses blindly – the dark tumours blotching his torso, each one a shrilly laughing replica of the Bokor's face as it would be without his mask of ash – the exception being the face between his legs, which was Lemaistre's own, the wiry hairs down there forming the goatee beard, calling out in short-lived relief as the nightshirt was raised…

Ah! that's better… I can see now!

~~~

The rain hammers down upon Carrefour's pate bringing with it more salt from the sea to increase his awareness. As the heightening wind blows it into his face he opens his mouth to drink it, thinking to imbibe more knowledge.

He remembers events before and after his death.

Before: the daily grind of the plantation and the arbitrary cruelty of the French plantation owner, making him and the other slaves watch as they meted out exemplary punishments to the insubordinate. Then of course there's the time of his own tongue's savage removal before an unwilling audience.

After: the period of unrest, revolt, finally the war of independence, Toussaint L'Ouverture leading rebel armies to challenge Napoleon's might, eventually triumphing, but only after his death in a French prison tower, the island San Domingo finally renamed Haiti. Toussaint was too much of a good Catholic himself to approve of the means that prolonged Carrefour's existence enough for him to dance away from the French troops, who beat him for a rebel spy.

But what of Carrefour's own death? It has been a blank space in his mind for so long, it never occurred to him before to question why he remembered events from so long ago as if they were yesterday. Though he dreads this memory he feels compelled to wander closer to the roiling sea stirred up by the lashing winds. Plunging into the brine will bring it back to him, a new baptism.

By the time he reaches the shore the storm has grown into a full-blown hurricane, but it is too late for him to turn back from the vast tidal wave sweeping over him, bringing his new life to an abrupt and final end – but not before it restores his memory of his first death, choking on the soil piled on top of him as he writhed against the twine cutting into his wrists and ankles, without even a tongue to cry out or block the dirt working its way into his mouth despite his attempts to keep it shut, making his throat gag uselessly, which it does now too, but at least this time it's on pure salt water, cleansing, rushing in, invading his lungs, washing out the mud that still remained in them from the time before.

The Lazarus Curse

The theories are legion.

A common thread running through all the various origin stories corresponds to the Christ Killer trope, which has always struck me as somewhat illogical because (a) it was the Romans who actually nailed him up there after lashing him to within an inch of his life; and (b) he was as Jewish as the crowd who supposedly opted for him to die over the other one. He even had the title "King of the Jews", uncrowned until the soldiers laid the hawthorn about his bleeding scalp. But when you've tried to kill yourself as many times as I have in ways that would surely have worked for anyone else, logic doesn't really come into it.

The first time you all know about, especially if you're a follower of his cult. But I won't go into that right now. Why assume I'm that guy? I could be... I don't know... Elijah. He got around a bit. Still does, like an ominous Pesach Santa Claus. I'm thinking of the tradition of leaving a cup of Kiddush wine out for the prophet. Kids find the idea of him lurking out in the yard creepy, and adults... What are they thinking? That giving him that muck's going to make him happy? Appease him if he's footsore and weary after his travels?

In any case, that doesn't fit with the most prevalent narrative of the man mocking and berating Christ on his final trek to Calvary and getting that sardonic gift in return. What would Elijah be doing, heckling Jesus? What would he be doing there at that time at all, unless he already had that gift?

So many questions.

Perhaps it's time I offered some answers.

~~~

What you people now call Jewish identity meant something quite different back then. Take Herod the Great, client Jewish monarch of Judea back when I was born there and named after my home turf – quite a lot of people did that of course. But Herod was ethnically an Arab and converted to Judaism. Not that he was the only person to do that. The entire Khazar Empire, stretching from the Black Sea to the Caspian, from the Caucasus to the Volga, converted *en masse*, but that was thirteen centuries later, in mediaeval times. In Herod's case, as the Romans' proxy ruler over the Jewish population of the place, it made sense to adopt the same faith, I guess.

Herod was a bit insecure about his place on the throne, so the one thing he didn't like – one of the many things actually – was other people taking on the title "King of the Jews". Hence the Slaughter of the Innocents. It wasn't all paranoia, and Jesus wasn't the only one to claim that title. Whenever there were unruly crowds around Jerusalem for high days and holidays they'd grab some poor schmuck and crown him King of the Jews. Kind of like the Jewish Lord of Misrule, a cheeky sideswipe at the official puppet-ruler of Palestine.

Speaking of which, I've had a gut-full of every putz going calling me a puppet-master over the centuries, as the walking emblem of my co-religionists, so maybe I shouldn't throw that kind of language around. Except in this case the Romans were the puppeteers, but this wouldn't be the first time my mispocheh got the blame for someone else's misdeeds. Or rather it would. The first of many. That saving of the other guy was the original sin of the Jewish people as far as many of the Goyim are concerned.

I'm just waiting for them to accuse us of antisemitism. That'll be the next thing. It's the next step from blaming me and mine for our own persecution.

Because when I say mispocheh, I don't just mean the

Jews. I mean those of us who have fought back against the Romans and their ilk. Like the Zealots – another bunch whose very name has become a dirty word, because we had the temerity to fight back against our rulers, rather than just hoping if we kissed ass hard enough we'd get away with twenty lashes rather than fifty or a hundred.

It was quite a coup getting one of our mob on the Jesus team. It wasn't easy. I had to undergo some pretty aggressive vetting, I can tell you. The Goyim would have you believing I made the grade because I was good with money – the classic trope originated in me. *Those horny-handed artisans and fishermen only took that schmuck on because he was a good fundraiser. How else could they pay for all the loaves and fishes?* But if I was such a wizard with the filthy lucre how come they could only stump up enough for five of each? Ah! they'll say, that was just creative accounting, prudence, the shrewdness that's come to be a shorthand for all the things the Goyim project onto my mispocheh.

Ah, yes!

From the Middle Ages to the Millennium you have insinuated we were footloose, never in one place long enough to put down roots in the soil so couldn't be trusted with it, or anything else solid, handmade. Money was all we were good for, protean shifty shapeshifters that we were, you implied. But how could we be anything other than rootless cosmopolitans? Whenever we tried to be farmers you drove us off the land.

I was the embodiment of that narrative, that self-fulfilling prophecy, with my thirty pieces of silver, while Jesus, the carpenter's son, scourge of the temple money-lenders, was the obverse, an un-Jew despite his hawthorn-crowned title. Yet even the Nazi caricature of the Eternal Jew looked rather earthy, with mighty shoulders and a giant cartoon hooknose that could have been carved from oak.

In real life, my nose is rather small and, as for the gambit with the loaves and fishes, my approach was more about practical solidarity and political strategy than trying to be frugal with the campaign war chest, such as it was. You give starving people too much to eat in one go and their stomachs will explode, but give them nothing at all, and no wonder they're too weak to fight back against the Romans! My reasoning was, we start small on day one, then gradually feed them progressively larger amounts until they're strong enough to start taking on the centurions. An army of five thousand marches on its stomach, after all!

But Jesus wasn't interested in a sustained campaign to build such a fighting force. He was just concerned with the grand gesture, the set-piece political stunt in securing his legacy for the history books. He didn't care what happened the next day, or the day after that, but only about what happened in the years and decades and centuries afterwards. I suppose he thought his father would be able to kvell about his baby boy's achievements to, I don't know, the Heavenly Host or something. And didn't it make an unforgettable spectacle? I've had to watch that tale told and retold time and time again, in a thousand different ways. I guess that's part of my punishment for jeering at that beautiful shining-eyed charlatan as he was on the way to Golgotha.

But before I get to that – how I became a gothic bogeyman, the model for Melmoth the Wanderer, maybe the Monster hatched on the shores of Lake Geneva too – a few words about how it came to that.

As a professional revolutionary, I'd cultivated contacts within the security forces. That was what we all did. There was plenty of discontent in the ranks which we could use to find chinks in the armour of the Roman occupation. There were two main problems with this. The first was, we didn't know who to trust; the second was that some of our informants expected payment in kind.

So it's possible, just possible, I might have let slip the secret location of our Seder supper that year.

I say "secret" but it's not as if we were hard to find. It's just that usually we moved around a lot. It's not as if my contacts were in the upper echelons of the army, either, but there was an element of *quid pro quo*, of *you scratch my back and I'll scratch yours*, even with the soldier-boys I shared information and sometimes a bed with. They liked a bit of local colour. This is why such liaisons were with Roman legionaries, not the Sanhedrin. The Jewish religious police were much too pure to get down and dirty with zealots. They took their Torah much too seriously. No sodomy for them!

The other disciples didn't get involved in this kind of thing. I didn't expect them to understand, simple Galileans that they were, good country folk smelling of figs and olives, more at home cleaning stinking fishing nets than plumbing the depths of the cesspit of Palestinian realpolitik. No, they didn't want to dirty their hands with that! The only unnatural acts they might contemplate were with sheep. They were true believers in God's golden boy. A lot of the time we were barely on speaking terms, not because they suspected I was a double agent. They just thought I was an up-himself Judaean who'd never worked with his hands.

When one of my contacts let slip to me that the Sanhedrin were going to move against him, I tried to warn him. Of course, the Goyim like to think the Romans were dispassionate observers of all this, above the fray of these petty Jewish squabbles, only graciously intervening at the end, giving the braying mob of wolves a choice of which scrap to devour. They just drove the nails in, doing what the Jews told them to do, right? But you've got your heads screwed on backwards if that's what you think. Did you never think it might be the other way around? That the Sanhedrin were the ones doing the Romans' dirty work? Giving them plausible deniability?

But when I gave him a chance to bow out in a face-saving way, he was having none of it. It was touching, his faith in both the Romans and the one he claimed was his father.

"So you think Daddy's going to save you?" I said. "Look how he treats his chosen people!"

"Ah, but that's because you've been doing it all wrong all this time."

He gave me that smile that infuriated and beguiled me in equal measure, arch and mocking, as if he knew how I felt and meant to teach me to do it the right way. I knew he'd never do *that* with me. He'd made that clear. But he wasn't talking about that kind of love anyway. He meant the divine kind, for something or someone invisible, intangible. That was the horror of it. I think he really believed his own propaganda!

"Okay," I said, "let's say the Sanhedrin let you off with twenty lashes, which I think is unlikely given the reputation you've earned yourself. What then? You'll be a marked man. Cain will have nothing on you. You've put a target on your back for the rest of your life."

"The Romans won't let anything happen to me," he said. "They'll save me."

I gaped at the klutz, open-mouthed.

"Why in the world would they want to do that?"

"Why do you think, Jude? 'Render unto Caesar what is Caesar's'. 'The meek shall inherit the Earth'. 'Love your enemies'." He laughed. "I always make sure I throw something like that in there when their troops or spies are listening. They think I'm their friend!"

I nodded slowly. "That's what you think?" I said.

He carried on smiling that stupid stunning smile.

He did. He really believed it. The trouble was, to a certain extent, so did I. It made sense, after all.

Here was someone who could pacify the masses, tell them to stop fighting for a bigger share here on Earth because their reward would come in the hereafter. The meek? Those schlimazels were part of the problem. Why throw this one to the wolves when he was saving the

Romans and their proxies the job of suppressing the kinds of meshugah there'd been here thirty years ago, by gentle persuasion and mystical bullshit? I only joined up with him because he brought people together, which meant there was a chance of stirring them up against the Romans. And they *were* stirred up. That's why the Romans didn't like it. Whatever caveats he put in for the ears of centurions or Sanhedrin, to persuade them he wasn't trying to rock the boat, were done with his fingers crossed behind his back as far as they were concerned, with a wink to the meshuggeners. He was trying to ride both horses. And anyone who has followed the history of execution methods over subsequent centuries the way I have will know, if you're attached to more than one horse galloping in opposite directions, you tend to go all to pieces.

The other reason they took him was because they could. Both he and I and all the rest of us grew up in the shadow of a big Jewish uprising, and after suppressing that the Romans weren't taking any chances. No point bothering hiding the iron fist inside a velvet glove anymore, if they ever did! That was why he said all the schmaltz about the meek. He wanted the Romans to think our movement was harmless. But I knew they were so paranoid now, they would never believe that in a million years. And they had a point. If you're an occupying force, people gathered in large numbers outside your capital are never harmless, no matter how meek they claim to be.

The kind of pacifism he advocated then has become more effective nowadays when states prefer to keep repression behind closed doors and don't want to be seen to be murdering people in front of the cameras. But back then, the rulers weren't ashamed of torture. They liked to put it on proud display, as a warning to others. Exemplary punishments were all the rage, tortured bodies hanging from wooden crosses by the roadside, making a mockery of the idea that you can appeal to the state's better nature by the nobility of your gesture.

Take Matthew and Judas (not me – a lot of boys had that name then), who pulled down an imperial eagle erected by Herod after they heard a rumour the ageing colonial gauleiter was dying. When it turned out the monarch was still alive he had them burned to death. That was the year Jesus was born. A few years later another Judas (that name again!) led another uprising. It was quite a time to be born into. No wonder the rulers liked putting troublemakers to death in spectacular ways!

Having said that, I was as shocked as anyone was by what happened.

Maybe not as shocked as he was though.

And the kiss? Well, when the Sanhedrin showed up I could see it was the last chance I would get – the only chance! To be fair, he was a bit of a captive audience though they hadn't actually picked him out of the crowd at that point, and in my rapture at the taste of his honey lips (he had just had a mouthful of Charoset) I moaned, "Oh, Rabbi!" Unfortunately, in doing this I'd let slip his identity to the enforcers of official Jewish law, as well as my true feelings. He was good about it though.

"Don't worry, Judas from Kerioth," he said with his usual pomposity. "You too shall live forever."

I thought he was speaking in riddles and parables like usual, and in a sense he was. My name would live throughout history, especially as the Greek translation of "from Kerioth" became corrupted to sound like "assassin". Sicarius – Iscariot. See? Over time I've changed my name so many times I've become nameless to avoid this deathless stigma. I had a lot of time for the original Sicarii, Jewish insurgents from back in 70AD, but these days Jews know being associated with back-stabbing is not conducive to healthy living.

But he meant literal immortality and he meant it as a curse. Strange that it should be one when the life everlasting was one of his selling points. Stick with me and you'll live forever! That was his mantra. However, his own experiments with actual necromancy were somewhat hit-and-miss, if you ask me. Lazarus was as glassy-eyed and emaciated in life as he had been in death, which made me wonder if he'd been in some kind of cataleptic trance the whole time, anyway, and when Jesus himself was released from his tomb he just wandered around a bit in a daze showing off his wounds before finally dropping dead. I often think he was unconscious but still alive when they took him down from the cross and just had a brief new lease of life once the stone was moved away from his tomb.

But he obviously had some kind of paranormal ability – some form of telekinesis certainly. I'm the living proof. It took me quite a while to get down from that tree where I'd gone to end it all after the trauma of dropping him in it with the Sanhedrin. At the time I just thought I'd made a mess of the noose. I wouldn't be the first failed suicide in history after all!

I went to demand an explanation from him but it wasn't a good time. He was on his way to Calvary, dragging the cross behind him, so he wasn't in the best of moods, blood pouring from his back and forehead. I thought about kissing his wounds better but it didn't seem like the right moment, if I'm honest. I was in a foul mood anyway, with a blinding headache after all that slow strangulation, so I launched into a tirade instead.

"This is the meek inheriting the earth? Well, you can keep it! This is what you get for failing. But it's worse than that. You didn't even want to succeed!"

He just turned his infuriating infatuating beatifically mocking smile upon me, those eyes shining even though he could barely even keep them open with all the blood pouring into them from his thorn-clasped head, and said it again, his blessing, his curse: "You will live forever, Judas from Kerioth."

I just stood there as he passed, my fingers tracing the bruising on my neck.

~~~

Well, it's not everyone who can say they've had a genus of plant named after them!

Admittedly only a houseplant, but who am I to kvetch?

Not named Judas, an appellation much overused back when I was a lad, as we have seen: Tradescantia (zebrina, pallida and flumensis) whose less prepossessing common names are spiderwort, inch plant and, of course, Wandering Jew.

It looks like the meek did inherit the earth after all, if by "the meek" we mean the followers of Jesus. Not that they stayed meek. It took about three centuries for it to grow from a despised Jewish sect to the official religion of the Emperor Constantine himself. Pacifism made its followers look like harmless cranks until they weren't any more – until the Jesus freaks ruled most the known world. If your rulers are throwing you to lions and nailing you to crosses left, right and centre, you might as well to try to suffer with some dignity and use the experience to build a mythology of martyrdom, which will stand you in good stead once you've got hegemony.

Once the Goyim took on Christianity and made it their own there was no longer any need for the pretence of weakness. There was nothing meek about the Crusades or the Inquisition. I should have converted to Christianity then and become a Roamin' Catholic!

Nothing meek about the Sicarii either, come to that. Not bespectacled Jewish intellectuals getting sand kicked in our faces. Well, not without a fight anyway. Or, as in the case of Masada, there were the times we kicked the metaphorical sand in our own faces!

Of course, Biblical scholars have debunked my involvement in this Zealot faction, but that assumes I died at the same time as Jesus, and given he'd condemned me to live I was no more able to die with the rest of them than I had been able to hang myself successfully from that tree forty years before. But up until that mass suicide atop the plateau, which seemed a perfect opportunity for me to have another go at ending it all, I'd wondered if it was just ineptitude rather than anything supernatural that had saved me from asphyxiation. Of course there was the fact I hadn't aged, but I put that down to clean living.

When the blood poured out of the self-inflicted gash in my throat and I still lived, it seemed more conclusive evidence that Christ wasn't talking metaphorically when he promised me eternal life, especially when it kept on pouring and wouldn't stop until I had to hold it shut as I staggered over the bodies of my comrades strewn about the fortress. Somehow I managed to evade the legions besieging it. It's easier to get around them when there's only one of you instead of almost a thousand, less so with an extra grin under your chin. I hid in a cave until the soldiers went. By that time the blood had dried up leaving a nice new scar on my neck. I wondered if I'd die of exposure but it seemed more and more likely that nothing could kill me now. Not even the Romans. For that reason I'm glad I didn't fall into their vengeful hands then. They couldn't have killed me but I'm sure they'd have had a lot of fun trying.

Since then it's been a long two thousand years, trying to avoid pain, punctuating the centuries with the occasional increasingly half-hearted attempt on my own life. Not that there has been any shortage of offers. There have been plenty willing to try and help Jews to a premature (or in my case long-overdue) end. They've blamed us for his death. They've blamed us for the plague. They've blamed us for capitalism. They've blamed us for communism. They've blamed us for financial ruin. They've blamed us for cultural Marxism. They've accused us of heresy, of conspiracy, of infanticide, of Jesu-cide, of blood sacrifice, of every kind of vice. For one reason or another, the pogroms have dogged us throughout history. There have been times when I would have welcomed them but they offer only pain without end, not even the relief of death.

If he was right about the afterlife and I could die I might

be able to meet him there, smiling that same damnable smile with which he first snared me. Maybe that's why he cursed me with life without end, the vain bastard. The ultimate punishment was never to see his face again except in my imagination, in my memory.

But there is hope.

Because come to think of it, he never quite made it clear what he meant by forever. My mortal cohabitants of this planet are currently busy making it uninhabitable. What then? When forest fires scorch the entire land and the oceans bloom red and swallow the coasts, will I remain alive? When the Earth dissolves into molten rock, will I still endure? My flesh burnt off, my lungs labouring in the cold vacuum of space, just a floating phantom nervous system drifting in ceaseless agony, an interstellar Flying Dutchman, only without a ship. Will the heat death of the universe precipitate my death? Will the end of time be the end of my time?

The promised Rapture has been slow in coming, leading me to wonder if it was all a fantasy and we were right all along, that he wasn't the Messiah after all. Or it could be that there's nothing after we die and that I'm the only human in history who will never find out if that's the case. If there is a Day of Judgement it might mean I'm cast into Hell forever but that's where I am now, and at least with a definite end to time and a possible one to my life there's a chance that one day he might favour me with one aloof and fleeting glance, one coldly distant smile.

One last thing.

Forget Elijah. Leave a glass of wine out for me – but make it proper wine, not that Kiddush muck.

The Topsy Turvy Ones

As fondly as he anticipated the Restoration, it seems likely that Sir Francis did not live long enough to see Charles II's triumphant coronation. I say "seems likely" advisedly for there is no actual record of his passing, though there are various unsubstantiated rumours about his fading from history in a manner most uncharacteristically quiet for this colourful figure. Certainly he was cruel, something of a local despot, and there must have plenty that wanted him dead and with the wherewithal to carry out such a wish with probable impunity in those chaotic and lawless times. There is a report, probably apocryphal, of him meeting the radical preacher John Pordage, something that again seems rather uncharacteristic for such a staunch Royalist. The only primary sources we have are certain papers he left to his heirs pertaining to some family curse, a tale drawn from shreds and patches of myth and legend, of Hydra's teeth and Mandrake roots, as luridly colourful as the man himself, and suggestive of some bizarre epiphany of interest only to medical practitioners in the field of mental illness.

From *Forgotten Figures of the Cromwellian Era*
by Sir Henry Hobday, Oxford University Press, 1954

1999

The fading ghosts of her dream danced in tatters before her eyes. Scraps of words and images that had formed part of an unbroken whole now splintered into disparate fragments; mercifully, she thought, for these remnants were bad enough, the tip of terror's iceberg, the thin end of its wedge. A man's voice howling of silver rust burning flesh. A hand inserting a finger through the hole in a tongue. Blood pouring from the toothless chasm a woman's mouth had become. Moonlit shoots sprouting pallid muddied heels and toes from grey soil, then ankles and shins and knees and…

But she mustn't think of what followed the strange fleshy efflorescence or she'd start screaming again. She hadn't even known she was doing it, thinking a shrill alarm had woken her until she felt Richard's arms around her, heard him calling to her over the noise that she now realised was her own voice, telling her it was all right, it was just a dream.

Once she'd calmed down, forcing herself to breathe deeply, she made herself remember what had frightened her into shrieking wakefulness. Something about the face that had followed the spidery legs and body out of the loamy earth…

"What was it, Marisa?" he asked. "A bad memory from … back home?"

"Richard," she said with a sigh on the edge of irritability, "it's not my home. I left when I was three."

She hated it when he acted all concerned and right-on about her past, like he thought he was the bus driver in that Ken Loach movie he'd taken her to see. Well, he wasn't a bus driver, he was a wannabe film maker with a trust fund, and she was from Chile, not Nicaragua. Her mother had got them out before anything really terrible could happen to them – bad enough to cause nightmares at least, though some of the things she'd subsequently heard or read about had induced them. Maybe this dream *was* linked to the horrors of her past. She had just heard the old general was holed up in some privately rented mansion in Surrey, awaiting a decision on extradition. She didn't want to mention that to Richard. He'd only get all worried and over-solicitous, and that would be annoying.

This was something different. The garbled words and images seemed disconnected both from reality and each other. Yet, she reminded herself, while the dream had been playing inside her sleeping brain, it must have had some strange internal logic. Somehow that passing thought was far from reassuring.

1649

A passing strange occurrence did take place at the crossroads near Iver on the first day of April, in the Year of Our Lord, Sixteen Hundred and Forty-nine. A crowd was gathering around a preacher, who did utter forth great sermons and prophecies. Not so unusual perhaps for there be all manner of strange doings hereabouts since the Body Politic lost its divinely anointed Head, but for one thing. This mighty testifier, whose words did impudently storm the very Heavens, was a woman! I wondered if 'twere some All Fools' Day jest, yet 'twas not so – she was in earnest. Some laughed at her and jeered at the impertinence of such as she thinking she could speak the Word of the Lord. Others, like this one – a man, mark you! – set forth an apology for her, saying unto me:

"Why should she not preach? Did not the Maid of Orleans take divine revelation and with it led men forth into battle?"

"Aye," said I. "And mark what happened to her!"

He turned his long pock-marked face away from me. I think him one of these pamphleteers that have of late been prating hereabouts of "Light Shining in Buckinghamshire". No wonder the world hath gone topsy turvy, for these "True Levellers" would have it so. Were it not for their ideas spreading abroad she'd have been hanged for a witch, I have no doubt. The times are so out of joint, I have betimes had to go abroad in rags or face the vengeance of the mob, and thus seem to level myself afore they level me into the ground!

1999

"There's a patch of flat ground over there," he murmured. "That might do." Glancing towards Marisa, he edged the car closer to the fence, tugged the handbrake into position and eased into neutral. As he turned the ignition off and started climbing out of the battered green and white 2CV, she called out to him.

"Hey! Richard! Won't we need to get permission to film in this field…" Then she added, more to herself than him, as he'd already vaulted over the fence: "Especially if we're going to have them digging it up?"

Eventually she sighed and got out of the passenger seat, leaning over the fence and glaring at him. He seemed oblivious. He was standing in the middle of the field grinning his stupid grin under his stupid golden-blond halo.

"Richard!" she called, dark eyes still irritated but with a half-smile tweaking a corner of her mouth. "You must be trespassing." He turned round, smiling back at her, probably at the way she put the stress on the syllable "pass". Though she'd lived in England since she was three she still had a few odd inflections, maybe from her mother.

He walked, almost strutted, over to her.

"Kind of apt," he said when he reached the fence, kissing her on the mouth. "Yes," he went on, his eyes blazing with a kind of fierce humour, "the heartland of Tory England, once the home of primitive communism!"

"What do you know about communism, posh boy?" she snorted. "Anyway, didn't the Diggers set up their commune on some hill in Surrey, not a flat field in Berkshire?"

"Buckinghamshire," he corrected her. "St George's Hill's the one everyone's heard of. The Diggers just called it George Hill, of course – they didn't recognise the established canon of Saints. But—"

"Yeah, yeah, I know, there were Digger settlements everywhere from here to Northampton. They were spreading. That's why the Parliamentarians crushed them, etcetera, etcetera. You don't need to explain it all to me. I have read up on this shit too! I was just taking the piss."

He nodded, a little crestfallen at her outburst. Had she gone too far? She didn't want to go to Surrey anyway – couldn't stand to be in the same county as that sick old bastard. But she wasn't going to tell Richard that. She also knew he had his own reasons not to want to go to the site of the more famous encampment. Right now it was crawling with would-be latter-day "diggers" from the Land Is Ours group, who'd commemorated Winstanley's stand by setting up an "eco-village" on St George's Hill. That would hinder filming.

"You're still trespassing though," she added with a smile. "And you'll definitely be trespassing if you try to film here without permission."

"Will you forgive my trespasses?" He smiled, leaning over the fence for another kiss.

"I don't know why," she murmured, "but yes…"

1649

Such is the anarchy loose abroad since the King lost his head and thus deprived Albion of hers that the trespasses of these wretches do go unpunished. I know not why for Cromwell's treachery did not extend to depriving great ones of their birth-rights. Yet some of his rag-tag army have taken his declaration of a Commonwealth a little too much in earnest. The very day that Mistress Preacher did wander abroad proclaiming signs and wonders, Winstanley did establish his beggar's commonwealth, stirring up every yeoman and ploughboy hereabouts to defy the authority of his master, so that the cart doth draw the horse.

This morning I rode to Iver Heath and beheld men, some women too, some of them strangers to this parish, grubbing in the grey earth with picks and spades. I thought them mere thieves, seeking provender in the soil, thinking to glean turnips overlooked in the last harvest or some such, and drew closer to them, thinking to remonstrate with them. Yet watching them through gaps in the trees I saw that what I thought had been a mere half-dozen of the round-headed rogues had now swollen to thirty or more. Presently, they were joined by another twenty leading a horse that drew a plough, to a raucous cheer that stayed my hand upon the bridle. Something in their bearing gave me pause and warned me that they might not scatter meekly from my chastising tongue, nor yet doff their caps to me, even had I worn my most splendid garb, not the mean garments I was wearing. Besides, some bore arms, a few even wearing the uniforms and cage-visored helmets of the Parliamentarian army, though I'll wager their officers hadn't given them licence to dally here. So it seemed politic to remain in the cover of the poplar trees, watching the rabble set about its work, for these rascals did not mean merely to rob the unharvested fruits of the earth in a desperate and incontinent fashion, but to cultivate it according to Winstanley's pernicious levelling creed that deems it a "common treasury".

I turned in disgust from the sight of these mean creatures ill-using the land God had given to their masters, without a benign guiding hand to instruct them in its best employment. Did they think themselves great ones, to take possession of what was mine? The Lord of Misrule should renounce his garland of coltsfoot and cowslip when his day is done. Not these! They have made every day an All Fools' Day. As I rode through the woods I came upon the wench I spied preaching on the first of this month, standing feet apart before my mount, dark eyes issuing a challenge.

"Let me pass, Mistress Preacher," I said.

"Do not mock me, sir," she replied. "My name be Meg Henfrey. But why goest thou in beggars' weeds, my lord?"

"Why, I am but a humble one like yourself, Mistress," I said. "Why sayest thou that I am a great one?"

"By the way thou sits so haughty astride thy horse, my lord," she said, hands on hips, a slight smile upon her red lips.

"If thou thinkst me a lord," said I, "should I not have thee whipped for calling me 'thou'?"

"We do call all folk 'thou'," said she, with no trace of womanly meekness in her voice. "Didst see the diggers at worship in the fields?" she asked.

"At worship?" said I with a laugh. "Surely the church is the place for that, Mistress."

"They do the Lord's work there."

"They do trespass on their lord's land there."

"So thou art their lord, then," she laughed, "for only their lord would forbid them."

"And yet still thou givest me a clownish thou," I said. "I am but one that believes that what belonged to his ancestors should go to his issue. I am no more a lord than thee a priest. Who ordained thee a minister to preach at crossroads, as I saw thee doing?"

"Christ is in all of us," she said. "He is in Abiezer Coppe, in Jacob Bauthumley. Him they lashed to a tree and bored through the tongue, who suffered me to pass my finger through the hole like Saint Thomas did to our Lord's hands. Christ is in the seed they cast on the soil yonder, to rise again so that we may feast upon his flesh!"

"Jesus in John Barleycorn?" I laughed, though inwardly I was far from amused. "How is this so? Explain carefully, Mistress Henfrey, lest thou find thyself put to the question by the magistrate, or even Master Hopkins."

"Only a lord would make such speeches," she said, with an impudent snort. "If thou art a commoner as thou pretends, get thee down off that horse and speak to me face to face, not from that lofty perch. Then maybe I'll tell thee more of my gospel."

"Very well," I said. God help me, for I now saw her design in wanting to level me down thus. As I jumped down to stand before her, tying my horse to a tree, her eyes fixed upon mine, enabling the Devil that dwelt in those dark pools to take aim, finding it easier so at point-blank range.

I have heard tell of the lasciviousness of them as do claim to need no chapel. The body is where they do worship, so they say, and they do go naked when the spirit moves them.

"Now that I have descended from my horse, I needs must mount something else," were the words he sent forth from my mouth, and my hands were about her waist and delving below her rough garment to do the Devil's work.

"Away, sir!" she hissed, grabbing my jerkin but using her grip to cast me away not pull me closer. Then did she strike my face as if she were a fine lady and I an impudent vassal. "Thou wanted to hear what gospel I preach. Thou shalt not whilst thou use me thus!"

"I have heard that thy gospel is community in all things," I said, my hand upon my smarting cheek.

"Sir, I am no common treasury," she replied, "unless I wish

243

it, and I do not." Thus did she put on a show of injured virtue after her saucy words and looks, leaving me with Cupid's arrow poised and nowhere to shoot it.

1999

"What was that?" he gasped. As he'd sat up something had shot out of a gorse bush near where they had been lying.

"You're very jumpy all of a sudden!" she laughed, stretching languidly.

"And you're very relaxed for someone who was worried about trespassing a quarter-of-an-hour ago."

"Maybe I was just tense," she teased, trying to keep the mood light, though she had to admit to an underlying sense of unease. It suddenly felt cold in the woods. When they'd rushed in here to quench their mutual heat the shade of the beeches had seemed a relief from the intense heat of the sun, but now black clouds had bubbled up adding to the damp chill of the shade.

"But you've helped me with that..."

She gave a low, guttural laugh.

"Look, I'd rather get done for trespassing than public indecency," he snapped.

"All right, all right."

She straightened her skirt and buttoned up her blouse, thinking it was a bit late for him to be worried about his virtue! "Why are you so tense? Did my stress just go into you? Didn't you...?"

"What? Shoot my bolt?"

"Well, that's a nice way of putting it," she said, forcing a smile.

"You know I did. That reminds me..."

He picked up the used condom, hiding it inside his hand as if it was evidence.

She felt a dismaying sense of deflation at his brusqueness, as if he was trying to rub her nose in the sordid aspects of their impromptu outdoor coupling. Perhaps her face had fallen, though usually she was quite good at hiding when his tone of voice or his gestures made her feel small.

"What?" he asked, his tone still sharp and irritable. "I don't want to leave rubbish lying around, do I?"

From the way he was talking, and striding off ahead of her, forcing her almost to break into a jog in order to catch up, she felt as if "rubbish" included her! No, she was being paranoid, wasn't she? But he was already out of the woods and into the field they'd crossed to get here. She could hear more rustlings, more animals rushing from one cover to a safer one. Something in the noise gave her the impression they were taller and thinner than most of the wildlife she thought of, living in a place like this. But her imagination must be running away with her at the speed the unseen creatures were, for something in the rhythm of their footfalls suggested they went on two legs, not four.

1649

What is it plagues me? I have heard them in the woods at dusk, with the double tread of men but unshod like to basest animals, within a month after I brought Mistress Preacher to heel. When Troopers Holborn and Bagley presented her to me I asked her who I was, knowing there could be no mistake as I now wore the fine apparel that befits my station.

"Why, thou art Francis Hearn, sir," she said, with the same damnable impudence as she addressed me when I met her in the woods at Iver Heath and, I marked well, omitting my title and still addressing me as "thou", though this time we were within my portals – in the cellar, that is, where rank dew dripped down the damp walls.

"Very well, Mistress Henfrey," I said to her. Then I looked hard at the two men and spake to them. "Remove her shift."

They glanced the one to the other and at the implements ranged upon the table before me, hesitating to act upon my command, but they could see the very Devil that skulked behind my eyes, the one they had already seen at work when that round-headed knave refused to take off his hat before me. I ensured he would get his wish to keep his cap on always. Thanks to a hammer and several stout nails, he need never remove it again! It has had the unhappy effect of making him a worse ranter than before, as he wanders the woods howling and prating of how the silver he wears about him shall rust and sear his flesh when the Day of Judgement does come. Perhaps 'tis he that makes those weird noises at dusk, then.

No doubt the troopers also remembered what I had put to them, about the punishment Parliament metes out to deserters, for they did as I bid them. It must have been that same Devil that spake next through my dry cracked lips, as I looked hard at the two tremulous men and pointed at the great black-iron pincers on the table. She had but herself to blame for she put that Devil in me. And besides, if Satan bids me do God's work of afflicting heretics, why then, he is no Devil at all!

What I said was: "Hold her fast. Let us see if thou can still say 'thou' without thy teeth."

1999

"Richard!" she called. "Hold on! No need to go that fast!"

He was almost halfway across the field they had crossed to get to the woods. It was open land but for the gorse bushes growing throughout, in full flower, whose buttery-yellow colour and coconut fragrance disguised the cruel sharpness of their thorns. He had stopped so now was the best chance she had to catch up with him. But something in his stance, the way he stood so breathlessly still, made her hesitate.

"Richard?" she said.

Slowly, he turned.

She let out a little gasp of relief when she saw his cheerier expression.

"Come on then!" he called.

She almost bounded over the stile dividing the wood from the field, which looked so inviting with the gorse flowers glowing in the renewed sunlight and Richard's stupid grin beaming at her. He was like that, Richard.

"Sunshine and showers", she called him, though some of her girlfriends were inclined to say "moody". They asked her why a tough cookie like her put up with his bouts of sullenness, to which she would just give a secretive smile that made them laugh in half-envious embarrassment. One or two of them weren't her friends anymore.

"I'm coming," she called.

"What? Again?" he grinned.

"Oh, ha ha."

"Car's still there," he said, pointing to the 2CV. "Sorry for being moody," he said when she reached him. "Worried something might have bashed into it because of where it was parked."

"So you weren't really worried about getting caught *in flagrante* then?"

"No. If the worst came to the worst I could always get Uncle Percy to put in a good word for me with the local beak."

"Really? Your uncle's a local VIP then?"

"Well, sort of. Stockbroker anyway." They both laughed. "He's pally with the one of the magistrates round here anyway. He's got an amazing place, the old Tory bastard. Practically next door to Pinewood Studios. When my folks used to take us there for visits, sometimes we'd see movie stars hanging around nearby…"

"Wow," she said. "So you looked at them and thought 'I want to be in pictures when I grow up'?"

More laughter, though there was an odd scared look in Richard's eyes that made her feel as if she'd overstepped the mark.

"It was more the other lot over in Bray," he corrected her. "When we used to go on family outings to Black Park I used to love playing at being Count Dracula…" He hissed and made a playful lunge at her neck.

Squealing, she backed away and felt gorse teeth biting into her flesh through the thin fabric of her blouse. "Hands off!" She laughed. "It's virgins you vampires like, isn't it?"

"I don't know that Christopher Lee was that fussy. Anyway, you know I see myself more in the mould of Michael Reeves than Terence Fisher."

With an inward rolling of her eyes at his slightly pompous tone, she asked, "The guy who made that *Witchfinder General* film?"

He nodded. She gave a little exhalation of disgust. She hadn't been able to sit through the video and he'd spent the rest of the evening sulking. It had taken some doing to get him to understand why: that the chaos and savagery portrayed was too close to home – to the place and time she had been forced to flee as a child. It was all very well for him, born into a comfortable background, in a country where the last time something like that had happened was the seventeenth century. She hadn't said that then of course. She'd chosen her words more carefully, the mood he'd been in.

Later they'd both read the Christopher Hill book, *World Turned Upside Down*, and discovered that there was another side to the English Civil War; more than two sides in fact, not just Roundheads and Cavaliers. New ideas were fermenting and ordinary people were trying to use the breakdown of traditional authority, not just to give vent to their worst instincts as suggested in the Reeves film, but to test alternative ways of living and create a better world.

That was why they were here. They'd both started work on a tentative film script, working title *Jerusalem*, and had come out here to scout potential locations. Well, that was one way of putting it, she thought drily...

"Look, I know you're not keen," he said, "but the way that guy used the English landscape..."

"Richard, I get that we can save money using real locations, but we still need *some* money for this project. Are you going to ask your Tory uncle for that too? Somehow, I don't think it'll be up his —"

"Shh!" Richard hissed. "Did you hear that?"

1649

"Speak up, Mistress," I said again, "for I cannot hear thee!"

I would have her address me in the correct fashion but still she persisted in calling me "thou". Without teeth to harden the sound it did lend due deference to her speech, so that she did gurgle out "yow". But her haughty air of defiance did take the lustre off my triumph. Suddenly I did feel a terrible disgust at what I had wrought. Even she did blush for shame. Crouching on the crimson-stained floor she began to collect up the bloodied pegs my cruel instrument had ripped from her gums.

"Why, Mistress?" I asked. "Thinkst thou to fit them back into thy mouth?"

And I did laugh heartily at this, but 'twas a counterfeit of mirth, and I did glare at my two unwilling disciples to bid them echo my example, yet they did look away in shame at their part in my atrocity. When she had gathered every single tooth into a scrap of her rent shift and tied it up as 'twere a bag, she gave me a look, a most dreadful look of wrath, that made me turn away.

1999

They turned back towards the woods. It had all gone quiet again but she had definitely heard the sound, a rustling of soil shifting under her feet. She looked around in shock at the sudden absence of the bright-yellow gorse bushes that had punctuated the landscape, turning it into a ploughed open field from which small white shoots were poking out, wriggling like worms. When she saw from the nails that they were big toes, she shut her eyes tight to drive the image from her waking mind back into the dream-world it came from. That was where it belonged, not out here in the daylight. She screwed her eyes tighter. She didn't want to see the rest of the maggot-fleshed feet emerge…

Opening them again, she saw the gorse had returned but when she reached out to Richard to tell him about what she thought had to be some kind of hallucination, she saw he had strode back towards the trees. Her unease compounded by the vision she'd just seen, Marisa was more hesitant in following him. Anyway, she was tired of trailing around after him when he walked off like that. She could hear Karen's voice warning her about going along with "controlling behaviour like that". Marisa had been meaning to get back in touch with her friend and eat humble pie about the hurtful things she'd said back to her, but she kept stalling over how to phrase the apology. In any case, Karen's accusation smarted. How dare she call Marisa a doormat! But would following him now prove she was one?

Maybe she should head back to the car and wait for him there, though that prospect made her feel almost as irritated as the idea of running off after Richard again. What was he doing?

She could hear scuffling noises from the undergrowth around the trees.

"Richard?" she called.

The sounds weren't just that of movement. There were voices too, muttering some kind of gibberish that sounded like sentences said backwards, something like "Ours is land until... Again and again rise shall..." More hallucinations, auditory this time? But the absent gorse bushes and the weird shoots had been as vivid as life, and Richard had heard the noises. That was what he'd gone off to investigate, wasn't it? She wondered if he'd seen anything unusual too. She had to find him first, and he was nowhere to be seen. She moved closer to the dark shade of the trees, still hesitant. A pale shape danced before her in the shadows with a face she couldn't make out clearly, but there was something wrong about it, profoundly wrong.

It couldn't be Richard.

She gasped. The figure was naked, hairless, sexless, limbs spindly, like something not long born, half-finished. When her eyes focused on the face she grasped the thorns of a gorse bush near her, the pain screaming at her brain that she wasn't dreaming, that the black pools of eyes really stared out of the place where the mouth should be, at the base of the head, the nostrils pointed upwards towards a mouth gaping toothlessly in a frown that was a smile turned upside down.

But before she could confirm this, the figure cartwheeled into the darkness, turning its topsy turvy face upright for the instant the splayed hands touched the ground, then leaving her standing there, gaping at the silent trees.

1649

In the forest there is for the most part utter silence. That doth make for a yet more uneasy night as I lie there awaiting the next sudden furtive noise from the darkness. I should hire cottagers to hew down the trees that do close into my chamber window, but methinks none will work for me now. This watching at night began when I did release the wench I had so intemperately ill-used, thinking I did the Lord's work when in truth I obeyed the Fiend's commands. A tinker did discover her corpse at the crossroads where first I spied her preaching, all bloody at the mouth. She must have fallen into an endless sleep there while trudging the road. According to the report my steward brought to me, they found no parcel of teeth on her person. I did not fear that I might be arraigned for her death. She fell far enough away from my house that none might connect me to her, save those two deserters whom I think have fled. I do not think they dare accuse me for fear of bringing retribution on their own heads for assisting me in my misdeeds, and also for their absenting themselves from their own martial duties without leave. Nevertheless, they may yet do so out of spite or remorse. So, for safety, if they do remain in this parish I needs must accuse them lest they do likewise unto me.

I have but one servant remaining, the others having quit my service to join with the Diggers on the Heath. I sent him forth to ride out and determine if my two former associates were lurking hereabouts. He saw them not, he said, but this he did tell me.

"My lord," he said, "I did see that fellow whose cap you did nail onto his pate when in his impertinence he did forbear to

remove it before you. *Scraps of it still remained about the rusty nail heads, with patches of wild hair sprouting forth between them. He did caper and gambol about the fields hither and thither, gibbering like Tom a' Bedlam, casting what I took for seeds about him."*

"Were they seeds, sirrah?" said I, for he did seem doubtful when he spake the word "seeds". "Speak, man!"

"Aye, my lord," said he. "Seeds of corn, methinks. This chant he did make as he scattered them: 'Jane Barleycorn is dead' as he hurled one seed, 'Jane Barleycorn is risen' as he flung the next, and so on until of corn he had no more. It did not take long. He had not many seeds. Not more than I have teeth in my mouth!"

He grinned his foolish gap-toothed smile but stopped doing so when I asked him sharply why he prattled of teeth.

"I do think the rusty nails in the fellow's head have curdled his wits, my lord," my servant said. "It should be John Barleycorn, not Jane, should it not?"

"Indeed," I said. "Indeed."

But 'twas a week after his report that I began to hear the nocturnal comings and goings hither and thither outside my chamber window, those sounds that are like beasts, but beasts that walk abroad on their hind legs.

1999

Not a sound came from the woods.

She walked forward cautiously, expecting to hear renewed rustling in the undergrowth as she surprised some animal or worse, the thing she'd seen, or thought she'd seen. The silence was like someone holding their breath. The birds seemed to be holding theirs too. Come to think of it, she couldn't remember hearing them at all since she'd been here.

She stepped into the shade of the trees, trembling at her memory of that thing. She still couldn't believe it: that upside-down face! It seemed so unreal now, mere moments later, though it had seemed real enough at the time.

Most of the trees were still bare but for tiny spikes of young pale-green foliage peeking out of their branches and the occasional snowy bloom of hawthorn blossom. The exception was the gnarled overgrown horse chestnut, whose floppy leaves dangled like flat green hands.

Despite the undeveloped forest canopy it still felt damp and shady amid the vegetation, as if some invisible force repelled the heat of the day. She shivered. The involuntary reflex gave itself voice, becoming a gasp as she felt a hand on her shoulder.

1649

I clapped him on the shoulder. He turned with a little gasp. He wore plain clothes though I had heard tell he was once a man of the cloth until he fell in with the Ranters.

"Dr John Pordage?" I asked.

"The same," said he. His eyes were narrowed, and who could blame him in these treacherous times which have turned son against father, servant against master? "And who art thou, sir?"

"Sir Francis Hearn," I said, assuming a haughty mien, my chin held aloft. "I have heard, sir, that thou art no stranger to the esoteric arts."

He turned from me as if to take flight, saying, "I know not of what you speak, my lord."

"Fie, sir, come back!" I entreated him. "Be not afraid! Master Hopkins' harsh witch-finding wind doth blow in the east, not here. I wish to hire thy services, not chastise thee for them. I would pay thee well…"

"Think you I am of the Devil's party?" he asked, turning upon his heel, his pale blue eyes still narrowed against me.

"Thou art Doctor John Pordage, art thou not?" I did press him.

"Aye, my lord," said he. "I have never denied this."

"Wert thou not a curate in Reading and latterly rector of Bradfield?" I asked.

"Well, indeed," he said, his downcast eyes closing further. "What makes you of this, my lord?"

"Thy father was a merchant," I said, lowering my countenance to try to catch his errant gaze. "Bradfield is one of the richest livings in the realm. And yet thou art garbed like to a rude mechanic preacher. It must go hard with thee to exist so meanly after such high living."

"I have no regrets," he said. "I have followed my conscience wheresoever it has led me, while you, my lord, have followed my career equally conscientiously." He smiled thinly.

"Be not saucy with me, sir!" I said. Then I softened my tone, pointing out that I could help alleviate his straitened circumstances.

"I have no need of thy gold, sir," said he, adding an impudent clownish "thy" to his insult. "The Lord provides…"

His pale lips formed another faint smile as his long arm did trace a half circle about him, pointing to the trees whose leaves did begin to shrivel around us in readiness for Autumn's shredding winds.

"Herne the Hunter is said to ride forth in these woods protecting the King's game from the hungry poor. But the King is dead so poor Herne wants employment. Dost thou think to usurp him, Sir Francis?"

I would not be provoked into another rage by his sauciness but simply said, "I can see a long day's ride to the Eastern counties awaits me. It shall be hard and I shall be saddle-sore at the end of it, but not as sore as thou shalt be when Master Sterne has finished with thee…"

And I made as if to begin untying my horse.

"What makes you think I practise sorcery, my lord?" he asked.

"Were there not wondrous apparitions at your dwelling in Bradfield this harvest time just gone?" I put to him. "Noisome poisonous smells? Loathsome hellish tastes of sulphur?"

"Aye, aye, my lord," he confirmed, "but there were sweet angelic fragrances and ambrosial flavours as well as those devilish ones you mentioned. I saw a giant with a great sword in his hand, a dragon with great teeth and open jaws whence he hurled fire at me. These wonders have made me to take to the virgin's life, thus to avoid the kingdom of the Dragon. But these conjurations were none of my own doing."

"Indeed, sir," I said. "Then whose were they?"

"I cannot say, my lord."

"Very well," I said. "Thou sayest thou dost not need my gold, for the Lord provides. Or is it the Devil that does so? Hast thou discovered the secret of alchemy?"

At this he gave a strange laugh, and said, "Nay, my lord. Had I done so all your gold would be as dross for being commonplace, as someday soon all that lucre shall be!"

And with that, he turned upon his heel and trudged onwards through the forest.

1999

She turned to see him close at her heels, silently appearing from the forest like a sprite. There was a strange smile upon his face, where blood bloomed in a hectic flush on his cheeks and also in spots that welled from a scratch along his jawline.

"Richard?"

His anorak was torn and there were patches of sweat staining the t-shirt underneath. His walking boots were daubed pale brown with wet mud, which also spattered the ankles of his jeans.

"Richard, what's happened to you. You look—"

"Like I've been dragged through a hedge backwards? But come and look what I've found..."

Something about the feverish light in his eyes made her hesitate but she couldn't put her finger on what. Besides, she couldn't very well put her finger on anything with her wrist now gripped tight in his as he pulled her towards his discovery.

She stared at the fluffy pale-brown lumps flecked with straw.

"Horse shit," she said, rubbing her wrist, wondering if there'd be visible bruising on it, hating herself for worrying what Karen might think if there was. "So what?" She couldn't be bothered to hide the annoyance in her voice.

He blinked but recovered quickly. "I followed the trail though," he grinned. "Wait till you see what I found at the end of it!"

"I can't wait," she said drily.

"You won't have to wait long," he told her, in a tone of voice she didn't entirely like but tried to ignore. "It's not far. Come on!"

She pulled her arm back from his attempt to grasp her wrist again, saying, "It's all right, officer, I'll come quietly."

He must have sensed the reproof behind her humour for he said, "Sorry, did I hurt you?"

"No! Not at all."

"Don't know my own strength." He let out a forced nervous laugh.

"I'm not dressed for this," she said as he led her through a tangle of briars that caught on her skirt. "Is it really as close you said?"

"Yes, not far now," he said, an edge of irritation in his voice.

They carried on for a few minutes in a silence broken only by the snapping of twigs underfoot and the rustling of leaves as they pushed through the thick damp vegetation. To Marisa, this didn't look like somewhere anyone would want to walk let alone ride a horse. And yet the dung kept occurring at regular intervals. It was steaming.

"It's fresh," Richard muttered. "How about that...?" When she failed to reply he added, "Makes you think, doesn't it?"

"What?" she said with a sigh.

"All sorts of things could go on round here without anyone knowing, hidden away behind all this growth..."

"Yeah," she agreed, thinking of the old moustached man hiding in a rented mansion not far from here, as if he'd followed her from her homeland. He no longer strutted around in his braided general's uniform, and was pleading age and ill health to avoid extradition.

All of a sudden the space opened up. She saw the clearing and in its dim bluish light what was hanging there.

1649

Deep in the heart of the woods the trees do open up to form a glade where the sun's rays do penetrate but dimly. That is where he would have me meet him. Wherefore I can only guess. Perhaps this Everard, the true author of the apparitions visited upon Pordage, wishes to keep either his occult dabblings or his dealings with me a close secret, or both. I should have asked the man with the holes in his skull what spells he cast over those teeth that their issue plagues me, as I think they do. But he was mad, now dead. My cruel nails must have penetrated further than I did think. So I can but hope that Everard hath the remedy, that he might disconnect the strands of the web that begins to enfold me.

1999

"Everard was the link between the Diggers and the Ranters. Christopher Hill said so!" Richard hissed, a strange feverish lustre in his eyes in the dank shade of the clearing. "You've read it, Marisa. Do you remember those passages?"

But Marisa wasn't really listening. Indeed, she was wondering how he could ramble on about history books in a clearing hung with upside down corpses, though their faces weren't. She felt as if she didn't know him anymore, if she ever had.

"But don't you see?" he went on as if he couldn't understand why her attention was focussed on the freakish charnel display instead of his monologue. "Winstanley's God was Reason! Not so Coppe and his ilk… Their science was alchemy, prophecy! You did read Hill's book, didn't you? Didn't you?" His rant continued as she failed to turn her gaze back towards him from the spindly dangling arms turning slowly. "You do remember the bit about Everard's magic show at Pordage's place, don't you?" He grabbed her shoulders, shaking them with the same febrile energy that burned in his eyes.

Then they softened and he released her shoulders, leaving her wondering vaguely if they'd bruise like her wrist probably would. But not as much as she was wondering why the faces, each with a stark hole between the black eyes staring at her from the white sexless bodies, were the right way up unlike the rest of the creatures.

"I'm sorry," he said, and his voice sounded a little more like his old self, the one she thought she knew at least. "I know I've been getting a bit obsessed with this film, a bit too far into the research side of it. It's just... Well, there's a special connection for me, a family connection, I believe!"

"Richard," she said, her eyes widening at something out of his line of vision. "Look!"

She didn't mean the shrunken parodies of humanity festooning the clearing, though that had been enough of a shock for her, sickening her to the core of her being both with their bizarre facial abnormalities and the casual inhumanity with which someone had strung them up like prize partridges. That someone, she suspected, was the figure now towering before her, astride a black stallion, the branching latticework of a pair of antlers sprouting from his grimacing death's head, dark spots staining the huntsman's red coat, a rifle slung over the shoulder.

The clearing suddenly felt dreadfully isolated.

1649

As I wait in this dread and lonely place I feel a terrible burden upon my shoulders, for methinks I have indirectly become the progenitor of a terrible infestation upon the land. The nocturnal sounds in the woods near my house have increased of late, suggesting the creatures have multiplied, and this after I set about them with horse and hound. It may be that the measures I took to exterminate these pests have given them increase!

Where is this Everard?

The longer he delays his arrival the more I do suspect he hath lured me here to ambush me with confederates and do me foul play. Nor would it be undeserved, for methinks I have done deeds of darkness for which I must answer before Heaven ere long. 'Twas with this belief in mind that lately I set myself to setting my house in order, with edicts to my issue on dealing with the monsters, though I fear my instructions may not be precise enough so that they that come after me shall perpetuate the curse they mean to exorcise.

I hear noises now. Is that steel glinting in the shadows? I fear that whoever comes upon me thus shall leave garbed in scarlet.

1999

"Why's he wearing a red coat?" was all she could think of to say. She hoped that those weren't going to be her last words. What stupid last words those would be.

"Pink coat," he corrected her.

"Okay, why's he wearing a pink coat?" she asked. "And shouldn't he have dogs then?" she added by way of another irrelevant question since ignoring the dangling elephants in the room seemed to be the order of the day, though anything less like elephants she had difficulty imagining. What *were* they like then? That was the trouble: the slaughtered creatures with their topsy-turvy heads were like nothing she'd ever seen before, neither man nor beast. Neither man nor woman either, their blank groins suggested, nor born of man or woman, their navel-less bellies told her.

"Not dogs. Hounds."

It was the muffled echoing voice behind what she now understood to be an antlered skull mask. There was an odd look of recognition in her boyfriend's haunted eyes at the sound of the voice.

"It's traditional to ride to hound of course," it said, "but they proved rather counter-productive. You see, they're rather like bindweed – and after all, the vermin did grow out of the ground. When the pack ripped the creatures up you just got more of the damn things!"

The dam holding back Marisa's rising gorge finally burst. It seemed like an age since she and Richard had shared the picnic lunch, she now watched spatter the already sodden leaf mould, which had gone rank in the airless silence of the clearing at her feet.

The newcomer went on. "Tradition, ritual. These are important things for our sort, eh, Richard?" The young man he was addressing looked up, with a look of dawning understanding.

Somehow Marisa now thought of him as "the young man", a stranger, not her boyfriend. Something told her she must get away from this awful place, run, but which direction? There might be more of those things out there, and though she pitied these dead ones she couldn't face meeting a live one face to upside-down face.

"Our school had its initiation rites, though of course I imagine they'd watered them down by your time, my boy! That's political correctness for you... This particular ritual's been going on since the seventeenth century though we've had to ... not water it down exactly... Adapt it for more practical reasons. So no hounds, just a bullet between the eyes. Bit quick but far more efficient—"

"Uncle Percy!" Richard gasped.

The antlers shook as the huntsman nodded his head. "But I've always thought of you more as a son to me, not having children of my own. Listen, lad, not to put too fine a point on it – your old man's going to pop his clogs soon so how's this for an idea: why not come and join me in the family business..."

"What? Stockbroking?" said Richard with an incredulous laugh.

"No, no, no!" said his uncle, suddenly whipping his rifle from his shoulder, taking aim and firing at the source of a rustling from the edge of the clearing, the report followed by a mewling whimper like that of a beaten dog, a sound more terrible than anything Marisa had ever heard before, even in Chile.

Then silence broken only by Uncle Percy's muffled breathing inside the mask. "Pest control. You'd need a bit of training, of course. Reactions and a sure aim like mine don't come overnight. Sure you'd pick it up though. Right sort of stock." He slung the rifle back on his back then added, "Well, boy? What do you say?"

Richard lowered his eyes and Marisa saw him glancing nervously in her direction, as if for support or advice. Maybe he wasn't such a stranger after all. "Richard!" she whispered to him, instantly regretting it as the antlered death's head turned in her direction, as if the huntsman had noticed her for the first time. "You're not like him!"

"Oh, but he is. Same stock, you see. I'm sorry, we have not been introduced. Richard? Who's your lady friend? Not from round here, is she?"

She gave a contemptuous little laugh and was glad her fear was giving way to anger and contempt. She guessed he was directing his jibe at her hint of an accent and her dark colouring.

"She's right," said Richard, his eyes narrowed. "I'm not like you."

"Look, I understand the need to rebel. Everyone's a bit of a lefty when they're young. Even I grew my hair long and dabbled in a bit of pot during my misspent youth. But there comes a time when you have to put aside childish things, decide which side you're on. There's a war going on out here, you see. Our illustrious ancestor Sir Francis Hearn understood that, so he took steps to try to remedy the situation. These wretched creatures were the unfortunate by-product. They're not all bad of course. As long as you keep the population down and give the remainder what they want, some of them can even be quite useful."

"What are you talking about?" Richard asked.

"Come on," said Marisa, trying to take his arm though it felt unyielding. "Let's go, Richard. Your uncle is obviously insane."

"I wouldn't expect you to understand," he said to her, then addressed Richard again. "The Civil War never ended. It just went cold. As you probably know, Sir Francis went missing at some point around that time so it was left to his descendants to try to control their spread. *Noblesse oblige*, if you will! As I said, it's possible to domesticate some of them but they still need feeding. Now if you wouldn't mind helping me restrain your lady-friend..."

"You leave her out of this!" Richard said, his eyes narrowing, but his uncle just laughed at his heroics, a horrible hollow sound reverberating behind his skeletal mask.

"Come now, Richard," he said. "I know she's a bit of a looker in a swarthy sort of way, but surely you understand that ties of blood outweigh such considerations!"

The look of uncertainty in Richard's eyes was enough.

She gave up any thought of trying to persuade him to escape with her and bolted for it. She had to put herself first and couldn't be sure that he would choose her over his family with its terrible legacy. This thought drove her through the brambles and branches, tearing her clothes, until the foliage grew sparser. All she had to do was keep going, though her breath came in gasps and her skin stung in places where thorns had torn at her as if the long straggling pale-green blackberry shoots were themselves agents of Richard's unhinged uncle, devoid of human consciousness yet possessed of a weird intelligence. Didn't he say that the creatures had grown from the ground like "bindweed", whose roots their pale spindly limbs resembled, implying they were actually plants of some kind?

Now she was out of the passageway that had led to the clearing, she dismissed such thoughts from her mind. Whatever she'd seen or thought she'd seen must simply be the result of the huntsman's demented power of suggestion. She'd worked in mental hospitals in the past and knew how persuasive some of the patients with psychosis could be, drawing you into their delusions by sheer force of will.

But she had seen those creatures, hadn't she?

Nevertheless, now she was out of the clearing and his sphere of influence it all seemed so unreal. She couldn't even hear a hue and cry of pursuit. All she had to do was somehow get back to civilisation. Not that it was far away. London wasn't much more than a stone's throw away after all. It would seem a lot further on foot of course but she'd manage it. If her mother could escape from Pinochet's Chile, she could surely get out of some woods in the Home Counties of England! Maybe she could break into Richard's car and get that going but right now she just had to put as much distance as possible between her and that madman on a horse.

She climbed the stile and was back in the open field with the gorse bushes.

A man stepped out from behind one of them.

He was wearing a flat cap, a tweed waistcoat and a collarless shirt, for all the world like an old-fashioned gamekeeper. She assumed the strange paddle-shaped stick he was carrying was for beating pheasants out of the bushes or something. But the most notable thing about him was that his hat was perched on a chin that pointed skyward.

Then she remembered what Uncle Percy had said about "domesticating" and "feeding" some of the creatures. No wonder he hadn't bothered to chase her.

She was about to make a break for it to get past the man, whose grim frown was actually a terrible smile, when another one stepped out from behind a gorse bush blocking off that potential escape route.

Then another one appeared from another direction. And another one. She spun round to see others closing in on her from behind, all carrying the paddles, which she now saw were studded at the end, like meat tenderisers.

They'd need them, the last rational thought in her head

told her, with those toothless black mouths, which had now begun sucking in expectation, leaving her wondering what form their "feeding" might take.

Story Notes

Let Your Hinged Jaw Do the Talking: I'd long been thinking of doing a haunted ventriloquist's dummy story, when I went to a fairy tale-based creative writing workshop in Portsmouth co-led by the fabulous Victoria Leslie, which gave an extra story prompt, a variation on the Bluebeard theme. That's why the narrator's father is called "Derek Fox", after the Bluebeard-figure in the version I read, "Mr Fox". Of course, Angela Carter wrote a story around this myth, "The Bloody Chamber", and this story also owes a heavy debt to her novel *The Magic Toyshop*, which I only read quite recently, but I have strong memories of the 1987 Granada film adaptation.

Coffin Dodger: Unlike some, both the title of and the idea for this story came to me almost instantly and simultaneously while mowing around the tombstones of All Saints' Church in Patcham, incidentally the source of the Wellsbourne, the underground river that was the focus of my previous and first short fiction collection, *Last Stop Wellsbourne* (Omnium Gatherum Media). The John Deere pedestrian lawnmower in use at the time does indeed have a very rigid waste chute that gets in the way when trying to negotiate gravestones, but the protagonist's past double life as an undercover policeman is not something of which I have first-hand experience, at least not to my knowledge. The police officers who used to conduct surveillance on me at protests used to be quite open about it, and in full uniform and making a point of being obvious, but then I suppose if there were other more covert ones I wouldn't know, would I…?

Cuckoo Flower: Continuing the horticultural theme, I wrote this after undertaking a PA1/PA6 certificate in the safe use of pesticides, a skill I've never had to put into practice since the local council banned the use of the main herbicide, Glyphosate. However, as this story shows, I have the correct procedures for preparing and handling a backpack sprayer down to a fine art!

Professor Beehive Addresses the Human Biology Class: This is the last of three stories with a gardening theme, but also the first of three where I attempt to play around with the traditional "club story" framing device. I've got over my obsession with this convention but there was a time a few years ago where I would try to insert a raconteur in a fireside wing-backed armchair into a story, whether or not it was appropriate to do so. The characters in this one are reminiscing about their days at an English private school, albeit a co-educational one, so expect references to Latin, Greek and extensive playing fields, but also some insights into the grounds maintenance aspects of their upkeep and the tasks and machinery involved.

The Chiromancer: Originally an EC-style comic strip called "A Helping Hand" in *Brighton – The Graphic Novel* (Queen Spark Books), about a corrupt Brighton detective who uses occult means to forge signatures on false confessions. I felt I'd missed a trick by not having a failed writer use the supernatural to fake lost literary manuscripts, hence this prose variation on the theme. So, appropriately in a tale of literary forgery, I plagiarised myself! The Regina Club that frames the story was an actual illegal gay nightclub in 1950s Brighton.

Slaughtered Lamb: The final part of the trilogy of "tales from a smoking room" is more of a "tale from a toking room". Where your typical raconteur in these types of stories is an old ex-army officer telling of dark doings in the Dark Continent, the colonial outpost here is somewhat closer to home, leading into an Irish trilogy of terror. Most of it is true, almost autobiography, with the names changed. Over the years I've tried with varying success to wean myself off this dubious technique for creating authenticity in fiction, but I'll leave the reader to guess where the join is between creative memoir and pure fiction.

Creeping Forth Upon Their Hands: A key colonial outpost in Ireland during the Elizabethan era was the Munster Plantation, where the poet Sir Edmund Spenser held sway for a while. You can still see the ruins of his castle in Cork. I happened to hear Feargal Keane's earnestly dulcet brogue intoning a passage from Spenser's *View of the Present State of Ireland* on Radio 4 one day, a tract that's essentially a how-to manual on how to subjugate the Irish, and it gave me the title and an approach to a submission to *The Ghastling* magazine's call for stories about ritual signs and protection marks. I have to thank Dr Tracy Fahey, gothic academic and unheimlich manoeuvrer extraordinaire, for beta-reading help and pointing me in the direction of William Hope Hodgson's "The Whistling Room", which gave me a reference point for imperialist marital paranoia.

A Heart of Stone: The previous story, "Creeping Forth...", shares with "Coffin Dodger", "Face Down in the Earth", "Zombie Economy" and "The Topsy Turvy Ones" the distinction of being wholly or in part told in the third person, the only ones in this collection to have this viewpoint; the framing sections of "The Topsy Turvy Ones" combines both, with modern-day sequences in the third person, historical ones in first. But for the most part the reader may have noticed my comfort zone is first person, which is a problem from the point of view of writing horror because it somewhat negates suspense if the protagonist has obviously lived to tell the tale. The way around this is to make the narrator herself a source of menace albeit a sympathetically traumatised one, as here. I think I used the device of postcards because I was so taken with the Don Tumasonis story "The Prospect Cards", but this is a more contemporary take on an ancient myth.

Mum and Dad and the Girl from the Flats Over the Road and the Man in the Black Suit: I wrote this almost as an exercise when I was co-editing the anti-austerity anthology *Horror Uncut: Tales of Social Insecurity and Economic Unease* (Gray Friar Press) with the late, great and much-missed Joel Lane. We'd both agreed not to indulge in using our editorial roles as an excuse to publish our own work but given that he passed away during the editorial process I over-ruled him in his case, posthumously including a reprint of his story "A Cry for Help", which in any case was the story that inspired me to believe this was a suitable theme for a horror anthology in the first place. My own tale of the bedroom tax and a council estate bogeyman had to wait until the fine journal *Supernatural Tales* printed it a few years later.

Face Down in the Earth: The top tip about the best protection for midges came from a fellow camper on a Highland campsite that did indeed have some plumbing issues.

The Fall Guy: More Highland horror in a tale where I responded to a call for stories of doubles by wondering what if a person's doppelganger were his or her guardian or even stunt double? As with the previous story, real-life childhood holidays fed into this one.

In the Hold, It Waits: When I saw a submissions call for a gothic novelette I decided to pull out all the stops. The result didn't make the cut for that, but did so for Egaeus Press's *A Book of the Sea*. The editor Mark Beech said he'd not wanted pirates in the anthology but changed his mind when he read this tale of terror on the high seas, despite or perhaps because of its over-the-top language. There were a one or two geographical errors spotted by Peter Coleborn that this version remedies!

The Cutty Wren: My significant other plays in a ceilidh band which provides the background to this story. Rosemary Pardoe rejected it initially for her *Ghosts and Scholars Book of Folk Horror* anthology, but it scraped in after some rewrites. As it was a limited-edition print-run, now out-of-print, this is your only chance to read it if you haven't got a copy of that! I first remember hearing the song "The Cutty Wren" while studying drama at Exeter University, and the lore around it is fascinating. The Old Glory Molly Dancers still dance and carry out the ritual of the Cutty Wren on Boxing Day, otherwise known as the Feast of Steven, although they stopped doing such things during the height of the Covid pandemic.

Zombie Economy: I was hoping to sell the original version of this story to the anthology *Classic Monsters Unleashed* as a *White Zombie/I Walked with a Zombie* monster mash-up, with a large dose of C.L.R. James' *The Black Jacobins*. After its rejection and some very rigorous beta-reading by Colleen Anderson and Anna Schwarz, who both agreed it was a little too heavy on the pseudo-academic discourse and a little too light on actual story, I decided it needed an extra ingredient in the form of some Voodoo body horror in the tradition of Edward Lucas White and Henry S. Whitehead.

The Lazarus Curse: This reinterpretation of the Gospel from the point of view of one of its supposed villains owes its existence to the Leon Rosselson song "Stand Up for Judas", the perfect Easter hymn for left-wing atheists!

The Topsy Turvy Ones: When Paul Finch invited me to contribute to *Terror Tales of the Home Counties* I naturally thought of Caryl Churchill's seventeenth century plays *Vinegar Tom* and *A Light Shining in Buckinghamshire*. Surrey now provides the electoral base for the likes of Dominic Raab and Michael Gove, but back in 1649 it was the home of Gerrard Winstanley's Diggers Commune. My approach to this novelette was essentially to imagine what might have happened if Michael Reeves or Piers Haggard had read Christopher Hill's *The World Turned Upside Down* before they made their folk horror classics. Not that they could have done as it came out in 1972, after their legendary films did…

Short story collections from The Alchemy Press

Lightning Source UK Ltd.
Milton Keynes UK
UKHW011127280422
402190UK00001B/38